Famine's Punishment

Famine's Punishment

Arrival of the Four Horsemen Series

Copyright © 2023 By Marcelle Valentine

Contact information: marcellevalentine.com/

Published in the United States of America by Medusa Publishing.

Medusa Publishing is a registered trade name of Medusa Publishing, LLC.

First edition 2023

Famine's Punishment

Arrival of the Four Horsemen Series

Marcelle Valentine

Contents

Always dream big...they're easier to catch that way.

Chapter One: Convictions

And now these three remain: faith, hope, and love. But the greatest of these is love. Corinthians 13:13.

<u>~Death Summer 2026~</u>

ISOLATION.
DARKNESS.
CAPTIVITY.

THESE ARE my punishments for my transgressions. A penance Michael believed I should have given myself without our Father's involvement. Regardless, I'm certain it overjoyed him when he returned and discovered where he had sent me. This is my tomb.

Unlike the jail they held me for the last year, this place is... nothing. Nowhere. This realm exists in a plane all its own, separate from the others he has created. The goal of this place is to make you forget your past. To surrender to its authority. It's meant to break me, but what they did not account for is that I already was living in this hell without Avalon. A nothingness they forced me to walk through every day, which only grew worse when they removed her from my view.

By placing me here, they sentenced me to millennia of isolation, but in doing so, they also gave me a gift. I no longer have to hide my feelings or what she means to me because just as they removed my gaze from her, I am removed from theirs. A reward they did not realize they were granting me.

So I fill my time with all the sweetest memories of my Avalon. The woman who showed me a better way. A soul who demonstrated what true strength is. An attribute she taught me is not physical but is in the steel of your convictions and your unwavering love for the people you hold dear.

Whereas before, I would not allow my thoughts to linger too long on her, now she is all I think about.

Her smile and laugh.

The scent and feel of her skin.

Her courage and principles.

The woman this world shaped her into… a fighter, a survivor, and loyal to the bitter end. A woman who captured not only this horseman's devotion but my brother's as well. Because even though I know War abided by my request, he did so with a heavy heart. Had I given him a choice, he would never have walked away.

In many ways, I suppose my father got his wish because I learned what it meant to be mortal, and with it, I found love, but other emotions also plagued me. One of the worst to deal with was the one I fought the hardest. Jealousy. This is why I could not allow War to explore his feelings for her. I couldn't accept one of my brothers loving what I had walked away from. I was a fool. And if given the chance to do it again, I never would have left the home on the hill we made together.

What Michael did not account for is I am even more resolute in my determination to return to the one place holding the woman who owns every piece of me. He may have removed my gaze from her, but he will never take away my heart. I will never surrender no matter how long I am forced to stay here because if I do, I have truly failed her.

"Son."

"Father, have you changed your mind? Have you come to release me?"

"I am here only to inform you that your brother has been called to her world."

Famine. No, not Famine. He will not be as willing to give them a chance or as forgiving as Pestilence and War. "How did this happen?"

"By force of hand."

"I don't understand what you mean. Did someone hurt Avalon or someone she loves? Did she face losing one of my brothers?"

"It matters not how it occurred. It was only fair to tell you your brother's decay is set to begin."

"No!"

"This is not for you to decide, son."

"I have done everything you have ever asked of me."

"This was true...until the lamb's importance surpassed that of your task. I cannot have you interfering with her path more than you already have. This is the lamb's task to complete. I'm sorry you love her. It is hard to see one of my most loyal sons suffering, but I must ensure she fulfills what I have assigned her. Something she will not do if I allow you to return to her. And with Raum—"

"Raum hunts her still?"

"He does."

"I must warn Pestilence and War."

"No. We will provide no such warning."

"But how will she fulfill her destiny if Raum succeeds in his?"

"Raum wishes to see the riders released."

"Father, once she has completed her task, he will carry her soul back to hell to be tormented and tortured. You know this."

"Then this is to be the fate of the lamb."

"NO!"

My Father fades away, leaving me to consider what this means for Apple and my brothers. War and Pestilence will never permit our brother to harm the ones they love, which means my brothers will have no choice but to oppose one another with Famine on one side and Pestilence and War on the other. The issue is Famine is stronger. As is my father's way, each rider is stronger and more resolute than the last. Meaning he will not fall by their hand without bloodshed. Regardless, one of my brothers will meet their end if I do nothing soon to stop this.

Then there's Raum. He opposes us all, including our father. He represents a danger not only to Avalon but to all of humanity. But not just them, because he overwhelmed one of my brothers, from what I was told. This interaction resulted in my Apple breaking War's seal so she could save Pestilence. He is a wildcard who will learn of my wrath the instant I ensure Avalon's safety.

*****

I have roamed in utter darkness for more months than I care to contemplate, unable to view Avalon's world or know what fate has befallen her or my brothers. Regardless of the countless years I must roam in this obscurity, I will forever hold dear this exquisite spirit and her significance to me. And if anything has befallen one of my brothers, fate will not look kindly on the ones who did this. If I were there, I could be their voice of reason for all of them, including Famine. So for these reasons, I will search for an exit. Find a way out and fight my way back to them. When I am free, nothing and no one will stop me from returning to her world.

I dream of this day. The day she will be back in my arms, and when it arrives, I am never letting go again.

Regardless of what trials lie ahead, I will never surrender. She deserves no less. Because of my Apple, I know what it means to be alive and to have hope. Because of this, my love for Avalon will endure forever, and I will never cease fighting to be reunited with the woman who has captured every piece of my heart and soul. Something the beings who have stolen her from me will regret. Because as long as I have a soul, these three remain: faith, hope, and love. So you see, this simple truth remains… when it comes to her, I know now there has never been any other choice. Too bad I didn't figure this out sooner.

Everything else pales in comparison to the love I have for Avalon. Because she is and will always remain…

My beautiful Apple.

Chapter Two: The Black Rider.... The Bringer of Decay and Despair.

When He opened the third seal, I heard the third living creature say, "Come and see." So I looked, and behold, a black horse, and he who sat on it had a pair of scales in his hand. Revelation 6:5.

~Famine Summer 2026~

AT LONG LAST, I TAKE my first breath. I have toiled in darkness for centuries with only brief glimpses of their realm. Of the world these mortals our creator held in such esteem have been gifted. But now I am awake. The seal that kept me prisoner is no more, which means my brothers,

Pestilence and War, are already there. I hope the few glances they granted me are incorrect; otherwise, it means my brothers have failed in their mission.

I cannot fathom what could have swayed them, and since my creator opted to hold these moments from me, I am left with more questions than answers.

The one name that plagues my hazy thoughts is Avalon. I have no clue why this mystical place would hound me. Perhaps I can ascertain this information from my brother. Thanatos should be here to welcome me, since he is the only one among us not forced to sleep. It's worrisome that he still has not made an appearance.

While waiting for him, I prepare the instruments I will require for my arrival. The ones I will use to weigh their worth. An action that is done so I can show them how insignificant they are. I will demonstrate to the ones who plead absolution they are not as pure as they believe. With my tools prepared, I move on to my companion. It has been far too long since he has walked in the sun. I look forward to the moment we do so.

After I had completed all the tasks requiring my attention, he was still unaccounted for. If he does not wish to welcome me, he leaves me no choice other than to seek him out to greet him. I have questions, and I assume he possesses the answers I seek. Perhaps Thanatos can explain why a place I've never visited holds such a profound significance.

As I wander the hall to his quarters, I cannot help but notice how deserted everything is. Not to allude that they ever brim with activity because they do not. Because my Father's kingdom is vast, spreading most of his most loyal thin. Regardless of this, the circumstances I woke to are quite unusual.

I plan to confront my brother and demand he explain what was so important it would detain him from greeting me after all this time, but when I arrive at the place he last inhabited, I find it as deserted as the rest of this place.

I roam from one corner of his room to the next, searching for any clue of his whereabouts. But nothing. The only evidence of his existence was the book prophesying our arrival. Is it possible Thanatos has found a way to unleash his wrath upon their world before me?

This is the only explanation that makes any sense.

"It is so good to see you after all these millennia, Rider." I whip my head toward the voice, only to discover my father's chief warrior standing in the doorway.

"Michael?"

"Yes," he smiles while moving further into the room. "How are you, Famine?"

"Confused. I am trying to ascertain why Thanatos did not greet me upon waking."

"Oh." A pained look crosses his face, twisting his features. "I'm sorry to have to be the one to tell you this, but I feel it is only fair. Your brother–he… our Father has punished him."

"Why?"

"He strayed from his duty."

"Thanatos did such a thing? This does not sound like my brother at all."

"I understand you're upset, my friend. We all were by his actions and the punishment he now faces."

"Since when did we become friends, Michael? I should like to hear what egregious act my brother committed."

"Well, for one, he refused to ferry a soul to their afterlife. Worse, he restored it."

"This was after my other brothers had already awakened?"

"Pestilence had already been called to their world. War yet slumbered."

"I don't understand why Thanatos would do this. If Pestilence had passed his judgment, why would he restore what our brother took?"

"Somehow, one mortal did what no one thought possible and bewitched him. This mortal could cloud his judgment and affect his mind, so he no longer believed in your mission. Had our father not jailed him, I fear what he would have done to your other brothers."

I am stunned by what this angel is saying. Our purpose is so deeply ingrained in our creation that no one believes the riders could ever go against it. How could one mortal be capable of such a feat? This is something I would like to hear.

"Is our father certain this was a mortal? What if it was one of our fallen brethren? One of the damned who will never be welcome here again? Because I must be honest here, Michael, I find it difficult to imagine he would grant any of the cretins Father tasked us with removing this ability."

"We are certain."

"How? How can you be so certain? Have you captured the being? Removed them from their plane? What actions have you taken against the soul who would dare to attempt such atrocities?"

"None. The being remains in the mortal realm." Raw fury fills my every cell upon hearing this. Why in the seven realms of hell would any of them allow this abomination to remain free in the mortal realm? For they must know if Thanatos fell to such a being, my other brothers are also at risk. Lashing out faster than he can react, I take Michael by the throat and slam him into the wall. He will explain why our creator granted immunity to such a being when my brother toils in darkness.

"Enough talking in half answers. You will tell me why this mortal still walks within their realm, and you will do it fast if you wish to keep your soul intact." For a fleeting second, Michael's eyes shift from sympathy to rage. I suspect he does not like me handling him as I am, but almost as fast, the emotion disappears so he can sputter his response.

"Because the being who swayed him is tasked with waking the riders." My hands fall away as I contemplate what he told me. The being responsible for calling us to their world is the same one who swayed my brother. No. No, this is not possible. The lamb is there to aid us, not oppose us; however, Michael eliminates further doubt with his following statement.

"You must resist the lamb's ability to control the riders." Michael's choking gasps are but a distant sound to my confused mind. If this lamb holds so much power, could this vile, wicked creature have already afflicted my other brothers with the same magic?

"Tell me of Pestilence and War. How do they fare in their mission?"

"Failed. The-they, too, have become lost to the lamb's influence," he replies through each wheezed breath he desperately sucks in.

"I must find them and right this wrong."

"NO! I mean, it is too late to change their minds, yet you still have a mission to fulfill. Once completed, we must hope they will find their way back to us. Find their way home. The reason our creator blocked your view of their fall. He feared the lamb's influence might be capable of reaching you even in slumber. This is also why I came to talk to you without your brother's involvement."

"Is that so?"

"You must complete your task, Famine. You cannot allow yourself to be swayed as the other riders did."

"What is your end goal, Michael?"

"I wish to end the ones who have spat on their creator's memory. The ones who have fallen far from his grace yet still command a large piece of his heart. I wish to release him from the agony of watching their failures."

"And what's in it for you?"

"Nothing. I gain nothing but the knowledge I have ended his long torment."

"Hmmm."

"You do not believe me?"

"No, I do not. There is always something to gain, which means there is always an ulterior motive. Even for one of the grand warriors of this realm."

"Need I remind you—" Michael snaps as he approaches me. His clenched fist and snarled lip show that he intends to remind me what he feels I have failed to recall.

"You needn't do anything. I know my task. It seems maybe you are the one who has forgotten yours."

"So I can count on you to follow your duty?"

"You can count on more than that because I will find this lamb, make them watch while I obliterate their world, and then force this wicked creature to break Thanatos's seal. Only to be rewarded with me ending their existence. Where can I find this lamb?"

"The lamb is not your priority, Rider!"

"And when did you become the soul who determined my task, Angel?"

"You riders never learn. You will fall to this deceiver and, in doing so, will fail in your mission... just as they have."

"This is still not your decision to make. Now tell me where I will find the lamb who dared afflict my brothers in such a way to make them turn their back on their task."

"A heinous vile son of Adam has captured the lamb, but one who will aid you in your task."

"You wish me to work with someone you refer to as heinous and vile?"

"Consider him as nothing less than a tool to achieve your goal. One I assure you will aid you in your journey."

"Why? Why would any mortal aid the riders sent to remove them?"

"The group he traveled with punished this son of Adam."

"The question remains. What did this mortal do to his kind to garner such punishment?"

"He attempted to halt the lamb's dark magic from afflicting your brother." Fury once again courses through me. So one mortal attempted to aid Thanatos throughout his mission, and these others thought to thwart him. They will soon learn the folly of their actions.

Laughing, I walk away to the clips and clops of my horse trailing behind me as my scythe and scales return to their position at my side. These mortals have been weighed, measured, and found wanting. The lamb will not sway me from destroying everything they hold dear, nor will I permit my brothers to interfere.

Just as the lamb has done to my brothers, I will make them all pay. But I have other plans for the one who believed they could control a rider. The lamb will not get off as easy. Once I discover the identity of this son of Adam or daughter of Eve, I will make this mortal wish they never interfered with our task. I will find the lamb regardless of what Michael believes, and when I do, I will make them…. *Suffer.*

Chapter Three: Return of Sausage Fingers.

I've heard it said you should never cave to evil. That you should turn the other cheek and forgive. But how do you forgive a monster sent to torment you?

NO. NO WAY IS THIS man standing before me with his hand clamped around my throat. Death killed him; he told me as much. He promised me. How could Nevil still live when so many others have fallen?

But here he is, standing inches from me with the same smug goddamn grin he used to wear in Death's horde. And not just

Nevil has survived. It seems Cammie is alive, well, and still as useless as ever. I am beyond screwed right now. He will repay me every ounce of pain inflicted on him, and if the scars covering his face are any clue, the rider tortured him.

I should have run the instant Raum revealed himself to me. After all, I knew what he wanted. It's the only reason the damn Birdman keeps showing up. He wants all four riders released. Although, in reality, he may not want Death to come back since everything the other riders keep telling me is that he opposes their task.

One of these damn days, that demon and I will have it out. Prior to this happening, the only thing I have to do is figure out what his weakness is. So I can exploit it when the time comes. Right now, I have another asshole to contend with.

Even though this reunion should terrify me, what has my hands trembling is knowing another rider is on his way. My eyes move from the man before me to the scrap of paper in my hand. I know it's a pointless hope, but I can't help it. I have to see the name.

Famis.

Famine. I have released fucking Famine upon the world, and from everything Pestilence and War have told me, he is not too fond of the people I have been trying so hard to protect. This means they could all fall if something happens to the two riders I have claimed as family.

Shit!

I can't believe I released another damn rider. Unlike when I released War to save Pestilence, I had no intention of doing the same to spare my miserable life. Who the hell knew the seal only had to be in my hand when it broke to work?

With Wayne and Trevor in the wind, I don't know what happened to our camp or what forces Pestilence and War will have to face because it's clear these assholes had help and not of the mortal kind. The scary part is Nevil forcing me to break the third seal. What does this asshole hope to gain by this, and how did he even find the damn thing?

I suppose these are all questions I'll figure out. As for right now, here's hoping the riders I call family can pull my ass out of this shitstorm I somehow landed in. If possible, before I find out if Famine is a friend or foe.

The hand around my throat tightens, and Nevil brings his head in front of mine. A long, jagged scar now covers his face from his right temple to below his left jawline. Most of the tissue around his right eye is so damaged it is hard to conceive how he sees through the ragged flesh that once represented an eyelid.

"Miss me?"

"With every shot so far, but if you give me my bow and arrows, we'll see if I can rectify it."

"I see you haven't lost that sharp tongue of yours."

"Well, you already know my stance on the best way to deal with assholes."

"By informing them they are—"

"In fact, an asshole. Yep, that would be the one, and I can promise you it hasn't changed."

"You know Avalon, I wanted to cut your tongue out the last time we saw one another. I'm glad I didn't. I have such plans for the wicked wagging thing."

"Sorry, not interested. Lucky for you, you still have faithful old Cammie, who appears more than willing to quench your thirst."

"That she does. I might add that she does so very well, but Avalon," he leans closer until mere inches separate us. "the gratification I will experience while I torture you... well, for this, there is no comparison. Anything else you would like to say?"

"Lucky me. Another miserable prick who believes I'll cower to them. I'll enjoy proving you wrong."

"You will cower, and this time I promise…. I'll make you beg." He pulls back, eager to see my reaction, but like every other prick I've ever encountered, I won't give it to him any more than I gave it to them. If he wants to see fear, he'll have to look in the mirror when the third horseman arrives. Maybe then he'll get his damn wish. And if the whipping winds are any warning, I would have to say he won't have to wait long.

"Babe, should we be… um—you know?" Cammie asks, flicking her head toward the door.

"Offering a sacrificial lamb?"

"Yeah. It's what he said we should do. Right?"

"So he did. Such a shame my playtime will have to wait until he's had his fill of you. And looking at you now tells me it shouldn't take long. I want you to know, Avalon, that for what minuscule time you have remaining in this world, it will be fraught with agony, suffering, and loss."

"You think I'm afraid to die, asshole?" I snap my question.

"You should be."

"Too bad for you, I'm not."

"Would you change your mind if I told you a certain rider is not the one you will find waiting to collect your soul? No, I think it's only fair with how big of a pain in the ass you've been to him that a certain sleek black raven should have this honor." Of course, this asshole and the birdman freak would have to be allies because why wouldn't they?

"Well, Nevil, since he wants me to break four seals, I reckon I still have some time to spare."

"Who said he wants you to break the fourth seal? The last one should be able to do what the other two couldn't, and from what I understand, aside from our former failed leader, he's the one you don't want to see."

"Death never failed." I know I shouldn't let him rattle me, but I still have an overwhelming desire to defend the horseman I once considered my rider.

"Since he let a piece of ass—even a fine piece of ass like yours." He lowers his voice and moves closer. "Something I've seen up close and personal." He winks before bringing his finger to his mouth to suggest I should keep this between us. He doesn't have to worry about me saying anything… but hitting is not out of the question. "Shh, don't tell Cammie I said that because she's kind of the jealous sort. She might stick a knife through your heart on principle alone."

"Did you say something, sweetheart?"

Nevil leans away from me to kiss the idiot who wandered up next to us before finishing. "Just confirming something that Avalon long figured happened but was never really sure,"

This must satisfy the bobblehead, who strolls back over to investigate whatever stupid ass thing has captured her attention. With Cammie occupied once more, he brings his attention back over to me. "absolutely fucking happened." He presses his mouth against my ear. "And not by Bob alone. With all this in mind, Avalon, I can confirm Death failed on a monumental level."

As bad as it always was knowing Bob raped me, having Nevil tell me this is so much freaking worse. But I can't think about it now. Right now, I need to keep this asshole talking. I can throw up later.

"What the hell do you think you'll get out of this? When Famine comes, you can't be so stupid as to believe he will spare you."

"Are you worried about me, A?"

"Don't fuckin' call me that. My friends call me A, something you will never be."

"Or what? What do you think you can do to stop me, Avalon? Especially since you don't have the protection of a certain rider."

I could reply with one of my typical snarky comebacks, but what's the point? I don't have any desire to continue this conversation, and every time I engage, it only prolongs the misery of facing this asshole who still has my throat gripped in his beefy hand. The fact I can still breathe astonishes me since he has tightened his hold with each retort I utter.

"Um… babe, can we maybe move this party along? I'm getting bored, and this place stinks."

"Cammie, we discussed this already." I don't have to look at her to know she's pouting. I can tell by the way the asshole keeps rolling his eyes. "This is the safest place for us, at least for a little while."

"I know I sure as hell feel all safe and toasty in this shit hole."

"No one said you get to stay in here, bitch," Cammie snarls, her voice dripping with venom as she steps closer. The musty smell of the old, unused space mixes with the tension in the air, making it almost palpable, and the dim lighting only adds to the eerie atmosphere. The walls of this confined area seem to close in around us, taking this situation from shitty to suffocating in a matter of seconds. Cammie's eyes blaze with anger while her hands clench into tight fists. Her heavy breathing fills the room, drowning out any other noise.

"Now you've gone and pissed off my girl."

"Oops."

"I am so going to fucking enjoy this." I don't know what's more distressing: the glint in his eyes, the glee in his voice, or the wicked grin covering his face. Before I can register what the hell is happening, he yanks my restraints free, hits me hard enough to make the world swim around us, and tosses me over his shoulder. As I tried to regain my senses, I could hear the distant echoes of footsteps and the sound of dripping water in what I can only call a cement bunker. Something I see when he carries me out into a long hallway.

Looking around his body, I can make out a thin sliver of light ahead. With any luck, it's a door and an option for my escape. But when I hear his heavy footfalls on the metal grating of the stairs, I know he plans to take me outside. He's taken care of the first part of my escape plan, which means I'm one step closer to getting out of this shitty situation. Figuring his idea is to toss my ass in the first muddy patch of ground he finds. I admit to being confused when he doesn't but marches away from the door and further into a field.

Looking back at where we came from, I breathe a sigh of relief because unless you are on this side of the damn thing, it doesn't look like anything more than a mound of grass and dirt. Something a person or rider could miss easier than I care to admit. This is when I see the thing he's marching toward. A colossal ass pole in the middle of the field.

What the fuck is he planning?

Nevil doesn't leave me wondering for long when he drops me to my feet. If I have any hope of surviving this asshole, it's now or never. When he bends to grab me, I slam my head forward, catching him in the bridge of his nose, but I don't stop there…I can't. His first wave of discomfort morphs into howls of pain when I slam my knee between his legs. Nevil drops to the ground in front of me. I grab the back of his head to push it down while

I bring my knee up. My hope was it would knock him out, but when he remained upright, I balled my fist up and smashed it into his already mangled nose.

This puts him on his ass, giving me the chance to run. I waste no time sprinting for the tree line. The thick overgrowth should help conceal me if I can make it in there before he regains his footing.

Somewhere behind me, I can hear Cammie screaming for him to get up. He has to stop me. That I'm escaping. To which Nevil replies with a gruff, he has eyes, followed with a definitive bitch declaration. I guess Cammie isn't the important princess she thought she was. I could have told her Nevil's loyalty only goes so far. But the princess issue is her problem because I have issues of my own to contend with. My problem is, in addition to listening to her screeched caterwauling, I can hear his heavy footsteps slamming against the packed earth, and they are without a doubt getting closer, not further away.

Shit-shit-shit-shit.

I'm within ten yards of reaching the trees I thought could magically protect me from view when Nevil's hand tangles in my hair while he yanks me back. The abrupt shift from flat-out running to flying backward has me on my ass. This time, Nevil doesn't waste time throwing me over his shoulder. He drags me back to the damn pole by my hair. I never had issues with my hair being pulled, not that I like it, but it was also something I could handle. But right now, it feels like he is scalping me without a knife to help with the process.

By the time we arrive back at the pole, my head is pounding, my ass is throbbing, and if I didn't know any better, I would have to say my back is bloody from being dragged over the rough terrain.

Nevil yanks me to my feet, jerks my arms over my head, and chains me to the damn metal pole and my feet to something cemented in the ground.

"So… this is your big plan?" I pant while twisting my hands to see if I can break loose from the thick chains binding me.

"You'll see soon enough," he replies, looking towards the sky. A sky that isn't just gray but black from the coming storm. The coming rider.

"You know, Avalon, I can't wait to see what he'll do. It almost makes me wish I could watch it all unfold. Almost. But since I have no intention of dying today, I'll be returning to the safety that place can offer me. You, on the other hand, won't be so fortunate. And if by some incredible stroke of luck you survive this shit, I promise you this…I won't forget about the shit you pulled out here."

He runs his hand under his nose to remove the blood I caused from my attack. Just prior to him returning to the waiting dimwit, he gives me a parting gift when he spits in my face. Why the hell do people do this?

Shit, if he leaves me here, and another tornado touches down, I'll have no prospect of surviving this time. The damn thing will rip my arms from my body before tossing me aside like some damn rag doll. I doubt a barn will materialize out of thin air to shelter me.

Am I terrified? Hell yeah. I don't know any person who wouldn't be. Will I give this bastard the satisfaction of seeing my fear before I die? Hell no.

"I'd like to see you escape this time, Apple."

"Fuck you, prick." His laugh increases as he meanders back toward the door held open by the dimwit. The sounds from the whipping winds shift from a pending storm to a freight train, and I know my day is about to go from bad to worse. With my arms pinned over my head, I try to shield it from the flying debris the best that I can.

I lift my chin enough to see Nevil wave before he slams the door closed. The sun is all but blotted out by the clouds while the thunder rumbles toward me. Shouldn't this sound be all around this field? Because it's not... it's in front of me and coming in my direction.

I squint my eyes, hoping it will help me see better in the low light, and it does. The first thing I recognize is the ground vibrating under my feet. Followed by an unmistakable musk filling the air. The reality of what I will soon face invades my thoughts, so I struggle to break free from the restraints. If I wasn't living this nightmare, I would have told the person they are full of shit, but I am, and the hell I'm about to face is all too real.

For the first time since Nevil dragged my ass out here, I'm unsure how I will survive this shit. Because what I discover can only be described as a damn stampede, and these freaking animals are coming straight for me.

The closer they come, the more I realize I'm not the only one afraid because their eyes are wild with fear and panic. They aren't coming for me; they're fleeing from something.

Wonderful! Just bloody fantastic because I have a pretty clear idea of what they're running from.

While most of the animals surge around the place I'm anchored to, several of them try to go through me, and the impact is jarring. I figured the force would rip the pole from the ground and leave me trampled under their feet. It doesn't, and as ridiculous as this may sound, my stupid thoughts shift to wondering how far into the earth they imbedded this damn thing to withstand this.

Their paws claw at my body, their tails slash at my skin, and their fangs rip across my flesh, but none stop to enjoy the tasty mortal morsel left for them to devour. Nope, because they're smart enough to hightail their asses as far away from here as they can get before the damn rider shows up.

The next thing I notice are the trees in the distance, bending at awkward angles. What the hell could make a tree do that? My answer comes with a sound I've already experienced once. It's a damn noise I will never forget. A tornado. It has to be, and with it comes the damn wind pinning me in place and taking away my ability to move. And just my damn luck, not a barn in sight.

When the last animal scampers past, the freight train noises morph into the roaring of a crashing plane. The hurricane-force winds make it impossible to move, so the best I can manage is a small head roll, but it's just enough to realize it's not a tornado coming… It's a wall of water as tall as a three-story house.

Shit-shit-shit.

"Fucking hell!" I yell because what else can I do?

"Have faith, little one." The damn mystical voice is back, and now it's asking me to believe I won't drown. No helpful advice. No words of wisdom, just a simple stupid, have faith bullshit response. Well, I hate to break it to him. Faith is one thing I don't have much of, causing the first scream to rip from my lungs.

"Pessy, War!"

This is the only thing I get out before the wall crashes into me.

Chapter Four: Meet and Greet.

I DON'T KNOW WHAT'S WORSE, the freezing cold water or the pain I can only associate with running head-on into a brick wall. Panic overwhelms me as I watch the wave racing in my direction. Since I could barely handle the pre-wave hit I just suffered, how the hell will I ever survive the beast barreling down on the place I'm restrained?

"Take a deep breath, Avalon. You will need it."

"Gee thanks, Dick Tracy… because I couldn't deduce that shit on MY OWN!" I scream at the disembodied voice swirling in the air.

"Now, Avalon. Take it now." I suck in a deep breath as the wave pummels against me. Jesus Christ, I don't know how every bone in my body didn't snap on impact. I want to scream out from the indescribable pain, but I can't risk losing even a bubble of the precious oxygen I sucked in before it submerged my entire body. I struggle to break the damn surface, but the leg restraints hold me under. Fuck, I'm going to drown. No matter how I twist, turn, or struggle, the surging current keeps me tethered to where I know I will meet my end. All of this struggling is only using up the oxygen faster, but you try to remain calm in a situation that finds you swallowed up by a damn tsunami.

"Soon, just a moment more, Avalon. You will receive a respite soon." Again, I dare you to remain calm, cool, and collected in this fucked up situation.

The pressure on my head subsides just enough for me to look up. This is when I realize something is forcing the water apart.

"Take another breath, Avalon." The strain I detect in the voice of my invisible friend tells me they are the reason I can exhale before sucking in another lungful of the precious damn oxygen the water is depriving me of. I no sooner have what I need to last a few more minutes when the water crashes around me again. Hindsight being twenty-twenty, I think I prefer the damn tornado to this shit.

With my head directed towards the sky, I have just enough light to see bolts of lightning rip across the atmosphere and flocks of birds trying their best to avoid it. I don't know how long my invisible friend can keep this up, but I'm guessing not long. I don't even know how any of this is possible because we sure the shit aren't around any oceans. In fact, we're hundreds of miles away from it. Unless, of course, they moved closer while I was unconscious, but I don't feel like I was out for days. Hours? Maybe. But not days.

This time, I force myself to remain still to preserve the oxygen he keeps granting me. Is it easy? Hell no. But like I said before, I don't know how many more times he can part the seas. The thing is, the force of the water against my body makes doing this much more difficult. It's like the surge is trying to force the air out of my lungs. Desperate to claim me as one of its victims.

Jesus Christ, of all the things I thought would bring about the end of my life, water wasn't one of them. The roar of the crushing wave is a reminder of how far I have come since the day when all I wanted was to glimpse the ocean one last time. To smell the salt water and listen as the gulls cried. Damn, I thought my life was crazy then. Well, look at me now.

"Last time, Avalon," the voice whispers through panted breaths. I force my chin against the rush of water, only to have it catch me and slam my head back. The pain is almost unbearable, but I grit my teeth and keep my eyes open, waiting for the gap to appear and grant me another couple of seconds. If I could ask my invisible savior a question, it would be this: Is it the last time because the water will recede, or is it the last time because you don't have the strength to do it again?

This will be over soon, one way or the other, so in the end, I suppose it doesn't matter. I'll either run out of oxygen and drown, or the water will recede, and I'll have to face the next rider. Right now, I'm not sure which option would be better.

"Pull yourself out of the water, Avalon." How the hell does he propose I do this? I'm tethered to this pole with my arms bound to a heavy metal object that reminds me of a door knocker you would expect to find at a haunted house, and my feet are secured to the bar at the bottom of the pole. I can't move an inch, so I'm not going anywhere.

"Avalon, you must liberate your feet. NOW!" My heart races as I desperately try to release the chain from the bar. I kick and tug and use all my strength, but nothing works. I know if I don't get free soon, I'm dead. Something I'm not too keen to experience. At least not yet. I have an asshole I need to teach a lesson to first.

As I am about to give up, I feel a slight shift in the bar. It's not a lot, but it's enough to slip the chains around my ankles from under it. I don't waste any time pushing off the bottom; I launch myself upward in a desperate bid to escape. The damn water isn't done with me yet as it tries just as hard to drag me back down, but I don't let it stop me. With the last of my strength, I grab the metal ring and pull myself to the top of the pole, hoping it's enough to lift my head out of the surging wave.

The sun's warmth on my face is the first thing I register. It seems I'm not the only thing beating back the signs of this rider's arrival. For the moment, I'm alive, but who knows how long before the rider unleashes his next hell? I have to be ready.

My body burns with exhaustion as I struggle against the force of the surf beating against me. My legs feel like the weight of the world is anchored to them, making my arms tremble from the strain. But with my heart racing from the adrenaline and fear, it gives me a strength I didn't have before. Each breath comes in shallow bursts as I fight to keep my head above the water. The longer I stay here, the harder it becomes to stay afloat. My muscles ache, and I can feel my grip slipping. It's only a matter of time before I lose my hold.

My heart is pounding in my chest, my limbs trembling with fear and adrenaline. My fingers are clenched so tight around the metal ring that it hurts. I try to steady my breathing, but I can't seem to find the rhythm because I'm exhausted. My lungs are aching for air, and my throat is parched and dry. The water laps at my skin, making the cold seep in deeper, numbing my senses and loosening my grip.

"Shit." This is my only thought as my fingers slip inch by painful inch from around the ring responsible for saving my damn life.

Finally, the water recedes, and the last thing I hear before I sink below the surface is a faint, "Almost done with this part. A second longer is all you need."

"This part? This part! No more goddamn parts. I've had all the parts I can take for one damn day!" With my lips trembling, the sentiment came out, more stutter than the yell I was going for. Regardless, I've fought this much. What more could be in store for me?

Maybe I should have kept this thought buried deep because there's more. Lots more.

"You have got to be shitting me," I scream because as the water recedes, something new takes its place. The rushing flood has unearthed trees, grass, and a shit ton of mud. A landslide. Because why the hell not? "ASSHOLES!"

At least I have one thing going for me. The damn mud isn't as high as the water, so I hope to keep my head above the surface. How do I propose to do that? Well… with a bit of luck and a lot of hand strength.

When the landslide hits me, it's a hell of a lot stronger than the water. The unmistakable crunch of bones breaking is the first thing I register before the intense pain ravages my weakened body and has me howling.

The worst part is since my feet are no longer tethered, it rips me off the pole. So much for my superior hand grip. The only thing keeping me from being carried away is the chains still clamped around my wrist and secured to the metal ring I held until three seconds ago.

The mud and earth are so strong that they pull me away from the pole, and debris threatens to drag me under. When it covers my chin and creeps ever closer to my nose, the fear I felt moments ago returns almost as fast as it vanished. But this is when a strange thing occurs. The mud solidifies around me. The abrupt change makes it impossible to move, but at least it is no longer trying to drag me under.

This is when a familiar sound echoes around me. It is the unmistakable sound of a horse approaching. Ten to one, this isn't going to be a friend. A hundred to one, I won't find War or Pessy. A thousand to one, the individual I will discover when they move into view is none other than….

"Well, what do we have here?"

"Famine, I presume."

"What gave it away? The death and destruction I left in my wake?"

"No, more like that big ass horse, the clothes you opted to put on, not to mention the damn scale and scythe. Because none of these things scream human."

"These items alone led you to believe I am the third rider?"

"Let's just call it intuition." Or firsthand knowledge since I'm the dumbass who called you here. If everything I've heard is true, I need to use care when broaching this subject. At least until he pulls me out of the destruction left in the wake of his arrival.

Here's hoping I can keep my damn mouth shut long enough for this to happen.

Chapter Five: Unearthed.

~Avalon Summer 2026~

WHEN I MOVE MY FOCUS from the sky to him, the first thing I register is his eyes. They are forest green and so damn bright. Almost to the point of glowing, this alone would be astonishing, but with black lines running from the whites to the iris, shocking doesn't quite describe them. They're startling, scary, unique, and amazing, all in the same instant. Something I have never seen before and doubt I will witness again.

Just like I'm assessing him, it appears he is doing the same thing to me, and when his lip curls in what I can only describe as disgust, I know I'm in trouble. Because one thing is for sure....

It doesn't appear to be a promising sign.

There are numerous reasons he would have done this. I'm sure I'm not looking fresh as a daisy since I've been a prisoner of a sadistic prick for days, and now I'm entombed in this damn mud. On the upside, the damn tsunami washed away the stench of sweat and body odor, only to replace it with fish, dirt, and destroyed earth. Since I can't move anything below my neck, I'm stuck waiting for him to do what the others have done before him. It's up to this horseman to help me out of this mess.

Based on previous encounters, I realize the riders are hellbent on following their path when they first arrive, but I've always been immune to their mission. If we look at the other riders' arrivals, Pestilence saved my friends and me from strolling into an ambush set by Raum. War pulled not only my ass but Renny out of the wreckage of a destroyed barn, so it's not so farfetched to believe Famine will not do the same.

But he doesn't.

This damn horseman rides away.

"Hey, you can't just leave me here."

"It is precisely what I plan to do. After all, I'm here to end your life, not save it."

"Hilarious, Rider. Now help me out of this shit." I yell, but the sounds of the horse's hooves clomping on dry mud are moving further away, not closer.

"Rider. Get your ass back here and pull me out of this shit."

I struggle against the mud, trying to free myself, but it's like cement preventing any movement, encasing me in what the rider believes will be my tomb. But when the earth encapsulating me shudders, I know this day is far from over. The slight movement shifts almost to a steady vibration, and I strain my neck, trying to see what's coming. The only thing I can make out is a dark and ominous cloud on the horizon. Fear wraps its icy tendrils around my heart as I realize that whatever it is, it's headed straight toward where I'm stuck.

The cloud is almost upon me now, and the reality of what is coming my way sinks in.

Shit-shit-shit. It's a damn swarm of insects. Of course, Famine would bring a swarm of fuckin locusts with him. Because why wouldn't he?

As they close in, I can't help but laugh at the irony of this shitty situation. For years, I've carried the burden of being the one who set the riders free, and now with only one seal left—the one a year and a half ago I would have snapped without a second thought—I'm going to die before finishing the task assigned to me. My fate is to die alone, trapped in the mud.

Mud. It's laughable. I mean, how the hell could you not laugh? The entire situation is ridiculous. So this is what I do. I laugh.

"Look, dying mortal, you will not be alone for long, for I see two more of your kind have revealed themselves, opting to face my retribution now rather than wilting and dying a slow, painful death. Perhaps your kind is not as idiotic as we believed," he said, his voice carrying back to me from a distance that wasn't as far away as I had assumed.

If I were you, I wouldn't bet on that one rider if the two you're talking about are who I think you might be referencing.

The mental image of big bad Nevil and dimwit Cammie being devoured by a horde of teeny—tiny insects summoned by the rider is hilarious. I think my reaction to this situation is confusing to him.

The rider jumps off his horse and strides towards me, his eyes blazing with determination. He raises the scythe above his head and swings it down with all his might. The blade slices through the mud like butter before freeing me from my dirt prison. Since the damn bugs are still on their way, I almost want to ask him to put me back in until he lifts his hand, and as fast as the swarm appeared, they're gone. It's like they hit an invisible line, and as they attempt to breach this barrier, they just disintegrate in a fiery little display.

"Nice trick. Thanks for the save," I mutter while peeling chunks of mud clinging to my clothes and hair away.

"I didn't come here to save you," he growls. "I came to remove you from this realm."

"Damn, if I had a quarter every time one of you riders said this shit, I'd be a rich woman. Well, if you all hadn't wiped out our previous life when money was a thing." The rider narrows his eyes at me.

"Your defiance is amusing, mortal. But it will not save you from your fate."

I roll my eyes. "You riders and your obsession with fate. Why don't you try living in the present for once?"

The rider's grip on his scythe tightens. "You speak of things you do not understand. Our duty is to maintain balance and restore the natural order."

"And what about our free will?" I challenge. "What about the right to choose our own path?"

The rider snorts. "Free will is an illusion. You mortals are captive to your desires and impulses. You cannot see beyond your own selfish needs."

I scoff. "And you riders are any different? You act like you're above us, but you're just as flawed as we are. Maybe even more so, considering the mess you've made of things."

The rider's eyes flash with anger. "You dare to insult us? You will pay for your insolence."

*****

As you can guess, my stupid mouth got me in trouble again. More baffling is how the hell I ended up back in Nevil's bunker. Something I would love to hear, especially since I don't remember Famine hitting me, nor do I have any telltale signs of being struck.

"Wait-wait-wait, it's only because of me you're here." It seems Nevil is finally getting a taste of his own medicine since Famine has him by his throat, hoisting Sausage in the air. His feet dangling several feet off the ground. The only thing I can say is it couldn't happen to a nicer asshole.

"Doubtful."

"You better tell him, bitch, or I swear I'll throttle you."

"Let me give you some advice, Nevil. When you want something from someone, the worse thing you can do is to threaten the person you hope will pull your miserable ass out of the damn fire." His glare confirms I'm not the one he plans to make suffer if I don't speak up, which is the only reason I say anything. "He's telling the truth because I had no intention of breaking your seal."

"You are the lamb?"

"That's what you riders keep telling me, although my given name has nothing to do with the woolly little buggers." In a turn of events I didn't see coming, Famine stalks to where I'm chained, grabs my throat, and slams me against the wall. Once again, my stupid thoughts wander to the same pointless observation I've made in the past. Why do assholes always go for the throat?

"You will hold your godforsaken tongue, you wretched, vile beast."

"I'm wretched and vile? Damn Nevil, if he thinks this of me, imagine what he believes about you? Oh, and P.S. rider, I'm not an animal."

"He said shut your fucking mouth, Avalon!"

Famine whips his head in Nevil's direction. "Why did you call this creature Avalon?"

"First, I'm still not a creature. Second, don't you dare start calling me a daughter of Eve either! And third, he called me Avalon because it's my damn name."

"The mortals of this world named you after the mystical isle?"

"Don't know shit about no mystical island, but yeah, my dumb ass parents named me Avalon. Guess they were fans of King Arthur."

"Who is this king you speak of?"

"A fictional character, you know, the one who supposedly pulls Excalibur from the damn stone."

"No. You are not making any sense. Why did I dream of you?"

"You think I know why you riders attached yourself to me 'cause I can one thousand percent confirm I don't have the first fuckin' clue."

"I do not understand what your words mean. You will speak in the common tongue."

"I am speaking in the damn common tongue. Common for 2026, not 2000 BCE."

"Allow me to remove this garbage from your view, my lord."

"I am no lord. I am Famine, the third rider. The bringer of decay and despair. And you are not worthy of judging her, but my scales are," he growls, slamming his scales down on the table. I have to admit, what he does next shocks the shit out of me.

He slices his finger to place a drop of blood on one weighing tray, then yanks my hand up and does the same to mine, only putting my drop on the other side. When the scales do nothing, his eyes shoot to mine. "What did you do to them?"

"I don't know what you're talking about."

"How did you break them? Is it with the same magic you used to bewitch my brothers?"

"Bewitch? I assure you, I don't have a pointy hat or a flying broom."

"Cease all attempts to sway me!"

"Huh?" Okay, I have to admit I am all kinds of confused right now. Does he really believe I have magical powers? What the hell did Death tell this rider?

"You will answer my question. What sorcery did you employ to manipulate this?"

"Since you've been watching me like a hawk this whole time, I think you know I didn't do shit."

"You. Now!" He barks while looking at Cammie. She hesitates while she moves her desperate eyes over to the man she hopes will help her. An act he has no intention of doing. The dimwit should have known Sausage Fingers is only out to save his own miserable hide.

"Nev–Nevil," she says with a tremble. But Famine is done waiting. He snatches out and drags his blade across her finger while forcing her forward enough to make her offering to his scales.

The scales sink down, almost touching the table, but not quite. The rider looks at her with disgust before he throws her hand aside, wipes the blood from the scale, and demands Nevil step forward. Nevil, being the dumbass he is, declines.

"This was not a request. You will give me your hand so I can extract what I need, or I will grant you the privilege of meeting my scythe."

The second the drop touches the dish, the asshole holds his breath. Is it any surprise when the scale drops to the table?

Chapter Six: Brothers

I T HAS BEEN MONTHS SINCE the lamb went missing. We scoured the area she was last seen in, and nothing. As hard as War and I attempted to pick up her trail, we continue to come up empty. This is beyond concerning because War's tracking abilities are unparalleled in this world. It did not take us long to realize what had occurred.

One of our Father's fallen happened, and if we had to guess, it was the fallen who had interfered with our arrival this entire time. Raum. He has access to resources of his realm to hide her from us. Why our Father would allow such a travesty is something I cannot fathom, yet he has.

Ellie blamed herself for weeks after Avalon's disappearance, stating it was only because of her and Duck that Avalon was out there. She should have known something was not right when they discovered something left in the exact location Duck went to. It wasn't until War assured her it was the fault of the cretins who took the lamb, not hers, that Ellie stopped blaming herself. But it wasn't until he promised her it was a mistake he would make the assholes who were behind it regret the instant he discovered who they were that she smiled for the first time since the day Avalon vanished.

Then he did something that made it clear he still held a deep affection for the lamb. He pronounced Ellie and Duck under his protection. Which is all but declaring these two his family. Did he do it because he felt guilty he could not find Avalon? Perhaps, but I believe these two lost children touched his heart much as Wren captured mine.

War encourages Ellie to continue her lessons with me, and since procuring our new accommodations, they now live with him as his daughter and son. Something his chosen has embraced.

Ember is quite an extraordinary woman. She is the perfect balance for my militant brother and someone who has helped him move past his feelings for the woman Thanatos has chosen as the soul who holds his heart. Ember is strong and does not allow War to push her around. She fights beside him and his army, never behind them. Although, if any were to harm her, they would soon realize their mistake when he claimed their life. Just as I would do for Greer and Wren.

"Hey, handsome, you want to share the burden?" Greer asks me from the bedroom door of the home we took as ours. Within a month of Avalon going missing, War and I secured a more permanent camp.

It was a small town overrun with bandits. Did these miscreants build it? No, they stole it from honest people attempting to rebuild their lives. We learned about it when a family who escaped the raiders found our encampment. In what has become our custom, we offered them shelter. War and I assured them they could stay a night or until they were back on their feet or remain with our alliance and under our protection for as long as they liked. The choice was theirs and theirs alone to make. Something I believe shocked them, but what they did not know yet is that my brother and I had turned from our task. Opting to live among the sons of Adam and daughters of Eve with the people who chose us to be their family.

When they realized we were not the monsters humanity once thought we were, the man told us about the community. After hearing about the defenses he and his former allies had put into place, War and I decided it would make the perfect base for our growing group.

Guided by Zach, War and I exacted revenge on the raiders, who had committed the same atrocities against the former residents of this place that we had liberated from their control. Once done, we offered the men and women they held as slaves the option to remain with us. Without hesitation, they agreed.

We placed the eldest and those incapable of fighting in the innermost dwellings while the soldiers took the outer homes. War and I selected the residences on opposite sides of the entrance to this community. If anyone wishes to harm the ones who stay with us, they must get past War and me first.

Once the community was up and running, I returned to the State where I had met the woman I would choose as my future wife—a term I am still adjusting to—and my son. I had one mission, and I could not fail in it. Somehow, I needed to convince Noll and Hope to join us. I knew it would be difficult, but it is also what Avalon would have wanted… no, insisted. She would have insisted we offer them a place here. So, I did what I believed would make her happy. I ensured their safety.

It took several days of convincing and promises if this place was not for them, I would help him return to his rundown cabin. This constant assurance finally made him relent and pack his rickety wagon to follow me to his new home. Something Hope delights in, as she now has kids to play with. She has even given my militant brother a new name. Grumpy Gills. Although he pretends this angers him, I do not miss the grin he grants her each time she skips away. Noll also seems content since he has set up a store for the members of this community. The one thing he guarantees is that the sugary blobs that my Renny loves are always in stock.

We also know that Famine arrived a week after Avalon went missing. War and I both believed our brother would seek us out, but he did not. We would have thought we were mistaken if not for the news we received regarding his destruction. When we went out looking for him, we were met with the stench of decay from the rotting crops lost in his wake. Leaving no doubt the lamb had broken his seal. But what we don't understand is why she would do this.

We both told her that of the four Riders, our brother Famine was the most likely to fulfill the task our creator assigned to us. A bitter pill for her since Avalon knew without calling Famine here, Thanatos could never return. And even though she told us she had to move past our brother, War and I could feel the hurt consuming her heart at the thought of never seeing him again.

Turning my attention from the scenery outside our home to my chosen, I smile. "La meva bella temptació."

"After all this time, I still love to hear you call me this."

"And I mean it as much today as I did then."

"You know how to make a girl go all weak in the knees, handsome. But you already knew this, and now I think you are trying to distract me from the question I asked. So how about it?

Wanna tell me what has you leaning against the wall staring out our bedroom window?"

"We have to tell him."

"Tell who what?" Greer's hand on my arm pulls my focus from the fading light as day slips away to dusk. Without a second thought, I wrap her in my arms. Her scent invades my senses, and I inhale it deep, wanting to drink her in, hoping it will calm my racing thoughts. She and Wren are everything I love about this world.

"Thanatos. We have to travel to him and do the unthinkable."

"Which is?"

"Tell him his apple is no longer under our protection and most likely travels with our brother."

"But that's a good thing, right? I mean, if she's with your brother, she has to be safe, and if anyone can change the mind of you riders, she can. She's done it three times already."

"Famine is not like War and I. We never wanted to see humanity fail, not truly. Besides, it is distressing that Famine has not sought us out yet. It leads us to believe he has no intention of finding his brothers."

"After all this time, why wouldn't he want to see you two?"

"Because he does not wish to hear our thoughts on this subject." I should tell her that by doing this, he has all but declared he opposes our choice, which can lead to only one outcome. Something our militant brother knows all too well.

The simple truth is this… if Famine is set on his path, he will leave War and me with no other option but to meet him on the field of battle. Even with the two of us, our brother commands the very world around us. From the lands to the plants, insects to seas, Famine can call them to his aid should we overwhelm him. Meaning….

It is a fight we may not be capable of winning.

~War Autumn 2026~

THIS IS A day I have been dreading since she went missing. It's the day that Pestilence and I will tell our brother of our failure to protect what he values above all else. I allow my eyes to skim over her naked frame. Ember is everything I want, yet I still owe Avalon a lot. She is the one who showed me a better way. A way that led me to the woman sleeping in our bed. If I had my choice, I would climb back into bed and stay with her until the kids return tomorrow. But I can't.

Standing, I walk over to kiss her. "Be careful."

"Are you worried about me?"

"Always." She pushes off the bed, giving me a tantalizing glimpse of her perfect breasts, and kisses me in a way that makes it difficult to leave. "Try to come home before Ellie and Duck."

"Did you have something in mind, beautiful?"

"Lots of very dirty things, Rider. Now get your ass in gear so you can come home and make me scream your name before the kids return." After she says this, she lies down and pulls the covers over her perfect body. I must force myself to slip out the door before I say fuck it and join her.

But Thanatos deserves the truth.

So I leave her to do the right thing. As I make my way to Pestilence, I can't help but think about the consequences of our actions. If Famine is against us, then we will have to fight him. And it won't be an easy battle. I know my brother's powers, and they are not to be underestimated. But we have no choice. We must protect what our creator has granted us, no matter the cost.

He is already waiting for me when I arrive at the stables we established to keep our horses out of the elements. Another thing done with Avalon in mind. It shouldn't surprise me to find Pestilence here. He is as anxious as I am to complete this task.

His face is grim, and I can tell he is just as worried as I am. We exchange a nod before traveling to where Thanatos awaits word of his Apple. As we approach the cell they hold him in, I can feel the weight of our failure heavy on my shoulders. But when we arrive, Raphael, not Thanatos, is the one we find, and I cannot halt the sense of unease.

"What brings you two here?" he asks, his voice steady.

"We have news for our brother," Pestilence says, his voice barely above a whisper.

"What news?"

"We have failed to protect her," I say, the words heavy on my tongue.

Raphael's eyes widen upon hearing my rushed confession, and I can see the sadness and disappointment in his gaze. "What do you mean?"

"Famine's seal has been broken, and we believe he has taken her with him," Pestilence says, his voice barely audible.

"Where is our brother, my old friend?" I ask, taking a step closer to the angel I have no intention of having this conversation with. We meant to have it with Thanatos, and since I will only give these answers once, it will not be to anyone other than their intended audience.

"I'm afraid he was too honest for his own good, an act that sealed his fate and placed him in nothing."

"What do you mean… nothing?" I snarl, taking a step closer to him.

"At present, he is in between worlds."

"How is this possible?"

"Our creator cast him there. Thanatos will remain until the lamb breaks his seal, or they have stripped all memories of her from his mind, so he makes no further attempt to bring down the veil."

"Why would he do this?" Pestilence asked, bewildered by what this angel had just told us.

"I don't know," he says. Sadness laces his words, and his eyes refuse to meet ours.

"Bring him out!" Pestilence and I shout in unison.

"I can't. I have been looking since our father sent him there but have been unsuccessful in communicating with him, let alone recovering him from this place. It is the entire reason I am in this cell. I had hoped it would lead me to him."

Pestilence falls silent for a moment, his gaze distant before he looks from Raphael to me. "Then our task is simple."

"Dare I ask?" Raphael must sense we will do anything to release our brother from the void our father sent him to.

"We must find the lamb, retrieve the seal, and request she call him there."

"You are going to encourage Avalon to break his seal?"

"I see no other option."

"You willingly risk releasing the final rider upon their world?"

"I don't fear what Thanatos will do as long as Avalon yet lives; however, we do worry about our other brother. He is the anomaly in this situation. It remains unclear to us what his intentions are for their world."

"Has your brother not sought you out?" Raphael asks, coming to full height. I believe he now understands the gravity of this situation and how close their world is to falling.

"No, which is unusual and rather alarming."

Raphael's constant pacing around the room is unsettling. Showing any level of distress is out of character for him. His hand stroking his chin more than once demonstrates his level of stress and uncertainty. As loyal as this angel is to our father, he holds a soft spot for the ones who captured much of our father's focus. He does not wish to see their destruction any more than Pestilence and I do. Until this moment, I believe he thought the riders would each find the thing to halt their slaughter, thus ensuring humanity's survival... but now he realizes the danger they face.

"And you do not know where the lamb is held?"

"We think if we find Famine, we will either locate her with him or close by."

"You believe Famine is hunting the lamb."

"It is unfortunate, but yes. We believe he travels with her now; if not, he is hunting for her. Hence the reason we must find her."

"And what will you do if she is with him?"

"Retrieve her," I tell him without delay or uncertainty.

"But what if Famine doesn't want to give her up?" Raphael asks, his voice no louder than a whisper. Perhaps he fears who may be listening, or maybe he's afraid our brother might hear him.

"Then we fight," I say, my voice steady despite the misgivings I feel, knowing I may soon have to fight one of my brothers.

Raphael nods, and I can see the resolve in his eyes. "Then, while you fight to retrieve the lamb, I will continue seeking a way to locate Thanatos."

"If Michael discovers you are doing this, you know it will cause problems between you and your brethren."

"I can handle Michael and the ones who follow him."

"And if you succeed, what of our father? What will you do when he learns you released our brother?" Pestilence asks.

"Ask for forgiveness."

And with those words, we set off on a journey that will forever change us.

Chapter Seven: Following Our Path

THROUGHOUT MY JOURNEY, I COULD NOT help but wonder about my brother Thanatos. He has always been the most loyal of us all, and it pains me to think of him trapped in the void between worlds. I know he would never betray our purpose as riders, so why would our father cast him aside in such a manner?

This is not the case where my other brothers are concerned.

They must know something has gone astray. We each sense the other's arrival, so I have little doubt they know I'm here, and because I have opted not to seek them out, they must be wondering what my intentions are.

I'm also sure they are missing the lamb who has bewitched them. But I have no interest in what they want. My sole purpose is to carry out my duty as the third horseman of the apocalypse. My task is to find and destroy all the food sources in this area, leaving nothing for the humans to survive on.

As I ride through the desolate fields, I can sense the hunger and desperation of those I have left behind to tell their tale of failure. They are so frail that standing seems almost impossible, but they persist in their will to live.

Yet they are not my concern. My only focus is on fulfilling my mission, and as I ride through the barren landscape, I am reminded of the enormity of this journey our father has bestowed upon us. My brothers have failed him. I have no intention of following in their footsteps. Hence, this is the reason I do not seek them out. They will attempt to sway me as they have been... something they would waste their breath on. So, I am serving them by saving them the burden of such things.

Making my way through the desolate wasteland, I can feel the emptiness and hunger that follows me. The land is barren, and the air is thick with the stench of death. It is a place of desolation, and I am its master.

If I so choose... with a flick of my wrist, I could summon forth my powers, and the crops would wither and die. The animals would fall to the ground while their flesh rots away. And as I ride through the village, the people would fall to their knees, their bodies coming to terms with the simple fact I would soon leave it wracked with pain and hunger.

Nevertheless, I ride on, my eyes fixed on the horizon. My mission is not yet complete, and there are still those who must feel the touch of my hand. And as I ride, the world trembles beneath my feet, for I am the bringer of decay and despair, and my power is absolute.

I am not without logic and can sense my brothers' growing frustration. I know they will soon seek me out. But I am not afraid. For I am Famine, I am the harbinger of the end, including theirs, if they attempt to interfere.

When we round the corner, my horse snorts from anticipation because we approach what I came for, the small community coming into view. I can hear the shouts of the people raising the alarm of my approach. Though not yet weakened by hunger, the mortals show signs of desperation, which will only worsen with time. I do not need to act fast to fulfill my mission because each town is the same. When I ride in, they are alive and thriving; when I ride out, everything is rotting or dead.

"You don't have to do this, asshole," the lamb yells as she loses her balance and stumbles behind me.

I will not permit her to ride with me nor grant her a horse as I have done with the one who forced her to bring me here. She is not worthy of such luxury. Consider it penance for her actions against my brothers. So for this, her hands are bound and strapped to my horse, ensuring she is incapable of running. She is fortunate I ride at this slow pace, allowing her to remain upright rather than dragged across the terrain by my companion.

"They have done nothing to you to deserve what you're doing to them!"

"They exist."

"So do you."

"As is my right."

"As is theirs," she yells while spitting out a mouthful of dust and debris my horse has kicked up.

"Shut up, bitch!" the one named Nevil snarls before he kicks her from behind. Do I require him to intercede on my behalf?

No, but he saves me from more arguments than I care to have with the lamb.

He is semi-useful, the laughing mortal behind him not as much. If I had my druthers, she would be lying next to my other victims, not accompanying me on this journey. But this son of Adam claims he needs her body for his mortal desires. Something I neither care about nor want to hear about. Having to listen to her screaming his name is nuisance enough.

He advised once that if I would allow it, he could use the lamb in the other's stead, but I will not permit this, as the lamb yet has a purpose to fulfill. She will watch as they fall. So, I will not allow her time alone with the dullard because I know she could and would, with little difficulty, sway him to her side if given a chance. So the fatuous daughter of Eve remains to satisfy his baser needs.

"Get bent, sausage fingers!" The lamb snarls, displaying one finger for him to view once she regains her footing.

I turn to face her, my eyes narrowed. "It would be in your best interest to avoid speaking," I caution in a low and dangerous voice. "Your survival thus far is a result of my leniency."

The lamb glares at me, defiance dancing in her heated gaze.

"I'm not afraid of you," she says, her voice steady and determined. She is not like the other mortals who feign indifference in my presence. She is unaffected by who I am or what I can do to her. "You're nothing more than a coward who hides behind your power."

Yet I will not allow such insolence. "You hold little knowledge of what I'm capable of," I say, reaching for my scythe. "But I can assure you, it's much more than you can handle."

The lamb's eyes narrow as she sees the blade glinting in the sunlight. "You still think I'm afraid of you?" she demands with the same cool indifference she has maintained since I turned to face her. "I've dealt with monsters my entire life. You're just one more in a long fucking line."

When I swing my leg over my companion and drop to the ground, the world groans in protest of such treatment. Storming over to where she stands her ground, this mortal does something I never expected. If this was any other of her kind, now is when they would fall to the ground or whimper their apologies, but not this one. She squares her shoulders and lifts her chin further, showing her defiance.

"You will learn what happens when you cross me," I say, raising the scythe. "Any last words?"

The lamb gazes at me, her eyes devoid of any discernible emotion. "Tell your brothers I said goodbye."

"Do not speak of my brothers, beguiler. I will discover your dark incantation used against them and reverse this travesty."

"Mazel tov, asshole."

"Hit her, Fammy." Hearing her call me the name I have told her more than once not to say, I turn to face the imbecile behind Nevil.

"You will silence yourself, daughter of Eve, or you will take the lamb's place." I hesitate for a moment, then lower the scythe. "Consider yourself lucky," I tell the lamb. "But don't think I won't hesitate to kill you if you dare speak to me in such a manner again."

"Then you better swing that scythe, Rider, because I have no intention of changing who I am or the moral values I ascribe to achieve."

My reaction is fast as I lash out and grasp her neck to hold her in place while I call forth the plants I will use to keep her still.

For the first time throughout this interaction, her eyes grow wide while the vines twist and snake their way up her legs and around her waist, stopping when they replace the hand I held her steady with. With my vines in place, I step back to enjoy the sight of what once offered life to the mortals of this land, wrapping tighter since their purpose has shifted and is now to remove it.

"I suggest you do not push me on this."

*****

The delay allowed the mortals of this place the time to escape. They took what meager possessions they could grab and snuck away. Faced with a situation that should have meant their demise, thanks to the interference of the lamb, they ran. I cannot help but believe this was her intended outcome.

Since I no longer have any need to destroy this area, I can use it as a base. I need to replenish supplies and allow the humans I travel with time to rest and recover. My father made my companion and me for continuous travel. The mortals and horses of this land cannot do the same. And with the crops almost ready for harvesting, it seems like a waste not to collect them. So staying here until they can gather what the good people of the place left for us is what happens.

Fresh-tilled earth and wildflowers fill my nostrils as I survey the area. A once vibrant and colorful landscape is now desolate, the only movement coming from the gentle sway of the withering crops in the wind. As I wander through the deserted fields, an eerie silence engulfs me. I can hear my breathing, which echoes softly in the stillness.

Tall grass sways in the gentle breeze, rustling against my legs. I can smell the damp earth and decaying leaves in the air, making my nose tingle with each breath. The silence is almost palpable, and it feels as though the world has come to a standstill. The sky overhead is a deep shade of blue, with a few fluffy clouds scattered here and there. I bask in the sun's warmth, which penetrates deep into my muscles, recharging them with its rays. The breeze is cool but not cold, brushing through my hair as I walk.

I feel a sense of unease as I wander through the empty fields, knowing that the humans who once called this place home have fled in fear. Their terror and desperation lingers in the plants, the trees, and the grass like an echo. A sensation my father has determined I should experience.

But I push those thoughts aside as I focus on the task at hand. I need to gather supplies and make sure my companions are rested and ready for the journey ahead. As I walk through the fields, my hand skims over the crops left behind by the fleeing humans. And as with any other living plant, they hum at my touch.

If not for the pain in the plants around me, this place would be my very own slice of paradise. Perhaps when this ends, I will make my home here… on this tiny swath of land.

The sound of rustling leaves and the soft crunch of grass under my feet are soothing background noises as I amble through the place I will call home for a time. Despite the desolate setting, there is a sense of peace in the air surrounding this place. The muted stillness of the empty fields and the gentle warmth of the sun on my skin combine, making me feel almost content. Until the giggles of the one named Cammy steals this moment from me.

I suppose I should return to the home where I left the lamb chained. If I could trust her to make no further attempts at escape, I would allow her time to enjoy the sun. However, she has already proven that if given the opportunity, she will run. So if she wishes to behave like a prisoner, I shall treat her as one.

Walking into the room, I toss the apple I picked from the orchard at her feet. She would throw it back at me if she wasn't starving. Unfortunately for her, she is, so rather than doing what she would prefer, the lamb reluctantly picks it up before mumbling what qualifies as appreciation to her.

"Gee, thanks."

"You should be thankful I give you anything, but it is not your time to die. It is imperative that you observe as more of your kind succumb to my special gift."

"You're fucking starving people to death. I wouldn't call that a gift."

"Because you are too shortsighted to see the truth of my words. But I believe keeping you on the verge of starvation has prevented you from enchanting me, as you did with my brothers."

"I've told you several damn times I don't have any magical powers. I'm a mortal, nothing more, nothing less."

"And I am supposed to trust the one who could bewitch my brothers."

"Trust me, if I had magical powers, I would have turned your ass into a frog long ago."

"I look forward to the day I can do away with you."

"Wanna give me a time frame for this expiration date? Might give me something to look forward to."

"When the last of your kind falls."

"How does Death value human life more than you?"

"Because he is weak. Easily swayed and careless."

"You don't know anything about him, asshole."

"Lamb, you cannot possibly believe you know my brother better than I do."

"If you believe he's weak, then not only do I know him better, I know he's a better man than you."

"Rider."

"What?"

"He is a rider, not a man. Like the rest of us, he has but one task. Should our father demand it, he will annihilate every living being on this planet without a second thought."

"He wouldn't. Your brother told your creator—"

"Our creator. Meaning all of us, because my father is also your father, and it would behoove you to keep this in mind and speak his name with the respect he deserves."

"What has he ever done for me?"

"Gave you life, mortal."

"That was no damn gift, Rider. Besides, this conversation was about your brother, not your creator. We can debate him another day."

"Yes, I should like to hear your thoughts on my brother, who you believe you know better than I because the truth is… not only would he end all life, but he would also do it happily if only to finally be granted respite to sleep."

"Bullshit."

"Thanatos will do as our father commands without a second thought because he is the pale rider. He is Death, and you would do well to remember it."

Chapter Eight: Sit, Stand, Repeat.

FAMINE'S WORDS CONTINUE TO ECHO through my thoughts. Like who and what Thanatos is are things I could ever forget. But what this rider doesn't know is that Death isn't the uncaring bastard everyone portrays him to be.

He was the being I fell in love with. For a moment in time, he was *my* rider and someone I still miss… every damn day.

I figured the other riders would have come looking for me. However, I should specify that I don't expect them to do this, especially since I am not the only one they need to consider any longer. Choosing between protecting their loved ones and rescuing me must be a tough decision for them.

I won't be idle and wait for someone to save me, so I must determine a way to break free from the chains that bind me to this rider alone.

For now, I am as good as alone in this desolate place, chained to a freaking post like a common prisoner. At least Famine let me out of the damn bedroom he's held me in since he took over this area. I'm thankful for the fresh air but would have preferred being confined somewhere I could have moved into the shade because it seems summer has circled back around, and it's hot as hell.

With the sun beating down on my skin, beads of sweat are forming on my brow. I lick my dry lips, trying to ignore the gnawing hunger in my stomach. I can't help but wonder how much time has passed. Days? Weeks? It's hard to tell since one day bleeds into the next. All I know is that I'm hungry, thirsty, and my body aches from being confined so damn much.

I let out a frustrated sigh and lean my head back against the flag pole I'm secured to. Lucky for me, the people who lived here were patriots who wanted to proudly display old glory. To do this, they made sure the pole they strapped her to wouldn't be at risk of toppling over during a storm, so no matter how much I push, pull, or wiggle, the damn thing won't budge. Like I said, lucky me.

As I stare out into the empty fields, I can't help but wonder what has become of the world. The last time we were conscious of time was in the Spring of 2022. Now, to the best of our recollection, it's the Fall of 2026, and everything is different. The world is in chaos, and the worst part is that the riders are being blamed for it, but I am as responsible for it as they are.

The sound of rustling leaves catches my attention, and I turn to see a figure emerging from the trees. It's a woman, her hair wild and tangled, her clothes torn and dirty. She stumbles towards me, and I can see the fear in her eyes.

"Please," she gasps, collapsing at my feet. "Please, help me."

I reach out to touch her, but the chains around my wrists stop me. "I can't," I say, my voice just above a whisper as I crane my neck to survey our surroundings to ensure Famine and sausage fingers are nowhere around us. The last thing I need is for one of these two assholes to show up, only to discover this girl here. She wouldn't stand a chance. "You need to go right now before they see you."

"Who? Are there others? Can they help me?" She begs, clawing at my arm while her wild, frantic eyes search the landscape.

"No, they aren't the helping kind," I mumble while whipping my head from side to side, praying the rider, bobblehead, or asshole will not show up while this girl remains here.

"My family... they're starving. We just need some food."

"Listen, I would help if I could, but I can't. If they find you here, you won't be helping your family either. So you need to go right now."

The woman sobs, and seeing another living soul lost, alone, scared, and begging for help pulls at my heartstrings. I want to help her. If I could, I would give her all the food left in this damnable place, but I can't because I'm chained to this DAMN POLE.

This is not the world I want to live in, where even the simple act of helping someone in need is impossible. The sound of dead leaves crunching underfoot informs me one of them is returning. And this girl refuses to leave, and she isn't releasing me from my restraints to help her, so in about thirty seconds, she will come face to face with one kind of hell or another, and I won't be able to do anything to stop them. Damn, I hate myself for what I'm about to do.

"GET THE FUCK OUT OF HERE, YOU DUMB BITCH!"

"Please, my-my little sister, she's going to die."

Goddamn it, I hate myself. I fucking hate all of this. What I did, what I sentenced humanity to. I despise it all, and what I'm about to say makes me every bit as much of an asshole as I like to call Sausage. "I don't fucking care. NOW GET LOST!"

"How can you be so... so... uncaring!" She scrambles to her feet and backs away from me. The look of horror and disgust she's giving me is the worst part because the simple truth is I do care. I care too damn much, and saying this shit to her is killing me, but at least I know she'll still be there tomorrow to help her family. She rushes around the corner just as Cammie comes from the opposite one.

"Who are you talking to?"

"No one."

"Oh my god, are you like... talking to yourself? That. Is. So. Pathetic."

Yeah, I'm the pathetic one here. Dumb bitch. I roll my eyes and turn away from Cammie. She's Nevil's lackey, and if I had to guess, she played a part in keeping him alive when Death left him for dead.

She's always trying to get a rise out of me to report my wrongdoings to the asshole, hoping she'll get to watch while he knocks the shit out of me. Today I refuse to give her the satisfaction. Instead of being pulled in by Cammie, I keep my gaze fixed on the direction the young woman vanished. I hope she makes it back to her family in one piece. Without access to food and water, their chances of survival are slim, so I pray they find what they need. But mostly, I hope they can survive this world that's been turned upside down and thrown into chaos.

As I watch the empty fields, I can't help but think about what led us to this point. It wasn't just me. It was a collective failure of humanity. We ignored the signs. We didn't take action when we should have, and now we're paying the price. The riders are just a divine solution to a much larger problem. The issue is, I played right into the hands of the asshole who wanted to topple it.

I close my eyes and try to block out the noise around me. The sound of chains rattling, the sound of Cammie's annoying voice, the sound of my own thoughts. It's all too much. I just want to escape, be free, and live in a world without worrying about starving or being chained to a damn flagpole. I want to live out what's left of my life with my family and friends.

But that world doesn't exist anymore, at least not for me. This is the reality I'm stuck in, and I have to find a way to survive it. Pestilence once told me humanity needs to hold on to hope, even when it feels like there's nothing left to hope for. But it's damn hard when your life has been one steaming pile of shit. Yet this is what I'm going to do. I'll do it for him, for War, for the rider I loved, and for the others who are counting on me.

I take a deep breath and open my eyes. Cammie is still standing there, looking at me like I'm crazy. But I don't care because I'm done playing the part of the damn victim. I'm done pretending I'm not angry, hungry, and tired. I'm done feeling sorry for myself. It's time I find the Avalon who wasn't afraid to stand toe to toe with Death and came out on top.

Because I care, and I'm going to do something about it. Even if it means risking everything or facing my own demons. Even if it means I can never return to the riders and the people I call family. Somehow during the weeks I've been stuck with Famine and Sausage Fingers... when I've lived in the stupid ass pity party created by none other than me, I forgot one crucial thing. All the choices and paths I've undertaken over the last couple of years I did to keep them safe. And it's about damn time I get back to it. No matter what.

"Let's go. What the hell are you looking at?" She asks, jerking on the chains she's holding. If it wasn't for Nevil coming across the field right then, I would knock her ass out and be on my way, but with my legs bound, he would be on me before I made it down the driveway. So running will have to wait until these idiots drop their guard. Taking one last look in the direction the girl went, I return to playing the part of a compliant hostage and follow Cammie into the house to switch from prisoner to chef.

*****

Like every other night, I cook while Cammie paints her nails or flips through the same magazine she's read a hundred times before. It's like the community we found her in all over again when I was stuck on ditch duty while this loon played Snow White. While it was baffling to me back then why they allocated her to such a shitty task... now I understand why they assigned her as my partner. Nevil, Steven, and Bob couldn't carry out their plan to kill me with witnesses.

When she isn't giving herself a manicure or expanding her pea-sized brain, she babbles about anything and everything that pops into her pretty little head. Like I give two shits about what she thinks or has to say. If I had my choice, Famine, not the bobblehead, would be the one to watch over me. Which says a lot, considering my aversion towards him and his incessant "completing my mission" attitude.

Only after serving the three assholes am I permitted to sit and eat. Of course, I don't get to help myself. Nope, and here's why… the minuscule amount of food Nevil dishes on my plate is meant to keep me alive, nothing more. Not once since I found myself in their company, have I ever felt satisfied.

The thing that pisses me off the most is Famine doesn't need to eat, but he does. Because when he eats, it means less food for the mortals he has no love for. Such a shame Sausage and Bobble—my alternative names for Nevil and Cammie—hasn't figured this out yet. These two imbeciles practically fight each other for the serving spoon, eagerly doling out scoop after scoop to gain favor with the rider.

Morons.

If I like them, I might tell them it doesn't gain shit. Or better yet, if they had any sense in their head, they would figure out how wrong they were. The only thing this does is leave them almost as hungry as I am some nights.

But tonight, his gaze is fixed on me. Does he know about the girl? Shit, did he catch her… torture her?

"Tell me of my brother's time here."

I blow out an exasperated breath because we have done this song and dance before. "I'm going to take a shot in the dark and say the rider you're talking about is Death."

"Tell me what you did to him!"

"I didn't do shit," I reply, emphasizing the word *"do"* since we've also reviewed this subject—as Pessy likes to say—ad nauseam.

"Tell me."

"As I've told you a million times already, I. Didn't. Do. Anything! Death came, destroyed a bunch of shit, started a horde," Nevil grunts with this statement, which pisses me off, so I add him to the list. "Collected some assholes, followed me when I had enough of dealing with said assholes, made his choice, and left."

Nevil's narrowed eyes, tight lips, and flaring nostrils all confirm he knows the asshole I spoke of is none other than him and his cronies from back then. But I don't care because my stance on him and what he is has never changed. So there's no point in holding back or shitting fluff for the sake of saving hurt feelings.

"NO! You swayed him. This I know to be a fact. How did you do it? What did you hold over my brother to force him to change his mind?"

"Um, in case you missed it, we're talking about Death. He never did anything he didn't want to, and none of us had anything—"

"She was his whore."

"Whore? This word is unknown to me."

"She let him use her however he wanted. It's the one thing these bitches all hold over us. The power of pussy is a frightening thing."

"Once again, your words are meaningless to me," Famine groans.

"He's talking about…." Cammie points down at her crotch while rocking back and forth on the chair as if this is going to help the damn rider one fucking bit.

"For Christ's sake, what the two idiots are alluding to is a vagina."

"Then why not say this rather than puss see?"

"Because it's a slang term for that part of our anatomy, and since the word vagina scares the shit out of big badass men like him, they use slang words when talking about it. Isn't that right, Nevvie-wevvie? Vagina scares the shit out of you. "

"Shut your fucking mouth, Avalon. I'm not afraid to say vagina. I just prefer calling your cunt what it is… a goddam pussy." Well, this wasn't the brightest idea. First, he used yet another word the rider will not understand. Second—and, to be honest, the biggest misstep—he took the rider's dad's name in vain. Something I doubt this rider will take kindly. If I'm counting, that would be strike three.

Famine shifts his focus from me to the idiot talking. Did he really think this bro code bonding bullshit would work on this rider? The cords in his neck turn rigid while the veins pulse. In case Nevil doesn't pick up on his other cues that reveal how disgusted he is with his last comment when his lip lifts in a sneer, it sure as shit should.

"I did not request your dissemination of vulgar and offensive musings regarding the female anatomy. Should I wish to hear them, I will inquire. Until that time, you will withhold your thoughts. One other thing, if you speak of our father like this again, you'll meet my vines." Once he is confident Nevil isn't going to speak again, he turns back to me. "Concerning you, I made a query. One I expect to be answered."

"Too damn bad." His teeth gnashed together, and I swear one of his molars just cracked under the strain. Like the other riders before him, he is not used to a lowly mortal talking to him like this, which sucks for him because I won't bow or give in to this damn rider. Not now. Not ever. "If you want the answer to this, ask your brother."

"If such a possibility existed, I would have executed it long ago to spare myself from inane conversations such as this one with you."

"Pestilence and War never had issues talking to him."

"I suspect this is no more an option for my younger siblings than for me."

"Why not?"
"Because Thanatos is gone."
What the fuck did he just say?

Chapter Nine: Family.

ER EYES ASSESSING ME ARE almost as offputting as Pestilence's frustration at me when I demanded we return to our community and not just rush headlong out to find the lamb. But I knew all was forgiven when he saw Greer waiting for him. I doubt Ember will be as easy to convince.

"Do you really believe Avalon would want you to risk the safety of the ones who travel with you and Pestilence if it causes an all-out battle with your brother?"

"No, which makes this entire situation even more difficult. How can Pestilence and I leave her to face what I'm sure is not a friendly, kind, or caring rider while we continue our happy lives with the ones she brought into our world while she toils?"

"So we leave the army here to care for the residents while a handful of us go out to find her."

"No."

"I thought you wanted to find Ava—"

"We will. But only Pestilence and I will do this. I will not risk losing you, Ellie, or Duck, nor would my brother risk Greer and Wren. Besides, I want you to remain to keep this community thriving. While we are gone, Greer, Suki, you, and Xander will be in charge."

"War?"

"Yes."

"Is this the only reason you don't want me to come?"

"I'm unsure what you're asking me."

"Is it because you wanna be alone with Avalon?" I guess I have not been as careful with my lingering affection as I thought. I love Ember, and the last thing I want is for her to think I would ever do anything to hurt her or ruin what we have built together.

"La meva llum perfecta, you are my chosen, not Avalon."

"It was ridiculous. Forget I even said anything."

Ember nods, understanding the weight of the responsibility I entrust her with. She knows this is not just about finding Avalon, but also about ensuring the safety and stability of our community.

"I'll ensure everything runs smoothly while you're gone," she promises. "But you have to promise me you'll be careful. Because I don't want to lose you either."

The slight smile I give her only increases the one she is granting me. "I'll be as careful as I can. And I'll make sure Pestilence is too."

Ember's expression softens at the mention of Pestilence. Despite their rough start, she understands how much my brother means to me. It's a bond she has told me she wishes she had, but it was not in the cards for her parents.

"I hope you find Avalon soon," she says, her words closer to a whisper than spoken. "She deserves to see this. Deserves to see what she helped create. This community, the kids, our family."

I nod in agreement. "We'll find her. And when we do, we'll ensure she never has to go through something like this again. Then we'll find the seal and release Thanatos from the prison our father has placed him in."

"Are you sure that's the best idea? What if your father wants retribution for you interfering? I can't stand the thought of anything happening to you."

"First, my father is not the retribution sort—"

"Um, I beg to differ since it's kind of the entire reason you and your brothers exist."

"No, we exist as a means to an end, Ember. And only if he determined you were beyond redemption."

"But he sent you." I could tell her it wasn't my father's decision to wake us; Avalon's actions brought us here. But I won't. There's no point in making things tense between the lamb I still care for and the woman I have fallen in love with. Besides, Avalon did not realize what she was preparing to do would bring the riders into her world… at least not the first time. And even though she broke the second seal knowing what would happen, she did it to save my brother's soul, something I will forever be grateful for. No, I think it is best to keep these thoughts, like my feelings about the lamb, to myself.

"Second, I cannot leave my brother in the prison they sentenced him to."

"But—"

"No, Ember. You cannot understand where he was sent to. It is a place meant to hold the worst of us. It is meant to break you. Thanatos does not deserve this. He acted no different from how

I would have if you were in trouble or Pestilence would have if it were Greer."

"So you believe he loves Avalon?" I smile while running my fingers across her cheek. It still amazes me every day that she chose me. A rider with a single purpose: to destroy them.

"I know he does." My gaze settles on her while a gentle breeze billowing through the curtains carries the sweet fragrance of the late fall flowers while the chirping from the birds filters through the open window.

The entire scene creates a peaceful ambiance around us. But despite the beauty of this moment, my heart is heavy with regret. The simple truth is that Death's love for Avalon is the only reason I did not pursue what was blooming between the lamb and me. This thought, although overwhelming, was not meant for my chosen to know. I realize it would only hurt her, something I would never do. Not to the woman who healed my troubled heart.

Ember nods, feeling a sense of comfort in my response. She knows that Pestilence and I will do everything possible to retrieve Avalon. And in the meantime, she'll do her part to keep this community strong and thriving.

"Do you plan to leave right now?"

"No, we leave at first light," I confirm. I can only describe the grin Ember grants me as pure wicked. I admit her reaction, while sudden, is not unwelcome. Since she is removing her clothes while straddling my lap. The smile I give her grants me the explanation for this sudden reaction.

"What? I plan on riding my horseman. Do you object?"

"Quite the contrary."

"Good, because I would hate to make you watch while I take care of myself." Her lips brush against mine as she slides her shirt down her arms. As if on cue, my erection is immediate.

Jerking to life as my hands replace hers in removing the garments keeping her body from my view.

"Oh, and make it good because it seems like it will have to last me until you return."

"You have my word, la meva llum perfecta."

"One of these days, handsome, you will tell me what that means."

"But not today," I confess, as my lips attack hers in a fierce kiss. Her hand slides around the length of my arousal. Her fingertips caress the head as her hand works the shaft in slow, steady movements. Each stroke makes me forget about the task ahead of me until the only thing remaining is this woman, the warmth of her skin against mine, and the rapid beating of her heart against my chest.

When she throws her head back, it lifts her breast towards me, and I waste no time taking the taunt peak of her pebbled nipple between my teeth. Her moans of desire fill the room when my thumb circles the tight nub of her clit.

"Fuck-fuck-fuck."

"Do you like this, Ember?"

"Yes. Fuck yes."

"Would you enjoy it more if my tongue replaced the thumb circling you?"

"Oh, Jesus fucking Christ, yes. Yes, please do." I smile against her skin, feeling her body shiver at my words. Her hand continues its slow, steady strokes on my dick, urging me to give her the ecstasy she desires. In one quick movement, I flip her to her back and position myself between her legs, my mouth eager to seek the wetness between her thighs. Her moans fill the air as I work my tongue over her clit, flicking it back and forth with deliberate strokes.

Ember's hips buck against my face, and I hold her down, not wanting to let go of the sweet taste on my tongue. Her fingers tangle in my hair, urging me on as I continue my ministrations. Her body is writhing beneath mine, and I can feel the tension building as I continue to push her to the edge.

I slip two fingers inside her, feeling the tightness of her walls as I push them in deeper. Her moans turn to screams of pleasure as I work my fingers in and out, my mouth still latched onto her clit. I can feel her getting closer and closer, and I increase the speed and intensity of my movements.

She comes apart beneath me while she screams my name, her body quivering with satisfaction. The taste of her explodes across my tongue, but I want more. I want all of her, every godforsaken thing she can give me.

I crawl up her body, my cock pressing against her velvety thighs. She reaches between us to grasp my length in her trembling hand, and I groan at the sensation.

"As much as I want you to fuck me, I want to taste you more." She wiggles until she has escaped from under the weight of my gigantic frame. I watch as she sinks to her knees in front of me. Seeing her like this flush from her own arousal, tongue darting out to moisten the lips I know she will soon wrap around me. I become lost in this woman.

Her eyes seek mine, and the thought of her pussy pressed to my face bucking wildly when she found her release has me licking my lips in anticipation of doing it again.

Even though I offer her my cock, she surprises me by leaning forward and taking my fingers into her mouth, sucking them with a hunger that leaves me breathless. Tasting the sweetness of her climax still lingering on them. She moans when I shove them in deeper, wanting her to know the rapture I experienced seconds ago.

The swell of her breast grazes across the head of my thick cock. I'm consumed by the feel of her body against mine and her tongue massaging my fingers. The electric sensation has me grasping my erection so I can stroke it as she works my digits the way I want her to savor me. I watch in amazement as she devours them. Her moans of delight send waves of euphoria racing through me. My hand works faster, keeping in time with her movements.

"Do you like the way you taste?"

"Not as much as I love the way you do," she replies, releasing my fingers with a loud pop. Her eyes glide down my frame until they reach the part of my body I want her full attention on. The cock I continue to stroke. Her groans are soft, but watching her tongue darting across her lips to lick the last of her spent excitement away has me lifting my hips toward her.

Pre-cum glistens in anticipation of what I know she will grant me. Her eyes follow my finger as I gather it and lift it toward her parted lips. Like the perfect lover she is, she keeps her eyes focused on mine while she runs her tongue against it, gathering my offered release, making my dick twitch with need.

"Ready for more?" she asks. Ember's mouth moves from my fingers to the tip of my cock, her tongue swirling around the head. I groan at the sensation, feeling my arousal building with each rotation. She takes me deep into her mouth, her lips wrapping firm around my shaft as she moves her head at a perfect pace, pushing me past desire and soaring straight to fucking desperation.

I grip her hair tightly, urging her to take more of me into her mouth as I feel my release building within me. The sensation of her tongue swirling around the head of my member is almost too much to bear.

My release continues to build inside me, and I know I won't be able to hold on for much longer. Ember seems to sense this too, and she pulls back, a wicked smile covering her face and a mischievous glint in her eyes.

"Your lucky you can cum without losing this beautiful hard-on." When she sucks me into her mouth this time, I know she will not stop until I finish. My hips thrust up with each of her downward movements. My ragged breaths inform her how close I am.

Ember's mouth continues to work me, her tongue swirling around the head of my cock before she pushes me further down her throat, doing something I didn't think possible… she takes me to the base. I can feel the pressure building inside me, knowing it won't be long until I reach my limits.

Her hand reaches down to massage my balls, adding to the desire coursing through my body. I can feel myself getting closer and closer, and I knot her hair around my fist, urging her on.

With one final suck, Ember takes me as deep as she can. The sudden invasion causes her throat to constrict, and tears form in her eyes as she tries to swallow me whole. Watching my girl working so hard should make me relent, but I don't. I fuck her harder. I slam my hips up and pull her head down so I can force my cock in further, and I don't know if it's the lust-laced moans she grants me or the warmth of her tongue caressing me that finally pushes me over the edge and I explode into her mouth.

She swallows hard, her lips wrapped tight around my length, not allowing a single droplet of my release to slip away. I feel her tongue caressing while her throat contracts and relaxes, milking me of every drop from my climax. The slurping sound of her swallowing echoes in the room, accompanied by the faint scent of her arousal. I shiver with pleasure as I watch her eyes roll back in ecstasy, her cheeks extended with my essence. It's a moment of pure bliss, as if time has stood still, and all that exists is the sensation of her mouth on me.

Once she is sure she has consumed all I have to give her, she runs her tongue from the base of my shaft to the head, taking a second to ensure she has licked me clean.

"My turn again. But this time, I plan on coming with your cock buried inside me," she says while climbing onto my lap. Her hand encircles my length to slide it against her wet folds. If I thought she was wet before, she is soaked now. I piston my hips up to rub the head of my dick against her aching clit while I swallow up the moan she releases. When she can take no more teasing, she positions me at the entrance to her pussy and sinks down my length, taking me deep.

The warm, wet walls I'm sheathed in clench around me as I take her to the height of her ecstasy. We move together in perfect harmony, our bodies matching each other's pace. The sensation is overwhelming,

I let out a deep groan with every move she makes, riding me with such fierce determination. Her nails dig into my chest as she grinds against me, her body writhing under my skilled touch. We move together in perfect rhythm, our bodies pressed together in a passionate embrace. Lost in the moment as we give in to the passion consuming us.

I reach up to grasp her breasts, kneading them rougher than most women like, but my beautiful girl loves it. This explains why she grinds harder, riding me like she was born to do it. Our bodies are slick with sweat, and the air is thick with the sound of our moans and the slap of skin against skin.

"Oh god, you feel so good," she moans, her breath hot against my lips.

"La meva llum perfecta, I want you to fuck me until you can take no more," I groan in her ear, my hands gripping her hips tighter.

"I'm going to cum again," she screams, her movements becoming more urgent. The familiar pressure of her looming climax and the walls of her pussy squeeze my thick erection.

The air is filled with the moans from our ecstasy, and the wet slaps of my cock invading her pussy create an erotic soundtrack. I can feel her walls clenching around me, the tightness almost too much to bear. But I hold on, wanting to give her the same gratification she gave me.

Her pace quickens, and I know she's close. I grab her hips, helping her move faster and deeper. She throws her head back, her hair falling in a wild tangle away from her face, screaming with such sweet euphoria when she reaches the peak and her climax overcomes her.

I feel her release wash over my erection, her walls pulsing around me, and it's enough to push me over the edge as well. I explode inside her, my release mingling with hers. Ember collapses onto my chest, her breath coming in ragged gasps. Our bodies remain tangled in a sweaty mess of limbs.

I pull away from her, taking a moment to watch as she catches her breath. Her eyes are closed, and a small smile graces her lips. I am always captivated by her appearance when she is lost in the aftermath of our sexual bliss. It is something that never ceases to astound me.

"That was fucking amazing," she says, her voice still husky with desire.

"It was," I agree, pulling her close for a kiss.

"My satisfied pussy would like to thank you. While my throbbing clit wants to know, how long before we can do it again?"

"When I return, I plan to lock you in this bedroom and refuse to stop until you beg me."

"Oh, fuck." It's the only thing she can say as her pussy spasms at the thought.

She fits me better than anyone, confirming one thing. My father made this beautiful woman for me, just as I exist for her. I appreciate that this is just the beginning of our journey together. There will be more moments like this, more passion, more love. She is la meva llum perfecta, my perfect light, and I will do anything to keep her safe and happy.

As we sit there, our bodies spent and intertwined, I feel a sense of contentment wash over me. It's during moments like this I'm reminded how fortunate I am to have found her. To have this beguiling woman in my life. I carry her over to our bed and pull her frame against mine.

"I love you, War," she responds, her eyes closed in bliss.

I still find it intriguing that a mortal could feel anything other than contempt for me or my brothers, but these women in our lives prove us wrong time and time again. I know she only whispered these words because she was falling asleep. A state of consciousness that allows her defenses to drop enough to speak the truth. With a soft kiss pressed against her forehead, I whisper, "As much as I love you, Ember."

Laying next to her, I can't help but feel grateful for this moment. Grateful for Ember, for our love, and for the bond we share. I may be one of the Four Horsemen of the Apocalypse, but at this moment, I am just a man searching for my place in her world.

I remain with her until the first dusting of dawn graces the skies. I know I should wake her when I slip out of bed, but seeing her like this, I choose to leave her with the sweet memory of our night together, not me riding away from her.

When I exited our house, I discovered Pestilence gazing at the home he shared with his chosen mate and his son. The sense of foreboding hanging heavy in the air. We know what we will face. The fight we will endure. We acknowledge the chance of never seeing the ones we care for again. Famine is a force to be reckoned with and should not be underestimated.

If we were smart, we would grant him a wide berth. Knowing to trifle with our brother is akin to taking one's life in their hands. But it changes nothing. Because leaving him to his task threatens the ones we hold dear and endangers mouse's life. Something we would never allow, even if we didn't need her to release our brother.

With Pestilence by my side, I mount Red and ride toward our fate. An unknown outcome, but determined to find Avalon and bring her home.

The journey ahead may be long and fraught with danger, but I know that with my brother at my side, we can overcome anything. And with Ember's love as my anchor, I am ready to face whatever challenge blocks our path from achieving our goal.

We are Pestilence and War. Two of the four horsemen and nothing from this moment forth will stand in our way.

Chapter Ten: Bullshit.

What good is it to gain the entire world if you give up every part of yourself to achieve it?

NO WAY. SINCE I KNOW these riders don't lie, he has to be mistaken. Or perhaps I misunderstood what he meant. Death can't be gone. It's not possible.

"What the fuck do you mean, he's gone?"

"What I said. My brother is no longer within the realm of my father."

"He died?" I ask, my heart beating at a frantic pace. I had resigned myself to the idea we would never see each other again. At least not in my lifetime, but the prospect of him dying never entered my mind. I mean, how the hell can Death die? It's impossible. Or at least I thought it was.

"He is nothing. He is nowhere. If this is how you define your word died, then… yes, he died."

Marcelle Valentine

"Bullshit! And before you say anything about excrement not being a part of this conversation, it's a damn figurative saying, not a literal statement."

"You make no more sense than the rambling of those two. Irrespective of your beliefs, my statements provide an accurate recounting of the result of your actions. Only through your use of witchcraft have you brought a curse upon my brother, which has caused our father to abandon him. His inevitable end resulted from his inability to deny you."

Panic surges through me, and it feels like he tore my heart from my chest. How can he be so cold about the death of his brother? And let's not forget he is the rider responsible for ferrying souls to the afterlife. If Thanatos isn't doing this, who the hell is? The only thought plaguing me is how any of this could be possible.

But the more I contemplate it, the more I'm convinced it's impossible. No one, not even the almighty, can kill Death. Thanatos has said it before. He is the embodiment of it. Besides, wouldn't I know his life had ended? I mean, wouldn't I sense it? Because one thing I'm sure of, assholes like his father wouldn't waste the opportunity to make me suffer. All of which scream the same thing… Famine is full of shit.

Unwilling to hear more of his lies, I spin on my heels and sprint through the door. What he told me can't be accurate, but if it is, I have no choice but to help him. I need to find a way to wherever the damn creator sent him before I can haul his ass back from the brink or beyond it.

I didn't use magic to sway him, but it doesn't make his current situation any less my fault. I did this to him. By showing him what it meant to be human, and even if Death no longer wants me, I will not leave him to face such a miserable fate. He has to be alive, and if anyone can send me to the hellhole they trapped him in, I know just the being I need to seek out.

Someone Pessy and War will be pissed that I went to. I can just hear them now... Pestilence asking me what I was thinking while War threatens to tie my ass to Red. But he's the only soul I know who I can make hate me enough to end my life, sending me straight to his realm. Or at least this is my hope, as Raum's name dominates my thoughts.

I make it no further than a hundred yards before something, or it would be more accurate to say someone jerks my hair, and I end up on my back, staring at the starry sky. Stars I have looked at so many times over the last couple of years; I swear I know them almost as well as the lines crisscrossing over the palm of my hand.

"Now, where in the fuck do you think you're going?" Nevil, número uno in the realm of assholes, asks. A hard smile is plastered across his face while he cocks his head. I can't wait until the day this smug bastard meets the riders who will do anything to save their brother.

"As far as I can get from your dumb ass." My response is almost as sharp as the knife I wish I still had from the kitchen because this entire interaction would have had a different outcome if I had.

In a display of the physical prowess I learned from hours of sparring with the horsemen, I return to my full height. Had I attempted to just stand, Nevil would have knocked me back down, so the only way I achieve this feat is by rocking my legs over my head and flipping them underneath my body. I may not have a weapon, but I will not back down from this prick tonight any more than I did the last time we did this little song and dance. The difference is tonight, the asshole will have to face me alone, and I like these odds a whole hell of a lot more than I did when I encountered him with Steven and Bob.

If Nevil thought he would get a second chance to remove my sassy ass from this world, he was mistaken since Famine shows up before he gets the opportunity. The problem is not only does the rider appear, but so do his damn vines. The ones coiling around my underweight physique to anchor me in place. Another thing I can begrudgingly thank the rider for since he isn't too worried about whether I get enough to eat.

"Your aid is no longer required, son of Adam."

"Famine, this bitch—"

"I said you are free to go. It would be in your best interest to exercise this freedom before I change my mind."

I watch while Nevil backs away, his eyes darting between Famine and me. The scent of fear and sweat emanates from him, making me smirk. He may have thought he could take me down, but he knows better than to mess with one of the four horsemen.

The vines around me tighten, causing me to wince in pain. Even the slightest brush with Famine's powers is no small feat, and I count myself lucky to be alive. The sensation of being trapped is suffocating, and I can't halt my heart from pounding in my chest, but at least the damn things are not getting any tighter.

Despite the cool night air, my body continues to radiate heat. The adrenaline from the confrontation with Nevil is still coursing through my veins, and I feel like I could take on the world.

"You will learn your place in this changing universe."

"Yeah, and who's the one determining my place? You? Your father? Raum? Assholes like the prick slinking back to the house you stole? Tell me who, so I know which asshole I should kill first."

Famine proves my pushing will not rattle him when he turns, places his hands behind his back, and strolls back to the house I was fortunate enough to sleep in last night. Something I don't think I will claim tonight since his vines twist higher and threaten to squeeze the air from my lungs.

As I struggle to take my next breath, the vines constrict around my chest, causing my vision to blur and my head to spin. The pain is excruciating, and my heart races faster as my body fights to draw in even a molecule of oxygen. A bone-deep sense of panic replaces the fear and anger bubbling inside as I realize just how screwed I am.

Sweat beads on my forehead, and my muscles tense as I try to break free from the vines' grip, but it's no use. Famine's power is too strong, and I'm trapped like a fly in a spider's web. The cool night air feels like a distant memory as my body temperature rises and my skin burns like fire. Burning me from the inside out.

I close my eyes, trying to focus on my breathing, but it's hard to calm down when every inhale feels like I'm being crushed. I can feel the panic rising within me like a tidal wave, threatening to consume me entirely.

In the distance, I hear footsteps and open my eyes to see Famine approaching again. I try to speak, but my throat is too constricted to form words. I can only stare at him, hoping he'll release me from this torture. But he doesn't. He gives me a warning instead.

"I will make you pay for what you have done to my brothers. However, before I claim your soul, I will force you to watch as everything you hold dear withers and dies from hunger or the vines that once fed them."

"Fuck you." I wanted my response to convey how much I loath him, yet it didn't carry the bite I had hoped for. All thanks to his vines, which only grant me the slimmest of room for my chest to fill with the oxygen I am desperate for.

He doesn't reply to my goading. Opting to call his horse to play the part of my guard as the vines settle in for what I imagine will be a long ass night. A companion of the rider I have yet to befriend. But one that will do what Famine demands. So here's hoping his presence will keep the four-legged predators at bay when they come slinking by and discover the tasty meal the damn rider left out for them.

I look up at the starry sky once more, and a new reality forms. I'm just an insignificant speck in the grand scheme. The universe is vast and unforgiving, and I'm nothing more than a mortal caught in the middle of a war between beings far more powerful than myself.

Does this mean I'll sit on my ass and watch while the pricks who have captured me destroy everything I care about? Hell no. The thought of it makes my stomach churn. In fact, the choking stench of our burning hopes and shattered dreams fills my senses, while the deafening sound of destruction echoes in my ears. I refuse to be a mere spectator to these monstrous acts any longer. The problem is, I also figured out this rider is not like the others, meaning I need to exercise a modicum of self-control.

I let out a sigh, resigned to my fate. It's only a matter of time until I break free from the grip of this horseman. I'll have to keep my impulses in check and wait for a chance to appear. This is my only option if I want to help him. Something I can assure you I am desperate to achieve. But it won't happen tonight. When it does, I'll make sure Famine's promise never comes to pass.

That is if I survive the damn foliage he commands.

Chapter Eleven: Lessons to Learn.

THIS MORTAL REFUSES TO ADHERE to my rules. No matter what I do, she continues to stand in defiance of me. Her insolence only fuels my anger, and I am tempted to crush her like the insignificant insect she is. But something about her tenacity intrigues me. It's been a long time since I've encountered a mortal with such fire in their belly.

It began the day I watched her from a distance. The day she put herself between the cretin who travels with us and a daughter of Eve who stumbled into our camp. I could hear the mortal begging for help, pleading for food I would never permit her to walk away with. The lamb's initial attempts to send her away didn't work, so she became aggressive when she sensed the cretin's companion approaching. Most would have believed she did this when she grew tired of the incessant begging, but upon observation, her posture belied this assumption. She did it to save her.

A moot point since I followed the daughter of Eve to where she hid her family and gave them the gift of a quick death.

However, the fierce determination I could sense within her proved there was more to this mortal than I thought. For now, I will exercise patience, awaiting the opportune moment to uncover the means by which she gained control of my brothers. The vines that once held her captive now serve as my loyal sentinels, ready to ensnare her at a moment's notice. But she is clever, always on guard, always ready to fight back. She is cunning, but more distressing is this mortal grows more confident and resolute in her path.

Hence, I contemplate my next move with this in mind... I must uncover the most effective means to crush her spirit, thereby shattering her defiant resolve. Perhaps I will unleash my power upon her, forcing her to witness the devastation that hunger can bring. Or maybe I will toy with her, leading her down a false path, only to reveal my true intentions at the last moment.

*****

~Two Weeks Later~

My brothers still hunt us. It wouldn't be an issue if not for War. The human and celestial worlds consider Pestilence's marksmanship skills unparalleled. However, War shows equal mastery in combat strategy, making him an adept tracker.

Too often, I am forced to vacate the town I have commandeered because they are gaining ground. I am tired of their pursuit, so today is the day I ride out alone for a confrontation none of us want. If they are wise, they will heed my advice.

My brothers have grown complacent during their time on this plane, making it easy for me to sneak up on them. For several minutes, I remained concealed to listen to their conversation. Which should consist of how they plan to complete their mission; however, it seems their preference lies in discussing the mortals they left behind. The damnable forsaken, who should be nothing more than dust and fading into oblivion by now.

When I had heard enough to know Michael was correct, I knew there was no point in confronting them. My brothers remain under the influence of these daughters of Eve, who have convinced them to abandon their mission. So before they sense my presence, I leave them to their fate while I return to the task the lamb awoke us for.

Though we may eventually meet on the battlefield, today is not the day. Although I know what I should do, I remain hopeful my brothers will come to understand the error of their choice and return to their mission before I am forced to do what no sibling should ever have to…kill my brothers.

*****

Despite the constant threat of War and Pestilence, the mortal lamb continues to surprise me. She has not faltered in her determination, and her resilience has proven to be a thorn in my side. I have tried to break her spirit, to make her succumb to my will, but she remains steadfast. It's almost as if she has embraced her fate, accepting that even if she does not survive our ride, it will not be from a lack of courage or her determination to save every mortal she can.

As we travel through the wilderness, I can't help but feel a sense of admiration for her. She may be insignificant in the grand scheme of things, but she possesses a strength many would envy. It is a trait that has been absent in the mortal realm for far too long.

As the night settles in, I watch her from a distance as she tends to the fire. She appears lost in thought, staring into the flames. One need not be divine to sense the weight of her burdens or the fear and uncertainty she carries. If I wish to gain the upper hand with this human, perhaps understanding her would be the best way to achieve it.

I approach her, keeping a safe distance, not wanting to startle her. She looks up at me, and for a moment, I see a glimmer of uncertainty in her eyes. It is a fleeting moment, quickly replaced by a guarded expression.

"What do you want?" she asks, her voice laced with suspicion.

"Tell me why you continue to fight when I have shown you all is lost," I reply, my tone even. I don't want her to detect the curiosity swelling within me.

"Because it's not." Avalon's response resonates with certainty. It's a sentiment that baffles me. How can she be so confident when she must see their end is near?

"You have defied me at every turn and remain unbroken. What drives you?"

She stares at me for a long moment, and I can see the war raging within her. Part of her wants to trust me, to believe that I am like my brothers. But a larger part rightfully stays wary, knowing that I am nothing like them, and the truth is I remain a horseman with a singular purpose... their eradication.

"I don't know what drives me," she finally says, her voice unwavering. "All I know is that I can't give up. How can I when so much is at stake? Besides, I would like to point out you haven't fucking won yet."

"Goals aside, it seems we are more alike than we care to admit."

Her chin lifts while her shoulders pull back, which juts her chest out. Her unwavering glare is challenging. Almost judging. In what reality does she believe she has the right to do this? To judge a rider sent to remove her.

"Let's get one fucking thing straight. I am nothing like you."

Thus bringing an end to our conversation.

*****

When the lamb believes she is alone, I hear her talking to herself, but I dare not linger long for fear of what enchantment her words could inflict. Until one night, as I watched her, she spoke a name few would dare utter. Thanatos. Is she trying to hex my brother, or could she be trying to save him? My memories transport me back to the night I informed her about his fate. She seemed… pained. Does she care for him? Blame herself for his circumstances?

Something shifts within me. A tiny seed of doubt takes root. Is it possible that I have misjudged her? That there is more to her than meets the eye?

I dispelled the thought, reminding myself that my centuries of existence have taught me she does not differ from the ones she is attempting to protect. Mortals are weak and easily manipulated. Often, they allow their emotions to guide them, which will be their ultimate downfall. I will not let this one break me.

Marcelle Valentine

Although it would have been my desire to remain in the home Nevil seized, I detected my brothers approaching. Since I still have no aspiration to fight them, I will try my best to avoid them, but if they continue this endeavor, they will leave me with no other option.

For now, I will capture the next village and the residents within it. I have discovered the lamb is much more amendable when the fate of the mortals she hopes to save is threatened. Especially when they are younger than the lamb.

She believes she can keep them safe; she is mistaken. I strike when she least expects it, sending my vines to wrap around her ankles, pulling her to the ground. She struggles, but it's no use. My flora's grip is too strong, which allows me to drag her through the dirt toward the heart of the village like the insignificant nuisance she has proven herself to be.

The residents scream and scatter as I approach, but I am unstoppable. My vines lash out, trapping them in place. They are like insects, squirming and wriggling, but they are no more capable of escaping my grasp than the foolish mortal who thought she could control a rider.

The lamb fights back, struggling to break free. But it's too late. I have already begun the ritual. The ground trembles beneath us, bringing with it a swarm of locusts, obscuring everything from view.

I hear her screams and their pleas for mercy; however, I ignore them. This is my domain, and I will not be defied. The ritual reaches its climax, and the air crackles with energy.

And then… blissful silence.

When the swarm clears, I look around, satisfied with what I see. The village is now mine. Its surviving residents are under my control, and the lamb lies at my feet, defeated.

"Now you understand my might."

But as I turn to leave, she struggles to find her footing. Her voice is stern with a hint of steel. "This isn't over because I will never stop fighting you."

I smile to myself, amused by her stubbornness. But deep down, I know she's right. This isn't over.

It has only just begun.

~Avalon Late Autumn 2026~

ONE THING THAT never ceases to amaze me is how many assholes will flock to aid a rider who holds no value in their lives. The worst part is that Famine could give a shit less if he has a following or not, so the decision of who joins his ranks is left up to none other than the king of the pricks himself, Nevil Sausage Fingers Asshole Extraordinaire. If his name gets any longer, he's gonna need his own zip code.

And if I thought he was on a power trip in Death's horde, he's ten times worse now with no one to keep him in check.

I get it. I look like a hypocrite since I wasn't as vocal when people flocked to join War's army. It surprised me at first, but I soon realized why when I saw his charismatic leadership style. Besides, unlike this rider, I don't think he ever wanted to end us.

The idiots who sign up for Famine's little uprising are the worst of the worst. The only thing I can think of is that they hope it will give them more time to continue being the miserable jackasses they have proven themselves to be. Lord knows most of them won't be strolling through the pearly gates anytime soon. If anything, Raum will have a plethora of playthings when Famine is done with them.

The solitary upside to this little adventure with the one rider I dislike is his insatiable craving to break me, rendering me off-limits to Nevil and the rest of the penis posse. To be honest with you, Famine's daily ritual of forcing me to watch as he judges the people who somehow survive his initial attack is grating, but there's no way in hell I'll let him know it.

Although he came close today when the assholes, not him, passed judgment on a girl who couldn't have been much older than twenty. A recommendation by the prick sitting next to him stuffing his face with his fucking fat sausage fingers.

"It doesn't surprise me you swayed my younger brothers to your side. They always had a soft spot for humanity, but Thanatos… now that is a story I should like to hear. After all, he is the strongest of us."

"If you think I'm going to tell you shit about my time with Thanatos—"

"I also found this odd."

"Seems to be a running theme with you."

"My brother permitted no one to call him this except a chosen few. Mortals were never among this group, but you…. Not only did he permit it, but from what my guard has told me, my brother enjoyed hearing you say it. He preferred you call him this rather than what the other mortals know him as." I don't reply in part because I don't feel he deserves this information any more than the other information and because my throat is constricting after hearing him confess how Thanatos felt about me. If I try to speak, my throat would strangle the words before they ever cross my tongue.

"Apologies, I interrupted you. Please continue."

Swallowing the lump forming in my chest, I clear my throat, hoping he will not detect how much his confession affected me. "If you think I'm going to tell you anything, you're sadly mistaken."

"Oh, Avalon, I have no doubt you'll tell me everything I want to know." I drop my gaze from him, preparing to show him how wrong he is, until he claps his hand, and crying snaps my head back up.

"You will if you wish to save this mortal."

I tried to help her, but Famine's damn vines thwarted every attempt I made. I don't know what I dislike more, the damn rider, the stupid vines, or the prick always at his side—no strike that I hate the asshole at his side more.

No matter how hard I try to get her pleading cries out of my head, I fucking can't. After Nevil and his elite thugs carted her off, Famine had some newer recruits return me to the room he sleeps in. Like this fucking rider didn't get enough sleep over the centuries

Even when I attempt to find the solace I used to know when the world was dark and silent, I can't shake off my frustration with myself. I should have done more to help her. If I had a damn knife, I would have, but they no longer let me around anything sharp or pointy. This is a lesson Nevil learned the hard way since he walked with a limp for a week when they still had me doing the cooking. Such a freaking shame I missed my mark.

Now I'm just left wondering why she is no longer crying.

"One of these days, you will learn your place, lamb." Why does it always sound like he's spitting when he says this stupid nickname?

"One of these damn days, maybe you'll learn I don't bend."

"You will comply, or they will continue suffering." This comment pushes me past the point of frustration to blood-boiling irrational fury. I whip away from the window I've been staring out for only god fucking knows how long and storm as far as my chains will allow in his direction.

"You would have thought you damn riders would be smart enough to learn early on that if you want to keep people obedient, you should always hold something they value more than they do themselves, like the people in this community. Had you not allowed your men to torture her, I would have complied to protect her. But because you and the rest of the pricks in this camp are too damn dumb to see past the point of your own nose, you lost your leverage, so you don't have shit to hold over me."

"Pain may change your mind."

"I wouldn't bet on that. After all, I have lived a lifetime with pain inflicted by others. Split lips, broken bones, and cuts strategically slashed into my skin so as not to be detected. Hidden horrors no one was aware of unless I revealed them. An act I discovered early on only made my punishments worse. And the people who were supposed to love and protect me were the first assholes to heap this generosity on me. Yeah, they loved me right up until they traded me to their child-molesting drug dealer for two fucking crack rocks and a dime bag of dope. They handed me off like yesterday's trash to a man who took cruelty to a whole new level. So you see, there is very little you or anyone can do to me that hasn't already been done. Asshole!"

I expect him to bark some stupid retort back at me, but he doesn't. Instead, he strips off his goddamn clothes, lies down, puts his hands behind his head, and tells me it's past time for me to go to sleep. Knowing what I am preparing to do will not be pleasant, but I don't care, nor do I stop as I launch myself at the damn bed he's reclining on. My hope was the damn chain would break, leaving me enough length that I could strangle the fucker, but the only thing that happens is my feet come flying out from under me, causing me to slam against the floor back first. And fuck does it ever hurt like hell. I'm pretty sure I did permanent damage to my damn tongue.

If this wasn't shitty enough, while I am attempting to drag my sore ass back to my corner, the asshole has so generously granted me... Cammy and Nevil go at it again. If the bitch moans his name any louder, I won't have to worry about Pessy and War not finding me. Her dumb ass will lead them straight to the front door.

"Tell me what they are doing in there! These incessant sounds are maddening."

"Oh, what's the matter is the old bump and grind stirring something under that skirt you're wearing."

"It is called a sub—"

"Subligaculum. Yeah, I know Death told me." My comment doesn't come out with the bite I intended since I'm still trying to suck in the air I knocked out when I landed.

"My brother apprised you of the accurate term?"

"If you mean, did he tell me the name? Then, my answer remains the same. Yep, he sure the fuck did."

"Despite this, you persist in calling it a skirt."

"Pissing you off is more fun than giving you what you want."

"If you gave me what I desired, you would all cease to exist."

"Is that supposed to bother me, asshole?"

"I meant it as a warning. Now, I will not ask you again why this daughter of Eve continues to scream his name. It is infuriating."

"They're having sex."

"Explain this."

"You don't really explain sex. You do it."

"Then show me. I aspire to understand their present activity."

"Hell no!"

"This was not a request. You can either show me or tell me, but you will do one of them."

"I thought you damn riders were supposed to be watching us during your time in limbo."

"Each of us is only granted the ability to see certain things. This appears to be one of those things my father did not grant me access to."

"Well, I don't give a shit because I'm not telling you what sex is, and I sure as shit ain't showing you. If you want to know, ask your brothers, or better yet, march your ass into the next room and ask them if you can watch."

When he storms out of the room, I believe he is doing precisely that, but when the front door slams shut, I know he left. Since he refuses to meet with his brothers, it seems this is one thing the rider will have to remain in the dark about.

Score one for Avalon.

Chapter Twelve: The Truth Unveiled.

My mother always told me to keep my mouth closed if I didn't want flies to make a home in there. It's a lesson I should have kept in mind.

~Avalon Late Autumn 2026~

HE RETURNS HOURS LATER. I know this because Sausage and Bobblehead kept me awake with their damn obnoxious sex sounds. If god had any compassion, he would render Nevil a eunuch, or at the very least, cut his freaking libido down to nonexistent.

If the damn rider had a lick of sense, he would understand simple courtesy, like not plodding through the god-forsaken room while someone is trying to sleep on the hard-ass floor he relegated me to. But no. He's loud, obnoxious, and could give two shits less if he wakes the entire community, let alone the dumb pain-in-the-ass lamb he wants to torment.

Famine's heavy frame collapses on the bed. So the irritated groan I give him is almost as grating. I hope he finds my reaction every bit as aggravating as his stupid ass is to me. After the room falls silent, he mumbles, "All you needed to say was it is the act you mortals do to procreate."

"Who the hell did you con into telling you what they were doing?"

"No one told me."

"Wait, you convinced some dumb ass to show you? Jesus, now I really do believe the world is coming to an end."

"I assure you it is happening," he said, "but to answer your other inquiry, I would never allow a mortal pass to do such a thing."

"But you said someone showed you."

"Not in the physical sense. Unfortunately for the defiant lamb, you will soon realize your mistake was in not telling me."

"What the hell are you talking about, rider?"

"Since you refused to tell me or show me, which I now understand why you didn't want to do this, I had to ask someone else. This someone has a unique talent. He can show events that will happen in the future or anything that has happened in the past. It is how Thanatos knew War intended to bed you before my brother defiled himself with such a baser desire."

"What the hell are you talking about, Famine? War never bedded me."

"Only because our brother stepped in and stopped it before War could carry out what he longed to do. It seems my brother Thanatos didn't want to share his toy with our brother." My breathing increases with each detail he reveals. "Gabriel showed Thanatos your private time with War, hoping to force him to admit his feelings—emotions I will never understand—but my brother is smarter than those dullards. He knew if he acknowledged his feelings for you, they would use you against him to force him to do what he had already declared he would not. Destroy humanity. But he cannot hide his feelings from me."

"You spoke with Death?"

"No. I have already told you he is otherwise engaged at the moment."

"What does that mean?"

"Afraid he has forgotten all about you, little lamb? After what you permitted him to do to you."

"Fuck you, famine. You don't know shit."

"I am cognizant of the gratification he experienced upon witnessing you kneel before him. It seems you do possess the skill to bend your knee, although not in the manner I require."

"Your so off fucking base you can't see home plate any longer."

"Speaking of home, would you like to hear how he wished he never left the house on the hill you two shared? Or how much he loved the feel of your breast against his skin and the longing he held until you granted him access to slide inside—"

"Shut up!"

"I now know how you bewitched him. How all of my brothers have fallen to the daughters of Eve in this realm."

"What the fuck did you see?"

"All of it, Apple. Every sordid act you taught him."

~Death Date Unknown~

I HAVE BEEN lost in this place for so long that I no longer hold any concept of time. Has it been days, weeks, years, or centuries? I pray this is not the case because, if so, she is well beyond my reach, and I broke yet another promise. First, when I did not halt my brothers from arriving. Second, when I was not there to greet her and ferry her soul to her next life.

There must be a weakness, a break in the barrier that separates this realm from the others. If not, how would my father come here or place the souls he wishes to punish in this realm? The answer is he could not.

Many consider my father all-powerful, but even he has his limits. Entering something he has permanently closed would represent one of these. This tells me two things: he hasn't sealed it, and my father wants me to find the way out. Otherwise, he would never have come here to inform me of something he knew I would feel, the third seal being removed.

Fuck Famine.

How do I keep forgetting he has already been called to her world? It's still a mystery to me why she would call him there.

I cannot fathom what treachery would have forced her to open his seal, but Famine is not to be trusted. His loyalty lies only with ending humanity. I fear what he may do to her, what he may already be doing.

My mind races as I attempt to devise a plan to escape my prison and make my way into her world. I need to see her... to ensure her safety. To make sure she knows she is not alone. To beg her forgiveness for ever walking away.

But I must find a way out of here if I wish to do any of these things. The darkness is suffocating, and the silence is deafening. Perhaps using my celestial part is not the way. Could it be possible the answer is in utilizing my dark half? I try to remember the ways of the underworld, but it all seems so distant, so foreign. It is a piece I have always felt such shame in having. The irony is not lost on me if this is the answer.

I close my eyes and focus to drop the cage in which I have locked this portion of my essence. A wall I must now deconstruct brick by miserable brick.

After more time than I care to consider, I remove the last brick from the wall, and what happens is a surge of strength as my two halves become one.

A hard-to-describe physical sensation accompanies the flood of energy. It feels like my body is expanding, growing larger and more powerful. My body feels like a coiled spring, tensing and tightening, threatening to break at any moment. But with the physical changes comes something else... a sense of darkness... an understanding of danger and uncertainty.

As I open my eyes, I see that the surrounding darkness has lifted. I can now make out vague shapes in the distance. However, the oppressive silence remains, but it is no longer deafening. Instead, it feels like a comforting blanket, wrapping me in its embrace.

After taking several deep breaths, I try to focus my thoughts. I know I need to find a way out of here, but I am unsure where to start. My steps are slow and deliberate when I decide on my path as I try to sense any weakness in the barrier that separates this realm from the others.

Without warning, a faint tremor occurs beneath my feet, and I know that I have found what I am looking for. A small crack in the barrier, barely visible to the naked eye, but it's enough. I reach out to trace the fracture, feeling the energy coursing through it.

With a surge of power, I push my hand through the crack and feel a rush of air as I am propelled forward. I am no longer in the darkness, but I am not in the world I know either. I am somewhere in between, in an unfamiliar and strange realm.

But I am not afraid. I am filled with a sense of purpose, a sense of determination that comes from knowing that I am on the right path. Taking a deep breath, I continue forward.

*****

Once again, my sense of time eludes me, but it seems as though it's been dragging on longer than it should. I have been reluctant to embrace my dark side. Instead, I hold it at arm's length. I can't say why this concerns me, just that it does.

However, all of this changed when I came up empty-handed again. Since I have wasted far too much time already, I use my newfound gift and reach out with my senses, trying to find any sign of a weakness in the barrier. And then I feel it. A faint pulse, a glimmer of light.

I follow the pulse, letting it guide me through the darkness. It grows stronger with each step, and soon, I see a faint outline of a door. It's old, worn, and covered in cobwebs, but it's a way out.

As I walk, I can feel the power of my dark half growing stronger. It's like a flame that has been ignited, burning brighter and hotter with each passing moment. While it's a bit unsettling, I can somewhat manipulate it, thus providing me with the means to use it to my advantage.

Slamming my body against the door, it slowly gives way before splintering altogether, and a rush of cold air hits me, followed by howling winds. When I step through the doorway, I find myself on the edge of a cliff overlooking a vast, desolate landscape.

I take a deep breath and jump off the cliff, spreading my wings and soaring through the air. I fly towards her world, determined to find her and protect her from any harm that may come her way. But just as I am within feet of escape, the portal shifts before shimmering out of existence, and I find myself lost in the dark once more.

Leaving me cursing my father's name.

Chapter Thirteen: Lost in Thought.

WHENEVER WE BELIEVE WE ARE gaining ground on our brother, he blocks our path and disappears before we reach him. Does he do this because he is as reluctant to fight us as we are to face him?

The one bit of promising news is we can sense the little lamb still travels with him. We don't know if she does this willingly as she did with War and me or if he has made the choice for her. After all, we have all felt the pull to be near her.

Regardless, we can't afford to let our guard down. Our brother's unpredictable nature means we have to be prepared for anything. It's a constant game of cat and mouse, with the stakes increasing with each passing day.

The mounting tension building within War and myself is palpable. We are on edge, ready for anything, whether by attack or betrayal. Trust is a luxury we can't afford. Not if we wish to retrieve the little lamb and return to our families.

Amidst all this chaos, I can't help but wonder about Avalon. Is she safe? Is she happy? Does she know the danger she faces?

I try to push these thoughts aside and let my thoughts wander to my son. He has made so many strides over the last year. When he first entered my life, I was a very different person. A soul who was not worthy of his love, but over time, he has shown me what it meant to be valued, with no ulterior motives other than to follow his nature and give me his heart. While I credit Avalon and Greer for helping me become the being I am today, my Renny was the catalyst who began my transformation.

What do you want? The question he asks when he is hungry or thirsty, and my answer is the same today as when watching Thanatos carry him to his afterlife. "You. I only want you, son."

I find solace in these thoughts as I continue to search for my brother and Avalon. It's a comfort to know that even amidst all this chaos, there are still things worth fighting for, worth protecting.

But as the days turn into weeks and the weeks turn into months, I grow restless. My brother remains elusive, and the little lamb's safety remains uncertain.

With my thoughts consumed by the people we left behind, the distance between War and I grows until he is little more than a blip on the horizon. I suspect Ember, Ellie, and Duck occupy most of his thoughts these days as well. When we rode away from the community, we never fathomed it would take us this long. We believed Famine would charge into battle, ending our reign or his in one epic battle. But he didn't. Instead, he has avoided the fight none of us wanted.

We can only hope the community is thriving in our absence. The men and women who joined us are reliable and skilled in battle. Thanks to my brother's insistence that they hone their skill, I have no fear the ones we left behind are protected. And even if the rest of the warriors left, Xander would never abandon the ones we hold close to our hearts.

Perhaps I should have kept my focus on what matters because I am meandering along one second, and the next, Storm's unease has me taking notice of him. Between my companion rearing up and my brother galloping back in my direction informs me I have lived too long in my thoughts of the family I miss more every day. The unmistakable whizz of an arrow cutting through the air has me spinning Storm in search of the source.

"Pestilence move," War's distant shouts carry to me through our connection. Alas, his warning comes too late as another arrow finds its mark in the center of my chest. The one thought repeating in my head is, how did the fools sneak up on us without War or I hearing them?

The impact knocks me from Storm. A sharp pain spreads across my chest. With my strength waning, I cannot leave my knees, gasping for air, trying to fight off the darkness that threatens to consume me. Something is off because while an arrow that pierces my heart will pain me enough to halt any retaliation, it will not cripple me the way this one does.

I have only ever experienced this bone-deep ache once before. It was during a time in this realm that I would sooner forget since I faced losing my heart when they took the woman who yet holds it and my soul to the demon who wanted to claim it—the very one who forced our release. But forgetting is not an option.

"Well-well, looks like we meet again, Rider. Only this time, you do not have your little lamb to save you."

I look up only to discover a figure emerging from the shadows, a demon I owe some retribution to because of our last interaction. Raum.

Storm stomps the ground before he moves over me. He wants to protect me, but I fear what Raum will do if he remains.

His notorious reputation precedes him like a thunderstorm. For the mortals of this realm, his mere appearance would send chills down their spine. He walks like a predator on the hunt, his leather boots clacking ominously against the cracked and crumbling asphalt. His piercing gaze penetrates the soul, daring anyone to cross him. This leaves no doubt that his formidable presence commands respect, fear, and awe.

My attempts to stay conscious are met with a tumultuous storm of emotions. Disgust, anger, and the need for revenge all course through me, each one amplifying the physical pain from the wound caused by the arrow. My heart feels like it's being squeezed, and my breathing becomes labored. It takes all my willpower just to keep my eyes open and focused on Raum.

The rage is building inside me, but it's mixed with a sense of helplessness. I know with the demonic essence he coated the arrow in, I'm in no condition to fight him, and my brother is nowhere in sight. Is it possible War has also fallen to this angel our father cast aside?

Raum's approach is slow; his steps are deliberate and calculated. He's toying with me, relishing in my pain and weakness. His power emanates from him in waves, and I know that if I don't remove the arrow paralyzing me soon, I'm in trouble.

When he finally stands before me, I can see the twisted glee in his eyes. He's enjoying this, drinking in my misery. I grit my teeth and try to push myself up, but my body refuses to obey. The pain is too much, and I sink back down to the ground. But with Storm still standing in opposition, the soul stealer remains at a safe distance.

Raum's chuckle is dark, and his voice dripping with malice when he fially speaks. "You're pathetic, Rider. I thought you would put up more of a fight."

I glare at him, my disdain for him growing with every passing second. "Remove the arrow, and I will show you a fight while making you pay for this and all the other atrocities you have inflicted, Raum."

"Is that so, Rider?"

"I swear it."

His hand streaks out at me, snatching me by my shirt collar, his laughter echoing around us. "We shall see about that, Pessy. We shall see."

"Perhaps you will see it sooner than you anticipate, birdman." Did I pilfer a name the little lamb has called him during past encounters? Yes, and I did because I knew it would infuriate this being but also to....

"Shall we see now, demon? I believe I owe you a lesson regarding what happens when you threaten one of my brothers."

Allow War the time he needed to reach us. Based on his snapped head and wide-eyed expression, I believe my brother's arrival was sooner than the fallen angel expected. The world trembles when my brother drops from Red's back. His horse joins mine to form a barrier between our adversary and me.

If I could remove the damn arrow, I may yet assist my brother, but every second it remains embedded in my chest the darkness extends further as it consumes me from the inside. I am fortunate his archers did not strike the target he advised them to hit. Had it struck my heart, I would have been lost in darkness rather than battling to extract the projectile.

Raum's unwavering gaze locks on the rider he has yet to face. If I had not forced my eyes to remain open, I would have missed the slight dip of his chin.

"War. Move!" My warning is strained but enough to bring his focus to the woods at Raum's back, where several sons of Adam step forward with arrows nocked for round two of their assault.

War charges forward, his sword gleaming in the sunlight. The ground shakes beneath his horse's hooves as they crash into the first wave of attackers. Despite my effort to stand, the agony in my chest is unbearable, causing me to collapse against Storm, who remains steadfast by my side and will do so for as long as I draw breath.

Raum's laughter fills the air while he steps back to watch the battle unfold, but his amusement is short-lived. War is a force to be reckoned with, and soon, he has driven Raum behind the line of men who are ill-equipped to fight a rider whose sole purpose is battle and strife.

I reach for the arrow in my chest, gritting my teeth against the pain. I yank it out with a loud grunt, and the darkness recedes enough to allow some of my strength to return. My limbs are still trying to shake off the effects of the taint that coated the arrow, but I yank my bow from my back to join the fight.

The sound of metal clashing against metal fills the air as War battles the infantry while I focus on removing the air assault. Hatred and determination fuel each blow. Raum's laughter morphs into growls of frustration when he realizes how outmatched he is. His stiff posture and rigid muscles accent the incessant tapping his fingers are doing against his crossed arms. His bared teeth and clenched jaw are victory enough for me. When War strikes down the last of his guards, the reality he has lost forces him to do something I suspect he never believed he would do today. He retreats.

I turn to War, my chest heaving from the wound and exertion, saying the one thing I believe represents what his arrival means. We are getting closer to our goal. A goal Raum also seeks. The lamb. "Welcoming party?"

He nods, a smile spreading across his face. "It would seem so."

"Shall we greet our brother before returning to thank this being for such a warm welcome?"

"As if you need to ask, brother; however, you must rest before we face Famine."

I nod, knowing he's right. But for now, I savor this win and the camaraderie I share with my brother. Together, we can face anything.

The one question that refuses to vacate my troubled thoughts is: Why would Raum risk so much facing two riders?

My answer will come soon enough.

Chapter Fourteen: Submit.

~Sienna Winter 2026~

THE STERN LOOK COVERING MY mom's face when I huff my frustration has me offering her an apology. I understand why she feels we need to go, but she hasn't left the confines of town for almost a year now, so she doesn't know how dangerous the world has become. The least of our worries are these riders. Nowadays, the hazards of traveling these roadways far outweigh the risk that some random rider will show up in our little safe haven. No, we need to stay put, and somehow, I need to convince her of this.

"Mom, how will we feed everyone on the road?"

"How are we going to feed anyone when that damn rider shows up and destroys our crops?"

"We don't know he's coming this way."

"And we don't know he's not. Besides, I trust Jacob." It takes everything in me not to huff again. Jacob is a weasel. A weasel on two legs who showed up one day, claiming he was looking for a town his group could trade with.

They had weapons and medicine. We had food. I wanted to tell him to keep going or risk my size eight foot up his ass, but Mom feared his group would return and take what they wanted, rather than his current offer to trade. However, now I think it might have more to do with what's dangling between his legs and less about any imagined fear of them returning. Who knew some asshole could sway Mom by whispering only god knows what in her ear.

Since Mom runs this little community, she listened to my objections and then did what she wanted to do anyway. It's damn infuriating. I shake my head, trying to push the thought of my mom and Jacob out of my mind. I need to focus on the task at hand, convincing her that leaving town is not the best option for us right now.

"Mom, think about it. We don't know what's out there, and we might walk straight into the danger you're hoping to avoid by leaving here," I argue, hoping to appeal to her sense of caution.

"We can't just stay here and wait for someone to come and take everything we've worked for. We have an obligation to the people," she retorts, her voice firm.

"I agree about the obligation part, which is why—"

"Sin, I'm done talking about this right now. I'm meeting with Jacob's group, and if I think it's best, then we're going." When I attempt to interrupt, she throws her hand up to silence me like I'm five. The issue is I haven't been five for a long damn time. "This conversation is over."

"For now," I grumble while she gives me her patented, 'You're pushing your luck,' squinted evil eye. I let out a sigh, feeling defeated. I know my mom is just trying to protect our little community, but I can't help feeling like we're making a mistake by leaving. If we have to go, I would prefer doing it without the weasel's help. Before I can argue any further, the sound of approaching hooves catches our attention.

Jacob. Jesus, he would have to show up right goddamn now. I swear this prick isn't human since it seems like he has an innate ability to appear whenever we talk about him and his weaselly ways. Not to mention, he's become a thorn in my side since he and Mom slept together. He shows up whenever the hell he wants. Taking things I don't think he has any right to touch, but I suppose sleeping with my mom has garnered him free rein.

"Hey, beautiful. Ready?"

Ready? Ready for what? When I look at my mom, her entire body goes stiff. I wasn't supposed to hear this. What the hell is she up to?

"Mom?"

"I'm just going to meet with the other members of his group," she said.

"Right now? When you said you would talk to their group, I didn't think you met today." Since the only answer she gave me was a raised eyebrow, I tried to appeal to her sense of duty to the people we lead.

"By yourself? Without talking to the members of this community?"

"Sin." The way she said my name is meant as a warning that I'm pushing my luck. Well, too damn bad. If she thinks I'm going to stand by and let this shit happen around me, she's lost her ever-loving mind. I grit my teeth and try a different approach.

"Mom, we've been through this before. We don't have to rely on others to save us. We can stand on our own two feet. Hell, we've been doing it for years now. Why would we want to depend on outsiders?" Jacob scoffs. If I didn't already want to hit him, I do now.

My mom's face softens, and she sighs. The damn sound is like she has the weight of the world resting on her shoulders. "I know, Sienna. We can't afford to wait any longer."

I cross my arms over my chest, and she tries another tactic when she realizes I have no intention of relenting. "We need this, Sin. Before winter hits because we're running low on supplies."

What the fuck. Last I checked, we had plenty of supplies to make it through the colder months.

Jacob!

This bastard has been pilfering our stores, and Mom let him. I can't shake the feeling that something isn't right. Jacob has been acting a little too full of himself as of late—even more so than usual. I don't trust him. Hell, I don't trust any of them. They've never given me a reason to, and if I hope to convince Mom, I'll need concrete evidence to back up my suspicions. I guess the power of a penis has overridden any of her logical thoughts.

"Fine. But I'm going with you," I announce.

I know her initial instinct was to tell me no, but when Jacob sees I have no intention of budging on this matter, he nods in agreement, and of course, Mom follows suit. Damn, when did she lose her backbone?

We set out with a small group to meet with Jacob's people. As we walk, I keep a watchful eye on our surroundings, scanning for any signs of danger. But the journey is uneventful, and we make it to their camp without incident.

"You three stay here. Sienna and Gail, you two come with me."

"I think it would be best if—"

"She comes, Gail." I noticed the weasel has seemed to grow a pair during our trip here. I grit my teeth but hold my tongue. There's no point in arguing with him. We follow Jacob into a tent where a few people wait for us. They're introduced as the leaders of Jacob's group, and my mom wastes no time getting down to business.

"Jacob said your group is looking to add new members. I think we'd be perfect."

"Mom!"

"Sienna, you should have stayed back at the community, but since you insisted on coming, you will be quiet," she says, her tone firm and authoritative. I can see the desperation in her eyes, but I also see the glint of something else. Something that makes me uneasy.

"Of course, we're happy to help," the bigger guy sitting at the head table says, smiling. A grin that is just a little too damn friendly, if you ask me.

Jacob steps forward, his arm draped over my mom's shoulders. "But, of course, everything comes at a cost. We can't just give away our supplies for free."

"Jacob, this wasn't our deal," Mom hisses. "I thought we discussed this."

What the hell is this deal she made? And how has it changed in the time it took us to arrive at their camp? Mom's desperate eyes search the weasel's face before shifting to the two who run this shitty group. My fists curl into tight balls while anger boils inside me. I knew it. I fucking knew it. He betrayed us, Mom, and they're extorting us.

"What do you want?" I ask, my voice low and dangerous.

Jacob's eyes flicker over to me, and I can see the amusement in his gaze. He knows he's got the upper hand.

"We need something in return. Something valuable."

"And what's that?"

"Your land. We're tired of moving, and we've decided your little slice of heaven is the perfect place for us to put down roots.

Long term." My mom's eyes widen in shock, but before she can protest, I step forward.

"Absolutely not. Our land is not for sale."

The big guy smirks. "Then I guess we have nothing more to talk about."

He turns to walk away, but my mom grabs his arm. "Wait. Jacob, I thought we were in this together."

"He fucking used you, Mom."

My mom looks from me over to Jacob, who is still wearing that damn smirk he's had since we walked into this damn camp. "It's not safe for us to stay here any longer. The word is the riders are—"

"You don't need to worry about that. Trust me, we'll know long before a rider is within a hundred miles of here."

"Bullshit," I retort while the one who leads this group of misfits raises his eyebrows while he drums his fingers on the table. Arrogant asshole.

"Don't believe me?"

"Hell no!" I said in response to his ridiculous question.

"Well, darlin'..." If I rolled my eyes any harder at his stupid-ass darling comment, they'd be at risk of popping out of my damn head. "Let's just say I have a connection on the inside."

"On the inside of the riders. Do I look like an idiot to you?"

"You look like something," the dipshit sitting next to the leader said before blowing a kiss at me, making the men filling the tent laugh. This is the first time I realize Mom and I are the only two females here. Not a good sign.

"Jacob, Wayne, there has to be something else we can do." Damn, is that desperation seeping into her voice? And how does she know this Wayne asshole? I think she's finally figuring out that the daughter she refused to listen to regarding Jacob and these assholes might have been right this entire time.

The one mom called Wayne looks at her, and I can see the calculating gleam in his eyes. "There is, actually. I've been thinking about this for a while, and I think it could be a win-win situation for all of us."

I don't like the sound of this. Not one little bit. But before I can object, He continues.

"Your daughter."

"What about my daughter?" Mom asks, and like she used to do when I was a kid, she pushes an arm in front of me to put herself between me and the danger she didn't see coming.

"We want her," Wayne's sidekick said in a flat tone. It's like he's bartering for a piece of meat. Although in these asshole's eyes, it seems meat is exactly what I represent to these men. Seeing where this conversation is heading, I don't wait for anyone else to respond.

"Like our land, I'm not for sale, asshole."

"Fine, no deal, and we'll just take your damn land."

"You can't do that," I snarl, pushing past my mom's arm.

"You think you can stop us?"

"Yeah, I think I can."

"I told you," Jacob tells the other men in the room.

"Told them what?" Mom looks from Jacob to Wayne.

"Since your daughter doesn't want to play nice with the men in this room, she can be a different form of entertainment."

"Entertainment?" I ask.

"You're a fighter, aren't you?"

My mom looks at me, confusion and fear etched on her face. "What are you talking about?"

"I'm talking about a fight. A big one, and it's happening soon. Besides, we know a cop is, or should I say was, since the miserable prick is dead now trained Sienna." My fists clenched at my side, ready to strike them for talking about Dalton.

"You don't know shit about what my friend taught me!"

"I wouldn't be so sure because the extent of my knowledge might surprise you. At any rate, I had a fighter back out at the last minute. I need someone to take their place. And I think your daughter would be perfect. I hate to bust up such a pretty face, but…." Yeah, something tells me he doesn't have any issues busting up anything.

I feel the blood drain to my feet. A fight? I've heard rumors of underground fights happening in the bigger communities, but I never thought they'd come to our little corner of the world.

"I'm not a fighter," I say, my voice barely above a whisper.

Jacob just laughs. "Everyone's a fighter when they're backed into a corner. And if you win, we'll give you all the supplies you need. Enough to last you through the winter and leave you with your land."

"And if I lose."

"You won't like what happens if you lose."

"Courtesan or fighter, your choice, beauty," the smarmy asshole next to Wayne interjects.

"No option C?"

"Do Trevor or I look like men who give an option C, darlin'?" Wayne asks.

"You look like an ass—"

Mom clears her throat and grabs my arm while her gaze shifts to me. When I don't give an immediate answer, her eyes grow wide as she murmurs a soft plea. "Sin?"

Damn, is she asking me to do it, or is she pleading for me to tell them to fuck off? God, please tell me this wasn't the deal she made. My eyes slip closed as I try to calm the panic inside me. I don't want to fight. I don't want to be any part of this. Hell, I talk a big game, but I've never faced another person one on one.

In fact, aside from a few squabbles with passing raiders, I've never raised my hands against another person other than a few lessons Dalton taught me before he died. But I also can't bear the thought of losing everything we've worked for.

"Fine," I say, my voice barely audible. "I'll do it. I'll fight."

Jacob grins. "Excellent. The fight is in six weeks. I'll send someone to pick you up." The two, who seem to be the head assholes in charge of this little ragtag group, stand to leave, but Wayne stops short of the tent flap. His beefy hand stroking the stubble covering his chin while he looks me up and down. "You should have taken the first offer, darlin'. Don't even think about running. My fighters need the workout, and my coffers need the influx of shit I'll get from the other communities who will come to watch the beauty get her ass handed to her. You can take the supplies my men put out for you. You'll need your strength, beauty, but if you even think about screwing me over... I'll find you, put your ass in the ring anyway, and then take you the way I wanted to."

And with that, he turns and walks away, leaving us shell-shocked and helpless.

Fight or fuck? I don't like either choice, but it seems my mom has left me with few options. I'll pretend she didn't know this was the proposed outcome. It's best we leave this subject in the tent we just came out of.

We load our carts with food and supplies, but the entire time, I can't shake the feeling that we're being watched; yet every time I turn to look, there's no one there.

The return trip to our community isn't much better. I can't help but feel on edge. This damn daunting feeling that something terrible is about to happen won't relent. Hmm, it couldn't have anything to do with a fight I'm ill-prepared for or being fucked by some prick I don't want.

Nope, not at all.

Yeah, that's a load of bullshit.

Regardless, the damn thought plagues me the entire trip back. In fact, I'm so rattled I keep my hand on my weapon, ready for anything coming our way. But as we near our town, what I see has my heart dropping to my feet.

It seems Wayne's inside man isn't as inside as he hoped. Because if the big guy sitting on the horse isn't a rider, then I'm a monkey's uncle.

Chapter Fifteen: Careful What You Ask For.

~Avalon Winter 2026~

HAVE YOU EVER BEEN SO focused on something everything else just slips away? Well, let me assure you that's not the case for me. While I have been searching for any mechanism to get my ass as far away from Famine, Sausage, and Dimwit as possible, I am acutely aware of each damn second ticking by on the imaginary clock in my head.

There's one second lost with Renny, one with Ellie, and one with Duck. A big second I've lost with Suki, time missed with Xander, Greer, Sophie, and even Ember. There are two more ticks off the clock that I could have spent brushing Storm and Red's shiny coats rather than fiddling with these damn shackles. Time lost wondering if Pessy and War are feeling guilty for not finding me yet instead of teasing them or teaching them what it means to be human.

But this one here… well, this one is the second I lost that I could have used searching for Death. Because I believe something terrible has happened to him.

Famine has taken a lot from me, but he can't take away my thoughts—and lately, I reserve a lot of them for him— wondering if Death is okay. If he's happy or living the life he had hoped for, because while Famine can take the rest of my seconds away from me, he can't take the ones I let myself think about the rider I let go.

I wish this insufferable prick of a rider would tell me where he is, but no matter how many times I ask, allude to his whereabouts, beg, or threaten, Famine won't say anything beyond Thanatos is unavailable.

Have I told you already how big of a prick I think this rider is? And don't get me started with his horse. I thought Red hated me when I first encountered him and War, but compared to Famine's horse, Red was a big ol' teddy bear.

We've been on the move for three days now, and except for the occasional breaks to let the Dimwit piss and fluff her hair, we haven't stopped. Well, that's not true. We also get a break when she bitches enough to piss off the rider about her ass hurting from riding so long. I swear I want to kick her off the damn horse every time she does this since my ass is trudging behind their horses, not lounging upon one. If this wasn't bad enough, Famine still binds my hands together, and one of the three assholes riding the horses gets to hold the rope.

At least Famine is in charge of my restraints today rather than the asshole or his dimwit because when he has them, the worse I get is him giving me a dirty look when I slow down too much. When Nevil or Cammie is in charge of my bindings, they yank them, jerk them or snap the damn ropes so much that my wrists look like raw meat by the time we make camp. I will say the rope burns are preferential to the shit I'm stuck listening to now.

"Although wickedness should never be rewarded, our creator has overlooked humanity's propensity for such atrocities." This asshole rider has been droning on about how we mortals should have been offed long ago, and I've heard more than enough for one day.

"That's where you're mistaken because humanity isn't all evil."

"Said one of the mortals who prays we will spare their life."

"I could give a shit less what you do to me, asshole."

"There are no redeemable qualities to man."

"What about children? Children are innocent."

"There is wickedness even in the hearts of the young ones you seem so hellbent on protecting."

"You can't be serious? Children are not wicked. They're just… kids."

"Do they not covet what the others around them have?"

"What the hell are you talking about? Do you even know?"

"I have seen children steal a toy from another."

"That's not wickedness. That's a child who simply wishes to play with something."

"Coveting what someone else has is the epitome of wickedness and goes against my father's commands."

"These are kids we are talking about!"

"Mortals and your idealist beliefs. Your constant insistence you deserve more than he has already granted you is infuriating to many of his other creations. You covet what you do not have, while your body desires what you should not want." His eyes linger on me for a beat too long, and I swear my breasts are the focus of his unyielding stare. What a damn hypocrite.

"Are we talking about humans or you?"

He grunts but turns his attention back toward the road. The issue is he's picked up his pace, forcing me to jog to stay upright.

Filter Avalon: You need to discover one. Because if you had one, you wouldn't be running to keep your feet under you instead of risking them being dragged behind you. I'm beginning too long for the times when I actually got to ride with the riders rather than run behind one.

My goddamn legs hurt, my back aches, and my muscles burn to the point I want to beg him to stop, but I won't. Because I would sooner swallow my own tongue than ask him for anything. I've also lost so much weight from the lack of food and constant walking that my pants don't want to stay up on my hips. The last thing I want is to give Nevil a peep show. The mere thought makes my skin crawl.

Perhaps the better option would have been paying attention to my surroundings during this little forced march because when I look up, Nevil is sneering at me with a knowing grin, and it doesn't take long for me to figure out why. We're approaching a community.

Talk about Déjà vu.

Damn it all to hell.

Nevil mumbles something to Cammie, who replies with a mocking sneer, "Do it, babe."

"Announce him."

You have got to be shitting me! After all this time, all the shit that's happened to him, to me, to the world... this is the best this idiot can come up with. The same old tired shit he spewed back when we traveled with Death. He truly is an idiot. An idiot I have no intention of pacifying. I don't care what they do to me. They can all go screw off.

"Announce him, bitch."

"Yeah, bitch," Cammie echoes.

"Up yours, dimwit. As for you, asshole, I've already told you my thoughts on this once before, but since it still hasn't registered, I'll clue you in again. The people who live in this place don't need me to announce the goddamn riders. They are all too aware of the dark cloud looming over their peaceful lives."

Famine's lip lifts in a sneer before he tells me in no uncertain terms how much he dislikes what I said.

"If you wish to retain your venomous tongue, you will not take my father's name in vain again."

"Don't like it?"

"No, I do not appreciate the reference."

"And you think they appreciate your ass strolling in there and ruining their fucking lives?"

"I've heard more than enough from you today."

"Then stop doing shit to piss me off."

"When are you gonna learn you don't run things around here?" Cammie shouts down at me from her perched spot behind Sausage.

"Right around the time you learn to keep your fucking legs closed." Cammie's response is to gasp like I said something to offend her, but Nevil's is to ride up next to where I'm trailing behind Famine's horse so he can kick me. I should have seen it coming. It's one of his favorite pastimes. Something he loves to do to me anytime he's on top of a horse. Maybe if I had paid attention, I wouldn't be lying face-first in the damn mud right now.

The worst part is that Famine's horse is dragging me since I am no longer walking. This damn horse turns and looks at me like I'm the asshole in this situation. You would think rather than having to expel the extra energy to pull me through the muck and the mud, he would stop so I could get my damn feet under me, but no, he keeps plodding along, making it impossible for me to stand back up. Something Bobblehead finds over-the-top fucking hilarious.

After several minutes—and the safe distance between us and the people who are about to have their lives ruined removed—Famine stops, letting me come to full height. With my hands covered in mud and blood, I do my best to swipe the muck from my face. I figured I made my stance clear on the entire subject of announcing a rider, but Nevil has other thoughts since he's still glaring down at me while Cammie has some fake ass pouty expression directed at me. We're talking... bottom lip jutted out, quivering and all. I'm waiting for her to wipe away the nonexistent tears, and if she does, I don't see it since I have redirected my focus toward the town I want to bypass.

"Right. Now. Avalon!"

"You sure you want me to do this?" I ask the rider, who has thus far remained silent on the whole "announce him" topic. Famine's stoic demeanor makes it hard to read his thoughts, but I take his lack of objections to mean he likes the idea of me announcing him. He probably should have discussed this with his brother first. With Nevil still glaring at me while Cammie points at the community like I don't see where the hell it's at, I make my mind up.

Okay, if they want their moment in the sun, they'll get it. They should all remember they fucking ask for it. I march past Famine's horse, who snorts while I grab the rope Famine is still holding and give it a good yank. I want to have all the extra slack I can get to ensure everyone in this town hears my announcement. And since I don't imagine the three assholes I'm traveling with will like what I have to say, I'm going to need all the slack I can get.

Just as I'm about to begin with this asshole's herald, five more people crest the hill to hear his formal announcement. Excellent timing. The more, the merrier.

The new arrivals stand there in wide-eyed, mouth-gaped confusion. All except one who whips her bow up and aims it at us. Ballsy but stupid.

"Ladies and gentlemen. Boys and girls… gather around because we have special guests here today. It's none other than the prick, the dimwit, and the asshole. Of course, you might better know the prick as the infamous Famine. Yes, that's right, the third rider of the apocalypse is here to ruin your day. He and his band of merry idiots have come to spread death and destruction, to take what's yours and leave you with nothing. So, if you don't want your valuables ending up in the hands of a dimwit, your food in the belly of an asshole, or your life snuffed out by a prick who plays with plants, I suggest you turn around and run as fast as you can in the opposite direction. You'll find the quickest exits to the left, right, or directly behind you. Consider this your friendly PSA for the day."

I let go of the rope, bow to the community, and step back while waiting for the inevitable backlash from Nevil and Cammie. But it doesn't come. Instead, Famine just stares at me with an unreadable expression while the rest of his group looks on in shock. Maybe they didn't expect me to have the guts to stand up to them. Or maybe they're stunned stupid. Nah, strike that because Cammie and Nevil have always been stupid.

Either way, I'm ready for whatever comes next. I've been through enough to know there is nothing else they can do to me that I haven't already endured. So, I stand tall, waiting for their next move, ready to face it head-on. Because if there's one thing I've learned in this new world, it's that survival depends on your ability to adapt, to be strong in the face of adversity, and never give up, no matter how many times they try to break me.

And like I've told this asshole before…. *Better men have tried.*

~*Famine Winter 2026*~

HOW THE LAMB survived my brothers is something I will never understand. I know I have thought of killing her more times than not. She is obstinate, defiant, and refuses to back down in the face of danger. But there is also a fire in her I can't help but admire. She has a strength that belies her dwindling frame and a determination that rivals, dare I say, even my own.

I watch as she stands before me, unflinching, despite—as she likes to call him—the asshole's attempts to break her. And I can't help but feel a grudging respect for this mortal. She may be a thorn in my side, but something about her draws me in. Perhaps she has powers they did not make me aware of. Gabriel showed me how Thanatos fell to her. Yet, could he be withholding vital information?

I clear my throat, drawing her attention back to me. "Your audacity is quite apparent, lamb, and not appreciated," I say, my voice low and ominous.

"Thank you."

"It was not a compliment," I advise her.

She narrows her eyes at me but doesn't back down. "Well, too bad because I take it as a compliment," she said, her tone mocking.

"You would."

"Up yours."

"May I ask what that was all about?"

"You and the asshole wanted me to announce you. I announced you."

"You believe they did not comprehend who rode up to their community."

"My damn point exactly. Which is why I told them who you are in a manner befitting the prick you have proven yourself to be." Having enough of her contemptuous attitude, I flick my hand and send my vines to silence her. She struggles to break the thorny vines, but I only tighten them to ensure she understands her place in this horde. In a world I now control. She may have bewitched my brothers, but she is nothing to me. Just a mortal who has yet to figure out her importance while I remain an unwavering force in her world.

But even as I hold her captive, I can't help but feel a sense of unease. There is something different about her, something that sets her apart from the other humans I have encountered. And I can't shake the feeling that there is more to her than meets the eye.

To my amazement and Nevil's dismay, she doesn't flinch or scream in pain. Instead, she stands there, her eyes blazing in defiance as the vines wrap around her. It's as if she's challenging me to do more, to break what no one else ever has. And for a moment, I'm tempted to do just that. Until the most unwelcome voice of reason reminds me that I may yet have use for this lamb. Only by her hand can I—if I so choose—pull my eldest brother out of the prison our father sent him to.

With a quick flick of my wrist, the vines disengage, leaving her off-balance and scrambling to remain upright. "Despite being a thorn in my side, lamb, you still hold some value to me. An asset I cannot deny or remove at present," I state in a low and menacing tone.

She straightens up, her eyes still blazing with scorn. "I'm not a possession. Least of all yours, Famine. Whatever you have planned for me, you can shove it up your ass." Her declaration might have held more weight had she not panted throughout her tirade.

While considering my response to her derogatory remark, a commotion in the distance draws my attention. The group of humans who until now have remained at what they believed was a safe distance approach, armed and ready for a fight. When will the mortals of this world realize that any futile effort to oppose me will inevitably lead to their agonizing demise?

With the lamb busy catching her breath, I turn to face the newcomers, ready to unleash my power upon them. When I am struck silent by the fiery response from one daughter of Eve facing me.

"Step the hell away from her, asshole," the one who has held her bow at the ready demands. Does this foolish daughter of Eve not realize who she's made demands of? I am preparing to advise her when I'm interrupted by another irritant.

"Nah, he's the prick. That one over there is the asshole," the lamb mocks while rubbing the spot on her neck where the vines apparently did not squeeze tight enough.

Perhaps I released her too soon.

Chapter Sixteen: Incapable.

I once said I wished I had the ability to lie my head down and dream like a mortal. My rapacious reason was to become a man worthy of my Apple. I may have reconsidered if I knew what else lurked in that world.

~Death Time Unknown~

ANOTHER ATTEMPT AND ANOTHER HOPE shattered. Having another chance to escape thwarted leaves me frustrated and feeling trapped again, but I refuse to give up. There must be another way out of this darkness, and I am determined to find it. I feel a renewed sense of strength and purpose with my dark half almost fully integrated into my being.

I explore this strange realm, searching for any clues or signs that may lead me to an exit. I'm sick of living in darkness. Even during the brief moments I am teased with light, the landscape is barren and desolate. It's nothing. It's just a different nothing than the darkness I live in most days.

I would like to say one is no better than the other, yet if I'm truthful, I prefer the dark. At least when there is no light, I am not constantly reminded of time passing. Time is my worst enemy right now. But as I continue to explore, I sense a faint energy, a presence that feels familiar yet foreign. Something I should know but hides just beyond my grasp.

I follow it, my wings carrying me effortlessly through the darkness. I cannot shake the feeling of time running out as I get closer. It's a sense of urgency building within me. A nagging itch insisting I must do something. I must act now.

Finally, I find what has drawn me here.

A lone woman.

A welcome sight after all this time left alone and living in darkness.

She is standing in the distance, her back turned to me. Without hesitation, I fly towards her, ready to scoop her up and carry her away from this place. But as I get closer, I realize the folly of this plan.

She is not alone. There are other beings with her, dark, shadowy figures who seem to be closing in on her. I can sense their malevolence, their intent to harm her. What I don't understand is why she doesn't run. It appears she plans to fight these creatures. Is there something wrong with her?

I land beside her, spreading my wings to shield her from the attackers. My dark half surges forward, and I am consumed by a fierce, unrelenting power. My previous task no longer consumes my every thought as a new one takes root. Protecting the woman behind me. I am a force to be reckoned with and will shield her at any cost.

Although I cannot say why I am so struck by her. I just am.

The shadowy figures close in, their eyes glowing with an otherworldly light. I can feel their hatred, their desire to destroy us both. They lunge at us, their claws and teeth bared. I strike back my dark half and celestial powers combined with a blast of dark energy, sending them flying. The woman beside me joins in, her movements graceful and deadly. Together, we fight off wave after wave of attackers.

But they keep coming, relentless in their assault. One of them grabs hold of the woman, and I feel a surge of panic because something inside me is demanding we protect her. We can't lose her now, not after just finding her. I unleash the torrent of anger building within me since my father left me to face this hell alone.

I slash out, tearing the creature apart. One somehow sneaks in behind me, and she yelps as the damnable thing lashes out at her. With a roar, I whip around, my dark wings slashing the throat of the one who hurt her, but more are coming out of the shadows. The faceless beings lunge at me, their claws and teeth gnashing. But I'm too fast, too strong.

The woman looks at me, her eyes—familiar eyes—filled with gratitude. Yet there's no time for thanks, let alone the seconds to spare contemplating how I know her or why I feel so compelled to kill anything near her.

I strike the closest creature, my fist connecting with its face. It recoils, screeching in pain. Another leaps at me, but I dodge, spinning around to deliver a powerful kick. It staggers back, its form flickering in and out of existence.

Together, we are a force to be reckoned with. We fight, our bodies moving in perfect harmony. The creatures continue to attack, but we are relentless. We strike them down, one after another.

Each time I believe we have faced the last of them, a new wave emerges from the darkness surrounding us. We will have to continue fighting as long as they have shadows to appear from. This is something I have no issue with; however, her ragged pants confirm she is close to collapsing.

I reach out, taking her hand, desperate to take her to safety. We run through the darkness, pursued by a never-ending horde of monsters. Until I see a glimmer of light in the distance. It's our way out. Scooping her into my arms, we race towards what may be our only safe haven from the darkness creeping closer. The shadows are hot on our heels, but we won't let them catch us.

Unsure what will happen when we cross, I pull her tighter against my body as we break through the barrier and emerge into the sunlight. The darkness around us dissipates, replaced by a soft, warm light, and with the sudden beams of muted light, the creatures stop their pursuit.

Which is a good thing since the force I expelled pushing from one realm to another has sent her and me sprawling.

My heart races as I try to catch my breath while she lies beside me, panting and coughing. I'm sure the intensity she experienced during our journey between realms was overwhelming. Every muscle within me aches from the exertion. Yet when she struggles to sit up, I reach out to help her. We sit there for a few moments, gasping for air and trying to regain our composure.

"Did we just travel between worlds?" she asks her voice nothing more than a whisper.

"Something like that," I nod, still too winded to speak much more than these few words.

"Thank you," she says with the slightest of laughs. "I couldn't have done it without you."

I smile, take a deep breath, and let myself savor the moment. Satisfied for the first time in a long time. But before I can say much else, the woman turns to me, her eyes filled with familiarity. She gasps. Her body goes still, her eyes blinking as if trying to chase away the illusion before her.

"You," she whispers, her voice trembling, a mixture of awareness, awe, and fear in her eyes. "Death…. How—how… We–we've been searching for you."

I am stunned, unsure of what to say or do. But before I can react, she reaches out and takes my hand. "Come with me. We need to leave before it's too late," she says, pulling me towards a shimmering portal that has appeared in the distance. "I know the way out of here."

I follow her, my heart racing with excitement and anticipation. Filled with both a sense of relief and an unrelenting joy as we step through the portal. I have finally found a way out of this darkness.

The light chases away the last of the shadows, removing the hazy fog I've felt since… I can't tell you how long. But with this lifted, the sight of her now leaves my heart shattered into more fragments than I can ever piece back together.

No, I won't believe it.

It's not possible.

They cannot send her here.

Not to this place.

"Apple?" My voice cracks from the knowledge I did this to her.

"I'm waiting for you, Thanatos." With a smile, she recedes into darkness, leaving me with only a faint whisper echoing in my ears. "Do you still think about me?"

Raw fury fills me while I race in the direction she disappeared. Until a cage slams down around me, preventing me from following her.

"Apple!" Nothing.

"Avalon!" Only darkness.

"Come back to me!" She's alone out there.

"AVALON!" My eyes snap open, and I'm bathed in sweat. A thick sheen clings to me even as the vision and memory of her touch slip away.

Was she an illusion?

A hope?

Did Michael find a way to torment me even here?

"No, a gift I granted." I look up, only to find my demonic half leaning against the rocky outcrop I now remember sitting under to rest while contemplating my next moves.

"You did this to me?"

"I felt it only right since you have locked me in a similar prison for centuries."

"I never tortured you with the image of—"

"Someone I love?"

"I don't love the lamb."

"Reaper, I live inside you. I share your emotions, your thoughts, your desires. Of course, you fucking love her… just as I do."

"You have never met her," I said, leaping to my feet as the last of the fog from a dream I should not be capable of having melted away.

"Because you did not permit me to, yet I love her all the same."

I turn to face my demonic half, my eyes blazing with anger. "And I never will. She's not meant for this life and should never be pulled here. This place is a prison, a punishment for our sins. Showing me this has only made it worse! You had no right to make me think…."

My demonic half smirks, his eyes glinting with amusement. "And yet, you couldn't resist the temptation to see her. Couldn't resist the pull of her presence, the warmth of her touch."

I clench my fists, feeling the anger boiling inside me. "You have no right to talk about her like that. She's not some toy for you to play with. Avalon is—"

"Ours."

"NO. Avalon belongs to no one."

My demonic half shrugs, his expression indifferent. "Too bad because she's the key to our salvation. The only one who can bring you back to the light. Besides, you and I both know she has already made her choice. She has given herself to us."

I shake my head, feeling the weight of my guilt crushing me. "I won't let her suffer because of me. If others know how we feel, they could use her against us. They could put her in a place like... No! I won't allow it. She will never be trapped in a hellhole like this. She deserves better than that."

My demonic half chuckles, his eyes glinting with malice. "And what about you? Do you deserve better than this? Do we deserve to be locked up in this place for all eternity?"

I pause, feeling the weight of his words. "I... I don't know. Maybe I do. Maybe I deserve to suffer for what I've done to her and her world. For not staying with her or returning when I realized she was in danger. Instead, I tried to remain the dutiful reaper our father praised."

My demonic half shakes his head, his expression softening. "No, you don't. You've suffered enough. It's time to let go of your past and embrace our future. And the key to that future lies with the lamb. She's the only one who can set us free."

"I was a fool."

"Yes, you were. However, it's not too late."

"I will give her the life she wants if it is the last thing I fucking do." I turn to begin my search for an exit but want to clarify one thing to my other half. "If you ever pull a stunt like this again, I will lock you so far inside me you will forget your own goddamn name."

He clucks his tongue while the smirk returns. "We will give her a life we all deserve, but only if you stop taking our creator's name in vain. Because if you don't, we won't have to worry about the woman we love since he will lock us both away. It is past time for us to return to our Apple. Now wake the fuck up, and let's find a way out of this hellhole."

My eyes snap open, only to find I'm alone again in the dark. With a new purpose, a determination… to return to the woman we love.

Chapter Seventeen: Fast Learner

WHAT WAS I THINKING? THIS seems to be the question playing on repeat. But it's only logical since I don't know why I said yes. Why would I agree to enter the underground fights when I don't know what the hell I'm doing? Damn it, I wish I had never insisted on going with them. Had I kept my ass right here in camp, something tells me I wouldn't be facing a lifetime of pain.

But that's not me. I won't hide behind these walls and let others decide my fate. Let's be honest; I didn't make this choice to save my skin, but because what my mom went to discuss affected all the people who live here. I don't care if I've known them for twenty years or ten days. They are a part of the community I help protect, which means I also want to keep them safe.

I suppose offering yourself up as a sacrificial lamb fulfills this decree.

Speaking of lambs. I'm more than a little confused about why the rider, who isn't known for compassion, continues to let us live and why he's still here. For some reason, I can't keep my eyes from wandering to him whenever he's around. I don't know what I expected the riders to look like or how they should act, but the one who turned up, isn't it.

Of the three who travel with him, Cammie and Nevil are the epitome of what I expected. Cammie is whiney, demanding, and a princess in her own mind. Nevil is mean, unnerving, and someone I steer clear of for more reasons than I care to give.

Then there's the one he calls lamb. Avalon. I would be happy to have her remain in this community for as long as she is willing. She isn't like most people looking for a handout without being prepared to earn it. The way the other two treat her is reprehensible. I don't know why the rider permits their abuse or why he keeps Avalon in chains. One thing is for sure, I don't plan to ask. My ass is in enough hot water without adding a pissy rider to the mix.

So, the intelligent choice is to stay away and continue training for what will become my life in a few short weeks. I throw punches until my arms are on fire. I duck and weave while I try to remember to keep my hands up. All things Dalton taught me. Damn, I miss him. If Dalton were here, he would know what to do to get me out of this shitty situation.

Dalton was a police officer when the world fell around us. He wasn't just a good man. He was a great man. I looked up to Dalton as the dad I never had. I don't blame my dad for leaving. My mom can be…difficult. She is demanding and often times overbearing. She's afraid of getting older and, most of the time prefers to act like my friend rather than my mother. But she has an enormous heart. She cares about us, and I have to believe she thought what she was doing would help us and not end with her daughter as their possession.

Dalton was insistent about me learning how to protect myself. The month before he died, we began our training sessions. He had just finished teaching me how to escape if someone snuck up behind me, and the following week, he was going to begin sparring with me.

I can still hear him saying you can't learn how to fight by hitting a dummy because it doesn't hit back. To which I would laugh and tell him nope, we reserve this for assholes and cops turned fighting instructors. But some freak fucking flood stole him from this world. No one knows where it came from or even how it occurred since there hadn't been any substantial rain for weeks.

After we laid him to rest, I stopped training. I didn't have the heart to continue something I started with him. Hindsight being twenty-twenty, I regret this choice, and I bet if Dalton can see me, he's grumbling about me not keeping up with the training. He would have told me it doesn't matter if I'm there or here, kiddo, you need to be prepared for anything. Boy, was he right.

Two hours into my training session, I'm interrupted by a gruff question. "What are you doing?"

I turn to find Famine standing behind me, his legs shoulder width apart, his arms crossed over his massive chest with an intensity in his eyes I've never seen before.

"I… I'm training."

"For what?"

"To fight."

"Who is it you plan on fighting, Sienna?"

"You know my name?"

"I know all of your names. Now answer my question."

"The people who would try to hurt me."

"People wish to hurt you?"

"Well, not at present, but a friend once told me I should be prepared for anything. I guess I decided it's time to listen." No point in telling this rider I stuck my ass in hot water with a bunch of idiots who plan on putting these nonexistent fighting skills to work.

"What exactly are you teaching yourself?"

"How to spar?" I know my response is more a question than an answer, but he makes me nervous.

"And this is how you do it?"

"Um… Yes? I think so?" Okay, so definitely more questions than answers. The reason for my uncertainty is simple…I don't have the first freaking clue how to do it. Like I said, Dalton planned on teaching me; we just hadn't gotten there yet.

"Show me what you have learned, sparring yourself." This comment kinda makes me sound like a dumbass. I know when you spar, it's common to do it against an opponent, but since I don't have anyone volunteering, sparring by myself is the best I can do. Err…well…I suppose if the rider is volunteering to be the missing opponent, I think I prefer to spar myself.

"You mean like on you?"

"Is someone here I have not yet seen?"

"Nope. Just me. All alone," I tell him before mumbling the rest. "looking ridiculous."

Even with his confirmation, I'm still unsure if I should do what he asked. Until he presses further into my space, leaving me with no other option but to defend myself, like Dalton taught me.

I raise my fists, not knowing if the adrenaline rush is from the intense workout or the exhilarating proximity to the rider. Sweat trickles from my forehead down my cheek as my muscles tense, and I don't miss how his eyes track the tiny bead. The fine hairs on my arms lift from the crackle of anticipation. What the hell is wrong with me?

I lunge forward with one swift movement, ready to unleash a barrage of punches, before weaving and bobbing like a seasoned fighter. But the rider stops me with ease. Hell, aside from moving the arm he used to block me, his stance is the same as when I discovered him watching me.

I throw a roundhouse kick, my leg extending with explosive force. In my mind, the impact will send him flying. I'm ready to do my victory dance, satisfied with how much I have improved. Ha, who needs a real opponent? But the victory dance doesn't happen when he remains in the same position with my ankle held in his hand. Damn it.

This time, I unleash a flurry of punches aimed at a different location on the rider. This is it. No way is he walking away unscathed this time. My body moves with precision, my muscles fueled with sheer determination to prove I can do this. Only to have him move, dodge, and block all my attempts without his feet moving from where they have remained rooted.

Despite my efforts, the rider's experience and skills are undeniable. Even my agility doesn't help me. With his size and bulk, I thought if I continued moving, it might throw the rider off balance. But he anticipates each one, countering my efforts with no problem. If I wasn't fighting him, I would be in awe of his graceful movements. But I am fighting him, so I need to stop ogling him and get back to the matter he came in here for.

Me kicking his ass.

With a single, agile maneuver, he dodges another kick, causing me to lose my footing and land with a thud on the mat. The force of my back hitting the ground sends shockwaves through my body.

Okay, in reality, not so much me kicking ass as me flailing around like a fool while he stands here looking like some damn Greek warrior god.

I lay there for a moment, the taste of defeat hanging heavy in the air. It's humiliating and confirms I don't stand a chance in hell when I face a real opponent.

"Again, Sienna. You must use your size to your advantage and break my defenses without trying to overpower me. Because you will never win this way. You must use intellect to win."

I rise to my feet, a newfound determination coursing through my veins. The rider looks at me with a mixture of respect and understanding. Does he know this setback will only strengthen my resolve?

Time seems to slow down as I circle him. Since I'm no longer attacking head-on, it forces him to move if he wants to keep me in his sights. The energy filling the room crackles between us. I refuse to give up, pushing myself to the limits, determined to prove worthy of his challenge.

I'm not sure if he is taking it easy on me or if I'm doing this good because, somehow, I haven't ended up on my ass again, and I seem to hold my own against a rider. Until I make one mistake too many when my feet somehow get twisted up in the mat, and I end up in his arms.

I struggle to regain my balance, but the rider's grip is firm. I can feel his strength overpowering me, and a wave of frustration washes over me. How did I let this happen?

His eyes scan my face. I swear if this was any other man I was being held by, I would say he was preparing to kiss me, but it's not. This is a rider. A rider who told me to show him what my friend had taught me, so I did what I thought he was waiting for. I swing my arm around to throw him off balance.

It would have worked too, if not for his vines streaking in to hold my arms mid-swing.

"Hey, that's not fair."

"Who said I fight fair?"

He runs his fingers across my cheek, but he pulls his hand away like touching me caused him physical pain.

"Famine?"

"You should continue your session," he mumbles before leaving me with more questions than answers.

~ Famine ~

I DON'T KNOW why I went in there, nor do I understand why I offered my assistance other than to say there's something about this mortal I feel drawn to. I could pretend nothing happened between us just now, but it would be little more than a lie.

The prudent choice would be for me to leave. Move on to the next town, the next group who will fall at my hands.

Her laugh carries to me like a promise of what could be in the wind. When I turn, I find her talking with a son of Adam. Every muscle feels taut, wired to explode at any second, which only intensifies when his hand finds its way to her back. I would be within my rights as a rider to rip it from his body.

What in my father's name am I doing? If I harmed this mortal, it would not align with my mission. It would be from the surge of emotions she evokes. Nothing about what I want to do to this son of Adam follows my father's decree.

Yes, it would be best if I left. However, as my eyes track her movements, I know I have no intention of leaving until I understand what she has done to me.

*****

After two weeks, my interest in this woman has only grown, leaving me with only one option to remove all thoughts of her. I must prove she is not worthy. My scales will tell me what my mind has failed to do. Prove this daughter of Eve is attempting to bewitch me, just as the ones who tricked my brothers have done.

With my scales in hand, I storm into where she continues her training. I'm unsure why she continues such folly. Sienna is not meant to fight. She is meant to lead. Although I respect her for aspiring to protect the ones she cares for.

I would have delayed measuring her worth if I had realized the lamb was acting as her sparring partner today.

"Famine, what are you doing?" the lamb asks as if she believes she has earned the right to question me.

"It is time for you to leave, lamb."

"Not before you tell me why you have your scales." This mortal defiance will not go unanswered when I send my vines to collect her. With her secure in my cage, I flick my wrist, letting them deposit her outside before they block her from entering again.

"Famine, is everything…alright?" Sienna's apprehension further proves she will fail my test. There is no other reason she would fear what my arrival means.

"I will require your hand."

"Why?" she drags out this word, further establishing I am on the right path.

"The reason does not matter. You will consent."

"Okay," she says, and I do not miss the slight tremble in her voice. Without another word, I prick my finger before doing the same to hers. My chest tightens when a small gasp escapes her parted lips. I watch as her tongue slips out enough to moisten them. Forgotten are my scales while contemplating if her lips are as soft as her hands.

"Um…are you done?" I shake my head to clear the confusion this enchantress must have employed to distract me, but I am not swayed with so little effort.

My eyes drop to the scale, still awaiting its offering. In mere seconds, I will know the truth. It's a matter of placing one drop on the dish. This will give me the answers I seek, so why am I hesitating?

My thumb slides over the back of her hand. If this is the last time I will permit myself to touch her, I want to commit the feel of her soft skin to memory.

"Famine?" I squeeze her finger and place a drop of blood on the other side.

If I were mortal, I would believe the scales remain even, but I'm not. Even so, this slight descent proves the opposite of what I thought it would. My vines recede when I stalk toward the door. Without a word to the lamb who has remained at the door, I yank her over to the scales because I need to know. I remove Sienna's sample, lift my scythe, and jab the lamb's finger.

"Not this shit again. Didn't we already do this once, rider?"

"Silence yourself, lamb."

"What's going on?" Sienna asks.

"Oh, well, that's simple, Sin." The glare I give her when she mentions this word…a word I have already explained to them all, does not represent an accurate portrayal of the woman they use it for, should silence the lamb. It doesn't. Avalon's response was to roll her damn eyes before finishing what she wanted to tell Sienna. "He's testing our worth."

"What?" she asks as she looks at the drop of blood beading from the spot I stuck her finger. Like the last time I tested the lamb's blood, the scale does not budge. My gaze flicks from Avalon to Sienna, wondering if my travels somehow damaged the scales. Yes, of course, this has to be the reason. Again, I storm to the door. The first person I see is the mother of Sienna.

"You, come." I bark because I am losing my patience. Unlike Sienna and the lamb, this mortal does as I command without opposition. Her only objection comes when she sees the scythe approaching her outstretched finger. When the scales drop, I know I have my answer. The issue is I don't know what to do with it.

Chapter Eighteen: Dreams.

I SUPPOSE IT'S ONLY FITTING that Death occupies my dreams since he's overtaken most of my thoughts when I'm awake. I would stop dreaming of him if I could, because unlike my thoughts—ones often coming from memories of our time together—the dreams are beset with horrible images of him being lost and alone in the dark.

It's as if he's searching for me, but I can never reach him. So when I wake from these dreams, I'm left feeling helpless and frustrated, but I can't help but feel drawn to them. They're like a haunting melody that I can't get out of my head.

I try to push the dreams aside and focus on my life. I have an objective, people to protect, and a new way of life that I'm still getting used to. But even in my brief moments of normalcy, Death lingers in the back of my mind. It's like he's a part of me now, and I can't shake him off.

Three nights ago, my racing heart woke me covered in a cold sweat. The dream was different this time. It's no longer just the Rider lost in the dark. I'm wandering aimlessly, searching for something I cannot find. Until Death appears with his hand outstretched, offering me a way out. Then he's gone, and I'm back on a hard floor in the room Famine forces me to sleep in.

No matter how many times or how hard I shook my head, trying to clear the images from my mind, they remained just on the edge of my thoughts. But this was also when something else occurred to me as I lay coiled around myself on the floor in the dark. What if the dreams aren't just a memory or a wish? What if they're trying to tell me something? Warn me of something coming.

This morning, I refused to let my thoughts drift to him. I need one night where I don't wake up with my heart racing or sweat bathing my body, so I throw myself into the task Nevil and Cammie assign to me. I work myself to the point of exhaustion. But it's pointless because the dream begins the instant I fall asleep. Only this time, I'm walking among the graves of the people who have fallen along the way. Mr. and Mrs. Johnson. Mrs. Deniker. John. Jay. Calvin. People I killed. People the riders killed. And for the first time, I'm afraid of what this means for all of us.

While I spin to take in all their graves, one in particular catches my eye. It's almost beckoning me to come closer. As I inch step by step toward the headstone, a beam of sunlight illuminates it. I swipe my hand across the rough surface to remove the decades of dust gathered on it, and the name I find leaves me stunned.

"What the hell? Tell me this isn't true. You can't be dead." I step away, refusing to acknowledge what this could mean, whispering, "Thanatos?"

I stand there for several moments, praying for a response I know won't come. But as I turn to flee this nightmare, something catches my eye. Something has bloomed at the base of the headstone. A flower. One I've never seen before now. It's small, with petals as soft as velvet and the sweetest scent I've ever inhaled. The color reminds me of his wings. Beautiful. Mysterious.

While my fingers caress the soft petals, I'm struck by the certainty he meant for me to find this. I move to pluck it, and I feel a jolt of electricity. The world fades away, and I'm transported to a different place... back to the darkness.

It's oppressive, hanging around me like winter clothes. Wet winter clothes soaked through, and they're trying to pull me under the crashing sea of emotions consuming every part of my body. When I feel I can no longer tolerate the weight, the slimmest sliver of light invades the nothing filling my surroundings. It's like a beacon calling out to me. Beckoning me closer.

My approach is tentative at first, less so when I see who is waiting for me in the light. It's Death standing there, his hand outstretched.

But tonight, there's a subtle shift, something tangible. Something that allows us…. To talk.

"Death?"

"Hello, Apple."

"You can hear me?"

"I can, and while I have longed for the sound, you don't belong here, Avalon. You need to stop coming to this place," he says, his voice soft and gentle. "Come. I'll show you the way home."

"I don't have a home."

He tilts his head and draws his brows together. His focus is fixated on me as he waits for me to elaborate. "I'm not with Pessy or War any longer."

"Famine?"

"Yes."

"Is he... treating you well?" His thumb rubs soft circles on the back of my hand he's taken in his.

"I wouldn't call how he treats me good, but it's nothing I can't handle."

"Avalon?"

"It doesn't matter. Not anymore."

"Of course it matters. I'm sorry this happened to you. To your world."

"It is what it is. I know he's your brother, and I imagine you care for him like you do Pestilence and War, but I have to stop him and then ensure I release no other riders." He smiles, knowing it's his seal I'm talking about.

"Come, Apple."

Taking my hand in his, he leads me towards the light. However, the closer we get, the clearer it becomes that this is not just a light. It's a door.

Death pushes it open, but I hesitate to step through. His gentle assurance is the only reason I move. Once I enter, I reach for him again, but he's gone. Only empty space remains. Panic overwhelms me until I let myself look where he led me.

What I discovered on the other side is a garden. It's beautiful, with flowers of every color and trees that stretch to the sky. But what catches my eye is the figure standing in the middle of the garden.

It's Death, but it's not. He's different somehow. His eyes are bright, yet a darkness surrounds him. Or is it coming from within him? Is he the reason I'm plagued with these dreams of nothing?

When he looks down at me, he smiles before pressing something he's holding into my hand.

It's the same small, white flower from the graveyard. I curl my hand around it, and as my fingers encircle it, I feel a warmth spread through me. It's like a weight has been lifted from my shoulders, and I can breathe for the first time in days.

He raises his hand and points at another door. One I'm not so keen to walk through this time, but his expression seems to convey this is my way out. What bothers me is that if this is the way out, he could also leave. Right? So does this mean it's his choice to stay here?

"Where are we?"

"I'm sorry for my absences. I'm sure it has left you questioning everything." Of course, he doesn't answer my question. I should have known he wouldn't since it's an ongoing theme with these damn riders.

"You could say that. You've been gone for a long time."

"It was not my intention. You look tired, and you've lost a substantial amount of weight. Are you safe?" His eyes almost plead with me to tell him I am, but I won't lie to him, and I know telling him the truth won't help either, so I ask a question of my own.

"If you had the choice now, would you...." No, I refuse to ask this damn question. I don't know if I want to hear the answer this time. When I've asked him this before, I suppose I knew how he would respond, but time and space change things, even for a rider of the apocalypse.

After Pessy and War confirmed they would not leave, even if their creator commanded them to do so, it left me questioning everything Death told me.

If he cared for me like he claimed... like his brothers declared, why would he not choose to stay like they would?

Which is why it's hard for me to believe I meant as much to him as he did to me. I would walk through hell and back, if only to prove to him how much of my heart I gave him. I could lie to myself when he still spoke to me when he invaded my dreams, but it's been almost a year since the last time he came to me. And even then, it was to tell me War would not interfere with the task they had forced on me.

I've tried to move past him. To forget him, but I can't. The closest I came was before War found Ember. Once she entered his life, he found what Pessy had with Greer. I don't begrudge his happiness. He's important to me, so I wanted that for him and Ember as much as I wanted it for Pessy and Greer. If I am being honest, I only clung to War because I was desperate to replace the empty ache Death's absence left in the center of my chest. I know it wasn't fair of me to do. In fact, it was beyond shitty. Which is why I took a step back when War did. And since I know War deserved better than what I could give him when he found Ember, I encouraged them to explore what they could have together. Ember is the better woman for him, while I should only ever remain his friend.

I would like to think if Death found love with another, I would be every bit as happy for him as I am for his brothers, yet I don't think I could hide the hurt of seeing him with someone else. I tell myself that time will heal the wounds his departure left me with; however, denial disguised as truth only lasts so long. I can declare and pretend I would be happy for him if he makes his life with another, but it would only be another lie I tell myself to keep putting one foot in front of the other.

Despite my efforts to move on, the memory of him still haunts me like a ghost. So for all these reasons, I won't ask him this question again because I don't want the truth I suspect he would give.

"Are you asking if I want to return to your world or return to you?"

"No." It's the only answer I can give him and still protect my heart.

"It is the only thought consuming me, Apple."

"Will you please tell me why you call me this?"

"Because you—"

Something crashes to the ground and jerks me awake.

My heart drops when I realize I dreamt the whole thing. Thanatos is still gone. This was nothing more than my wish. Closing my eyes, I try to return to sleep, praying he will still be there waiting for me until another sound has me sitting up.

With the cobwebs of sleep shaken off, my head is on a swivel as I try to focus on the noise that stirred me awake. My heart leaps into my throat when my eyes come up to find him standing in the doorway, and I can't help the smile tilting my lips. And then he's gone. Vanished like a puff of smoke swirling in the gentle wind.

Only then do I realize it isn't my rider who woke me. It's the prick. Famine is sitting in the corner, watching me sleep. Talk about fucking creepy, and since he looks comfortable sitting there, it makes me wonder how often he does this shit. Before I can ask, he has a question of his own. "Dreams about my brother or nightmares about...."

"You?" I snap.

"Humanity's end. Because make no mistake, little lamb, it is coming. It's such a shame my brother will not be here to see it."

"What the hell are you talking about?"

"I have no intention of letting you break the final seal." Little does the prick of a rider know I've already decided this on my own. Still, why wouldn't he want me to release another rider? If

Death comes, wouldn't it complete his task faster, thereby spelling the end of the mortals he despises?

"But then your wish to eliminate us from this plane will never happen."

"I don't require Death's gifts to end humanity, and something tells me his intentions may have shifted. Which, as you have not so eloquently pointed out, would be of no help to me. So why would I allow it?"

"You don't know what the hell you're talking about. Of course, he'd follow his task." Why in the hell am I arguing with him about this? I can almost hear Suki yelling, Shut up, A. You're making everything worse.

"Oh, my brother's sweet little Apple. You are the one who lacks knowledge of the subject we're discussing. It seems you have twisted the unwavering Death."

"I think you give me far too much credit."

"And I think you protest so much because you care as much about him as he does for you. Who knew a mortal could love the being sent to end them?"

"I don't...."

"Love him?"

"Yes."

"Is this the lie you must tell yourself to help you sleep at night?" Sleep? Who the hell sleeps anymore? Certainly not me, and in all honesty, it's the lie I tell myself because the truth would shatter my heart and destroy me.

Chapter Nineteen: Unwanted Desires.

I HAVE RELEASED ALL THE mortals who followed me since I have no use for them. In truth, I never did, but the son of Adam, who still travels with me, insisted they would be a benefit. They were not. The ones who left without protest are alive. Those who did not meet my vines.

I'm confident this will come as a surprise to many. Yet I don't care, just as I didn't when Nevil questioned me or when the lamb made demands upon me. I will offer no explanation because it is something I don't understand myself.

We remain in the community where the lamb had made such an affectionate declaration about me, and I cannot fathom why. I can only say one daughter of Eve has somehow rattled me. If I had believed she would not flee, I would have killed the others and left only her, but if I had, she wouldn't be the same woman I discovered when I stumbled upon this place.

I am fascinated by this woman, which began when she first yelled at Nevil and then pushed me when we stormed their community and trampled several plants she has tended and cared for. Her exact words to Nevil and me were….

"Mind getting your big freaking clodhoppers off my flowers so I can fix them, and next time pay attention where you're stepping. These plants mean more to me than most people do." She supplemented her initial remark with a barrage of insults directed at us, including quite a few dumbasses, pricks, and some damn-its for emphasis.

She is fiery, yet compassionate. Serious most times, yet funny at others. She is akin to the light that feeds my vines and the moon that revives my soul. She is an inscrutable enigma I must figure out.

This daughter of Eve loves the mortals she has taken the role of caring for. She also thanks my father for providing for them. Yet it is how she treats the plants I control I find most appealing. There is only one thing I would change if I could: the time she spends with….

"Avalon. Come here. We have another plant budding."

The lamb's mouthy ambivalence regarding me and my task may taint Sienna. Something I am not fond of happening.

"Sin, I need your help this afternoon. Don't forget."

I also wish her mother would stop calling her Sin. This daughter of Eve is far from sinful. She is graceful and pure, Much closer to the celestial beings these mortals pray to than the one our father cast aside.

Mostly, I hate she so easily evokes these conflicting emotions within me.

The holiday these mortals celebrate is almost as ridiculous as the one called Cammie. Yet there they sit, drinking ale and wearing green. They all believe it's a day in which they honor a false saint. A St. Patrick. I can assure them no saint with this moniker exists. Based on what I overheard the lamb saying, this day was celebrated in what would have been mid-way through the third month of their new year. If they had asked, I would also have told them they are three weeks early for the day they believe they are celebrating. However, they didn't ask, so I didn't correct them.

I must admit I'm shocked by their behavior. Here I am, a rider living in a community filled with mortals, yet they act as if it is an everyday occurrence to have one of us among them.

"He won't." Another daughter of Eve, not much younger than Sienna, tells her in a hushed tone. Do they not realize I can hear them regardless of the volume they speak?

"I don't care. I'm still gonna ask. What's it gonna hurt? The worst he can say is no."

"The worse he could say is squeeze her harder when he sends his vines to capture you and your insolent ass."

"No, something tells me she'll be just fine," the lamb proclaims with a knowing grin. Her assumption that she knows me is misguided. I'm unsure why she has become so comfortable with her perceived knowledge of horsemen. I understand she has met all of us, and while Pestilence and War did precisely what she believes I will do, she doesn't know me. Nor has she ever met Thanatos when he is here for this task. When he last traveled her world, he did so to judge, not end. So she should not be so comfortable.

"Hey, Famine, we're celebrating—"

"A saint who does not exist. Yes, I am aware."

"Don't be the prick A likes to call you." I attempt to hold the grin, threatening to show my amusement at bay. I do not succeed.

"Why do you call the lamb this?"

"A?"

"Yes. It is not her name. It does not represent what she is. This means nothing."

"It's what her best friend called her. You know, before some asshole stole her away from her family." I contemplate telling her I would not be here without the asshole doing such, but I'm unsure if I want to hear her response.

"I can assure you the lamb has no family."

"That's not the way A tells it. From what she's told us, there are several people she met after the world took a shit. These folks are her family."

"None of the ones she traveled with are related to her."

"Nope, but it doesn't matter to Avalon. They are the people she would give her life for. In this post-rider world, if that isn't family, I don't know what is. I can also tell you she counts your brothers, Pestilence and War, among them." I know the lamb claims she cares for my brothers; however, if push comes to shove, I doubt she would offer her life for one of them. Still, I prefer not to discuss this at present.

"Are you certain you wish to spend time with a rider whose task is to end you?"

"Well, you haven't done it yet, and having you here has kinda kept the assholes away, so I call it a win. Besides, you should know that I don't scare easily."

I can't help the slight smile or the soft chuckle I grant because of her bravado. "No, I suppose you don't. But you should be careful. My leniency only stretches so far, and much of what they said out there is true. I should take offense at such insults, but their opinions are of no consequence to me."

"I'll risk it," she says. Her chin tilts, lifting her head higher in defiance.

I raise an eyebrow at her. "Is that so?"

She nods, the fierce determination in her eyes shining as bright as the moon on a cloudless night. "There's not a lot you can do to me, rider, that hasn't already been done."

"You shouldn't be so confident of this declaration." It is sound advice she would do well to heed. I study her for a moment, taking in the fire in her eyes, the set of her jaw. There is something about her that draws me in, something that makes me want to know more.

"You're a strange one, Sienna," I say, my voice low. "But I can't deny that something about you intrigues me."

She raises an eyebrow, her expression skeptical. "And what's that?"

I smile at her, a slow, dangerous smile. "You have a fire in you. One I can't help but admire," I tell her. "And a spirit that refuses to be broken."

Sienna grins back at me, the corners of her lips turning up in a mischievous way. "Well, if you're looking to break this someone's spirit, you'll have to try harder than you have so far, Famine."

The area they have selected for this gathering is filled with laughter and chatter, the clinking of glasses, and the occasional bottle popping. The air is thick with the scent of foods they all came together to make, but these things pale in comparison to her.

Sienna nudges me with her elbow, pulling me out of my thoughts. "You know, for someone who's supposed to bring despair, you're not that bad," she said with a grin.

I chuckle, the sound low and rumbling. "Was that a compliment, Sienna?"

She laughs, grabs a second beverage from a young woman balancing far too many, and thrusts it at me. With a drink in hand, she raises her glass and quietly says. "Here's to the nonexistent saint, leprechaun, pots of gold, and unexpected friendships."

I clink my glass against hers. "To unexpected friendships," I repeat, sipping the sweet wine.

For a moment, I forget who I am or what I am meant to do. I forget the weight of my responsibilities and the burden of my powers. I am nothing more than a being enjoying the company of another. And at this moment, it's enough.

Perhaps there is more to this world than I first thought. Perhaps this mortal can prove them wrong, just as the lamb has proven herself worthy to my brothers and, in just the slightest possible measure ... me. Something I have no intention of disclosing to these daughters of Eve. I smile to myself, relishing the challenge that lies ahead. For the first time in a long time, I feel alive.

An insignificant son of Adam calls her over to where he sits. I don't like it. What I would like is to remove the tongue he wagged to beckon her over to him so he could admire her many curves. What in my father's name is wrong with me? These emotions go against everything I despise.

While I continue to observe her, I cannot help but feel a sense of admiration for her resilience. It is a trait that I have not encountered in many mortals for a time beyond measure. In fact, only one other can claim this trait. The individual who makes it her mission to infuriate me. Today seems to be no different.

"I see you are not so immune to the charms of humanity as you proclaimed."

"Silence yourself, lamb."

"Yeah, I can work with this."

"Work with what?" I ask, turning my attention from the woman I want to spend more time with to the lamb who is hellbent on irritating me.

"This. You. Her." Each word is punctuated with a wave of her hand. Which looks ridiculous since her hands are bound by the ropes I still demand she wears. When she sees where my focus is directed, she lifts her arms before asking, "Do you think we could do something about these now?"

"No," I bark as I turn my attention to my horse, whom I have yet to tend to today.

"Come on, you know you secretly aspire to be nicer than the prick you've been since meeting me."

"Not helping your plight, lamb."

"Still, we both know you're gonna do it."

"No, I'm not," I respond, confident in my proclamation.

Until I retire for the night and take them off her for the last time.

"Now if I could just get my own room," she said.

"You should not press your luck on this, lamb."

*****

"Shit!" Sienna's mom growls as she looks at the approaching men. Ordinarily, this individual provides me a wide berth, something I am grateful for. So when she rushes to the area I have chosen for my horse, it's rather irritating. I am preparing to tell her space would be in her best interest until I discover what has her rattled enough to risk being in my vicinity.

"Who are these sons of Adam?"

"Assholes who came to collect what they bargained for."

"Explain."

"I made the mistake of trusting an asshole named Jacob, who turned out to be the worst kind of asshole. When I decided it would be best for us to join another group before yo—um… well…what I meant to say is um be—before…."

"Before I arrived." This was not a question. I offered the statement she refused to speak, only to speed up this inane conversation, yet she answered it all the same.

"Yes. I thought I was protecting the people who live here. Turns out I made a horrible mistake, and now they have come to collect the only thing they want outside my lands."

"I would like to point out these are not your lands." She glances at me from the corner of her eye. I'm unsure if she wanted to argue this point or not. Regardless, it would have been futile since what I said is true: these humans own none of the world around them. One would think they would have figured this out when we arrived to reclaim what they felt was theirs, but simple logic is not within their capability to grasp.

"Still, they think they have a claim to it unless we honor our deal. That's the only way they will allow us to remain here. I had hoped they heard a rider took over this place, and it would keep them away, but it seems either they don't know or they don't care."

"So give them what they risked my ire to retrieve."

"NO!" she snaps. My horse snorts before slamming his hoof on the ground when he senses my frustration, while the vines clinging to the crumbling wall slither closer to the individual who has garnered it. When I shift my focus from my horse to her, she swallows audibly, lifts her hand in submission, and backs away. "What I meant to say is I don't want them to take anyone from this place."

"I will assume, based on your statement, the item they have come to collect is a mortal residing within this community."

"Yes, and I won't let them take anyone. I made this mistake, so I should be the one to go."

She remains there, tapping the side of her leg with the shovel she holds at a relentless pace. Since the ones approaching don't seem to be in a hurry to get here, she remains rooted in place. I only appreciate this when I am the one doing the rooting. Perhaps I can speed this along.

"Who is it they wish to claim?" My plan is simple. I will pluck the individual they have come for up and deliver them to the ones approaching, with a message of course. This being any claim they believed they had on this community or the people within, I have fulfilled with the delivery. If any of them return, it will be to face me since I have taken what they thought they could.

This thought remains until she answers, and she is fortunate my attention shifts to the ones approaching; otherwise, I may have snapped her neck.

"They want my daughter. They want Sin."

A mistake they will soon regret.

Chapter Twenty: Sharing Is Caring.

While it's always best to learn from your mistakes, it's wiser to learn from the ones made by others and avoid the pain that comes with such blunders.

MAYBE SOMEONE SHOULD HAVE TOLD these idiots this simple logic. At least if you want to continue breathing.

The minute I witnessed him go rigid, I knew something was about to happen. When I made some inquiries, it didn't take me long to figure out what the hell had him so rattled. And since I'm a sucker for watching bastards get their asses handed to them—even if it is by a rider I dislike—I arrive at his side moments before they crest the hill.

The tick of his jaw, the cords visible in his neck, and the fierce way he is clenching his fist all tell me an ass handing might not be a strong enough word. These assholes will be lucky if they walk away from here at all.

Yeah, I'm gonna say showing up to collect someone the riders have taken a vested interest in is not the smartest thing to do. But one I'm happy to watch play out.

As the men approach us, I expect to see the fear in their eyes. They must have heard this rider was in the area, and if so, then there's no way they aren't aware of his propensity for violence. He's a strike first, ask questions later—or never—kind of rider. This means most people avoid him and this community, like Pessy's plague. The crazy thing is, fear is not what I find. Determination, indifference, arrogance, but the terror is nowhere to be seen. Are they stupid?

Famine's hard stance only grows more dangerous the closer they move toward the community he has let live. I know their survival has everything to do with a specific redhead who has captivated this rider.

I keep waiting for the new arrival's calm demeanor to falter; however, with their confident approach never wavering, I realize how fast this whole shitshow can go wrong, so I step forward. If I can save these people the stress of a pending battle, I'll try to convince the approaching jackasses to step back.

"Who are you, and what do you want?" My voice is cold and commanding, leaving no room for negotiation.

"We have come for what the woman bargained. We gave the three weeks promised. She belongs to us now," one of them speaks up. His voice is gruff and unyielding. Didn't they get the memo about who the hell this being to my right is? Should I clue them in or let Famine open the can of whoopass I'm confident he is preparing to unleash on their unsuspecting backsides?

"Where's Jacob?" Gail yells.

"Apparently not fucking here. Don't worry, Mom, he plans to greet her in person when we take her back." Gail continues to scream her protest, but my focus is on the rider, who gets more irritated with each word they utter.

"So chop-chop, we can't wait to return to camp with her sweet ass in tow."

With Famine's furrowed brows and clenched teeth, I know the ass whipping may be closer than I thought. One thing I can assure these idiots is this rider is not amused by their boldness or their demands. "If you are referring to the daughter of Eve known as Sienna, then you are mistaken. She belongs to no one but herself."

They better pray they take his advice and leave Sin right where she is, or things will take a nasty turn fast. Thank god she's training and remains blissfully unaware of this entire interaction.

"She belongs to us." One idiotic big mouth shouts at us from atop a horse who seems to understand who it is facing since it keeps neighing and stomping the ground while the asshole attempts to hold him in place.

"She is under my protection. As such, she will not accompany you anywhere, least of all your encampment."

"Do you know who the hell you're talking to, asshole?" The big mouth asks.

"Do you?" Although only two words, Famine's retort is laced with the deadly venom he is preparing to unleash.

"From where I'm standing, a soon-to-be-dead man." Yeah, this guy is so fucking dead. If I'm being fair, Pessy and War were easy to pick out based on the big-ass sword War carries and the shiny fucking bow Pestilence straps to his back, whereas Famine is a little more understated. He has a sickle… that looks better fitted for harvesting wheat than lopping off heads and scales, which could be for weighing said harvested grain. They sure as shit don't scream tools for assessing your worth; however, Famine doesn't need big, ostentatious weapons. The reason for this is, like Pessy and his plague, Famine doesn't need weapons to complete his task. He has his....

Vines shoot from all directions, closing in on the loud mouth quicker than he or his horse can react. His horse rears up, neighing in terror, as the other men try to pull him free. But it's too late. The vines have him, and they're not letting go. Once they have him entwined past the point of release, they pull him off his horse and slam him to the ground. His screams fill the air as thorns dig deeper into his flesh.

The other three invaders draw their weapons, but Famine is faster. He raises his scales and blows on the dish, causing a gust of wind to carry a wave of decay and rot. They first appear as nothing more than tiny bugs; however, by the time his response to their act of aggression surrounds the men, it turns to ash, allowing them to inhale the death famine sent their way. The newcomers reel back, clutching their stomachs almost as if Famine himself delivered the blow.

With these men dealt with, Famine returns his attention to the one writhing and screaming on the ground. The vines wrap around his limbs. His screams echo around us as thorns dig further into his flesh. Dots of fresh red blood appear with each inch the vines advance up his body, squeezing tighter with every passing second.

Famine steps forward, his cold eyes focused not on the man struggling to break free. They're on the nervous men searching for his next wave of attacking vines. With a swift motion, he twists his hand. The vines react to this motion by following suit.

His neck snapping could be heard over his screams before everything grew silent once more.

"You will tell your people that Sienna is under our protection. Let it be known if any of you attempt to remove her from this community, there will be consequences."

The certainty of this being's identity standing beside me seems to have fully registered, causing their calm, relaxed demeanor to dissipate. The men nod, their eyes wide with fear. They know that Famine is not one to be trifled with.

"Can anyone here claim to be the leader of this regime?" In a matter of seconds, these three individuals have displayed a significant increase in cognitive ability in the moments since Famine dispatched the talkative one. As a result, they respond with vehement head-shaking to avoid his wrath.

"Who is?" Famine asks, crossing his arms over his chest. When they decide the best way to answer his question is by looking at one another with stupid, you tell him expressions covering their faces; I step in to move this along.

"It would be in your best interest to answer his question. Quickly. If you relish drawing breath." I give them a respectable ten count, then push again when it becomes obvious my first warning wasn't enough.

"Faster, assholes," I say while snapping my fingers. "Speak now or forever hold your tongue, kinda like the pin cushion over there. Now repeat after me... we're happy to take you to our camp, Mr. Kill 'em all and let god sort them out later, rider who wants to end us."

Phew, that was a mouthful. And quite possibly the longest name known to humankind.

I don't know if it was the name or Famine taking a step towards them that finally shook them out of their stupor. Yeah, I know their answer has more to do with the angry rider and not the stupid name, but after the last couple of shitty months, I like my version of the events more. When they see they have no other choice, they nod their agreement and back away, their eyes never leaving mine.

With their agreement in place, I turn to leave until Famine snatches my arm to halt my retreat. "Since you inserted yourself into this situation, you shall come with me as I clarify their misstep to these mortals."

"Um... hard pass."

"It is not a request, lamb. You will come. Now!" With his demand delivered, he mounts the horse I still won't be riding and follows the men who keep a respectable distance between the rider and them.

I can't help letting my frustration shine through since these dumbasses just ruined my day. I'm not sure if I'm more infuriated at myself for stepping in to save their sorry asses or them for making demands of a rider. Something they thought they could get away with and live to tell the tale. They're incorrect, of course, because I have no doubt Famine isn't done with his lessons yet.

Nothing like leading the damn wolf straight to the sheep's pen. It's a massive mistake on their part, and for at least one of them, it's a mistake they'll never make again.

*****

If trudging behind the four men riding wasn't bad enough, it had to rain halfway through our trip to their camp. So now I'm soaked through, tired from having to jog to keep up, hungry since I didn't get to eat yet today, and pissed as all hell for the shift this day has taken since these morons showed up at camp.

I contemplated running several times since I doubted the rider would choose to chase me over protecting Sienna, but if I'm incorrect, running will end one way, with me in chains again. Which is something I don't aspire to revisit.

"You are much too tranquil. What are you planning?" Damn, how does he manage to do that? Every time I'm thinking about something he would disapprove of, I swear it's like he hears my thoughts because he asks me what I'm doing. Screw it if he already knows my thoughts, there's no point in trying to hide them or lie.

"Running." He stops his horse and glares down at me.

"You're falling behind the other assholes," I tell him, lifting my hands to point at the men moving further away from where we stopped.

"Must I chain you again, lamb?"

"What is it with you damn riders thinking you have the right to do this shit?"

"If I must respond, it indicates a failure on your part to listen. Which also means you are not nearly as intelligent as you believe you are."

"Clearly, I'm not that smart. If I were, I wouldn't keep finding myself in the same shit situation over and over again. Yep, pretty sure this covers the definition of insanity."

"You will not test me on this, lamb."

"Or what, rider, because let me tell you something, if it wasn't for your damn vines, I would have run a long damn time ago."

"You believe my companion would not run you down?"

"I'm working on the horse!"

"I fail to comprehend the intended significance of this statement." Sucks to be him because I don't plan on saying shit. He can figure it out on his own. If he talked with his brothers, they could have told him about my affinity for naming their horses. Since he refuses to meet with them, he can ponder the meaning of what I said all by his lonesome.

I have been trying to get his horse to like me. Of course, this is only when Famine is busy flirting with Sin. Otherwise, he wouldn't let me within a hundred feet of his damn horse. So far, I'm finding it might be easier to get a rabid badger to cuddle up with me.

It's taken me weeks to get to where we are today. The horse will finally allow me to brush him, and he quit trying to bite me when I talk to him. I call that progress. We only accomplished it by slow conditioning of day after day Avalon therapy—this is what I'm calling it—where I exposed him to me a little more each day.

I've tried several names during our therapy sessions, from Onyx to Shadow to Wraith to Phantom—he hated this one. Hell, I even thought about Raven, but I don't want to associate him with the asshole who caused all this shit.

Yesterday, we made a breakthrough. I'm not sure if it's right for him or not, but at least he didn't huff and slam his foot on the ground when I mentioned this one. I'll have to let it sit for a minute and get to know him a little better before I settle on it, but it's looking more and more like his name will be Eclipse.

Had I known what would happen when we arrived, I might have reconsidered everything I had done since climbing off the floor this morning.

*****

He sticks the damn things out and shakes them again. He can rattle them until his head falls off. Not gonna freaking happen.

"You have to wear these," the dumbass gate guard repeats because he thinks I didn't hear him the first five times he said it.

"What about him?" I ask, snapping my head in Famine's direction. Word must have spread quick about who was coming to call. The guy looks from me to the rider, whose expression is almost daring this dumbass to say he needs to be handcuffed to enter the camp.

"If you think I'm telling him to put them on, you're fucking crazy. You, on the other hand...." Okay, clearly this prick doesn't realize I'm not opposed to shoving knives in the chest of assholes.

"Put them on, lamb. I grow tired of his incessant demands."

"You have got to be—"

"I am not shitting you. Now, put them on. I want to conclude this and return to camp to ensure everyone is accounted for."

"Sin's fine, Famine."

"I have also instructed you already to refrain from calling her this. And I am still waiting."

"Horseshit. If you didn't bring me to help, then why make me come at all?"

"The pleasure of your contemptuous company."

"You're planning on handing me over to these assholes, aren't you?"

"The thought has crossed my mind, and while tempting, it is not my current plan. However, if you delay any longer, it may come to pass."

Throwing my hands out so the prick blocking our path can restrain me, I see another way to bypass this since he looks between the rider and me. He doesn't want to come any closer, and since I have no intention of walking over to him so he can slap the damn shackles on, he has no choice in the matter. He either has to approach the rider to put them on or let me in without the bindings. Let's see if brains or balls are bigger in this asshole.

I believe this entire captive conversation will be a moot subject when he swallows harder than necessary prior to looking down at the object he is supposed to put on me.

"Her arms will not grow any longer, and since this is your rule, I will not force the lamb to approach. You will put them on her yourself, if you wish her to wear them. Whatever the choice is, make it now, son of Adam. I grow tired of this entire affair."

Balls must have won out since he approaches, but common sense has him scrambling to slap the shackles in place before backing away almost as fast.

When we enter the tent in the camp's center, my mouth falls open with who I discover sitting at the table.

"I have to say I enjoy seeing you in chains."

"You!"

"Me."

"You fucking gave me to Nevil."

"I did. It was all a part of the deal we made."

"Deal? You do realize the entire reason you're facing a rider right now is because you made a deal with the asshole who forced me to break his seal?"

His nostrils flare, and his eyes narrow. I don't think this idiot realized who he had when he took me. Based on the glare he's giving me right now, I'm gonna say he might not have taken this deal if he did. The entire thing makes me want to laugh at his stupidity.

"So the horseman whore—no offense, rider—is also the one to break them out of their prisons. Fucking figures." Based on the glare Famine gives him, I'm going to say offense was taken, but since he doesn't respond, I let the woman-beating asshole—also known as Trevor—in on my thoughts about his comment.

"Up yours, asshole."

"I see you've forgotten the lessons we taught you the last time we met." Yeah, I remember those lessons. My ribs hurt for weeks. "What do they call you, sheep? Yeah, sheep fits you. If you want to keep your fucking teeth in your mouth." Trevor stands. I imagine he plans to give me a recap of their previous lessons. "I suggest you shut that fucking mouth of yours, sheep."

"The lamb," Famine's emphasis on lamb is his way of telling these assholes he's not happy with my new title. Even if he doesn't like me, he respects the "task" I've been given, so calling me anything other than lamb doesn't sit well with this rider. "Is not yours to punish. I suggest you remain where you are if you wish these negotiations to proceed with your tongue in place."

"Fair enough, Rider," Wayne said as he placed his hand on Trevor's arm to halt him from making a huge, monumental mistake. One that would have this rider putting him six feet under.

"I suppose I owe you a debt of gratitude for releasing me."

"Seriously, you would focus on this part of the conversation. But just so we're clear," I wave my bound hands between him and me, "It was still my damn hands that broke your dumb seal."

"Did you wish me to thank you as well?"

"No, I don't want you to thank me! I just don't want you to thank these assholes."

"As you wish, lamb."

"Not that I'm not enjoying this little show, but care to share why you're here rather than the person my men were sent to retrieve?" Famine looks at me. Okay, I guess my role is to speak for him since it appears he lost the ability in the last five fucking seconds.

"You're not getting her."

"Why not?"

"Because we said so." He scoffs at my response but keeps his thoughts to himself.

"What do you want?" A woman standing next to Wayne asks. Her question and how she said it hurt my heart a little. I miss my little buddy Wren. I suppose the look on my face must reveal my emotions, because she brings her full attention to me.

"Why are you looking at me like that?"

"What you said… it reminded me of someone."

"I assure you whatever backwoods buffoon you want to equate me to couldn't be further from the truth."

"Yeah, you're right about one thing."

"Why don't you tell me what that is, Lamb?" The way she says this pisses me off. I'd show her how much if I didn't have these damn cuffs on.

"You are nothing like the little guy who says it. Wren is hands down a better person than you will ever be."

"What did you say?"

"He's a better—"

"No idiot, the name. What did you say his name was?"

"Why?"

"Because my son's name was Wren, and there's no fucking way you can be talking about the same kid." No goddamn way this bitch is my little buddy's womb and egg donor. If she is, as the asshole who saddled me with calling the riders here is my witness, I'm gonna kill her. I don't care if I have shackles on or if they beat me to death because before they do, I'm going to wring this bitch's neck.

"Definitely not. I know Renny's mom. She's also a better person than you."

"Who did you say his mom was?"

"I didn't."

"So why don't you tell me her name, idiot!" The chick demands in a pitch high enough to make dogs howl while she takes a definitive step closer to me. I don't know if this was supposed to intimidate me... it doesn't.

"Why don't you fuck off? Who the hell are you anyway, and why are you even here?"

"What I'm doing here is none of your damn business. As for my name, it's—"

"Lynn. Right?"

"How did you know that?"

"Greer. Wren's mom told me."

"That woman is not Wren's mother. I am! That bitch stole him from me!"

"The fuck she did. You left him, you miserable cow."

"What are you talking about? I left to get supplies, and when I got back, she had taken him."

"If you think I believe anything passing through your lying lips, you're crazier than the over-inflated fat fuck sitting next to you." Wayne's reaction to me calling him a fat fuck is for him to growl. I don't care. He can fuck off too. "If what you're saying has any basis in reality, why in the hell would you leave your son with some random ass stranger?"

"She wasn't a random ass stranger, she was his teacher. Someone I thought I could trust. Someone I plan to have a long discussion with when I retrieve my kid."

"Lady, if you so much as make a move to leave this tent, I'll beat the shit out of you," I snap.

"You believe you can stop me from claiming what belongs to me?"

"Try me," I confirm before moving to position myself between the exit and the bitch who thinks I'll let her anywhere near Renny. The men at the table all stand, but if they believe they will stop me from killing this chick if she moves one more inch toward the exit, they're as dumb as she is. I square my stance like War taught me and bring my hands up, ready to use the chains binding my hands together as my weapon.

"Enough!" Famine's booming voice halts everyone dead in their tracks. "This matter has no bearing on why I'm here. Go retrieve your son, daughter of Eve."

"No," I roar, once again moving to position myself between her and the exit. "You don't know who Wren is."

"I don't care, lamb. Now move, or else I will move you."

"I bet you will care."

"Doubtful."

"You will when I tell you who Wren is to Pestilence." This gets his attention.

It's time to clue in the clueless rider who refuses to talk with his brothers. Here's hoping Pessy doesn't get pissed at me. I wonder if it would be too brazen if I start with....

Well, Uncle Famine, it's like this.

Chapter Twenty-One: Replacement.

WAITING OUT THE DRAMATIC PAUSE the lamb gives us is unnecessary. Does she believe anything she can tell me about this child named Wren will change my mind? If she had asked, I would have told her it would not, and if she does not get on with this tale, I will allow the female mortal respite to retrieve what she claims is hers. I may have a self-serving reason. By bringing the child here, I will not have to travel as far to end his life.

"I'm getting my kid."

"Like fuck you are," Avalon replies.

"You tell the rider everything he wants to know right fucking now so I can get about the business of retrieving my son, or I'll slit your throat."

"Does it appear I require your assistance?" My demand alone would have been enough to quiet her shrill screams. However, my set jaw, stern stance, and unrelenting glare are enough to ensure she remains this way.

"Wren is Pessy's son." Avalon delivers her response in a rush. My initial thought was that the lamb misspoke, but after observing the hard lines of her face and rigid stance for several seconds, I realized this was not the case. Regardless, the entire statement is ludicrous and one I will rectify straight away.

"First, Lamb, you need to refrain from calling my brother Pessy. Second, Pestilence has no son. We cannot produce offspring, a blessed gift our father granted us."

"Yeah, well, don't tell Pessy that shit. Unless you relish the thought of your windpipe crushed in his hand," the lamb huffs.

"Alright, explain to me how my brother, Pestilence, counts this child as his son."

"Do we really need to listen to any more of this shit? Wren. Is. My. Fucking. Kid!"

"You will remain silent while the lamb provides me with what I have asked."

"Short story. Pestilence didn't want to admit how much he cared for Wren, but Renny wouldn't let him be. He liked your brother despite himself and loved Storm."

"This child likes inclement weather?"

"No. Jesus. Storm isn't important right now."

"Then why bring it up?"

"Do you want the reason, or do you want to keep asking dumb questions?" Avalon's inquiry is punctuated by her crossing her arms over her chest.

"Do you plan on getting to the part where my brother declared this child his son soon?"

"You're really pissing me off, rider," she grumbles. Nevertheless, my comment makes her refocus on providing facts without the fluff.

"Some jackass who wanted to join up with these assholes burnt down Greer's cabin. What the moron didn't know was Wren was inside."

"Yet the child survived."

"No, Wren died." When she says this, her bottom lip quivers, a movement so subtle one might miss it if they were not looking for a lie, and her voice becomes thick. "The asshole killed Wren."

"My son is dead?" Lynn screams.

"Still not your son," the lamb said with a growl.

"Since I can't get the brat back, the first thing I'm going to do when I leave this tent is kill the bitch who took him." A flick of my wrist silences this daughter of Eve, so I may continue my conversation with the lamb.

"You are not making sense. Explain to me how my brother considers a dead mortal child his son."

"This would be the part where he became his son." Her vague answer seems to allude to her reluctance to say much more in front of the other mortals in this room. If what I believe transpired is true, I understand why. Michael's comment makes sense now.

"Thanatos. He took him to Thanatos," I said.

"Yes."

"And Thanatos restored what was taken." It's not a question. I already know this is what happened. Pestilence ferried the child to our brother, who disobeyed his role and restored the soul of the child Pestilence loved. Michael all but confessed as much when I woke. Thanatos did this for our brother, not the lamb, as Michael insinuated during our conversation. So this is the choice that contributed to the sentence they have imprisoned my brother for. It seems the lamb is not to blame for all of his circumstances. However, this does not exonerate her from the rest.

"Yes, but it wasn't just Death. Pess," the look I give her halts her from calling my brother this inane moniker. "Pestilence gave a piece of his mortality."

"Thereby binding this child to him. Making him his—"

"Son. Yes."

"And my brother cares for this child?"

"No, Famine, he doesn't just care for Renny—"

"His FUCKING name is Wren, not Renny. What the hell is it with you idiots and this stupid goddamn name?"

Avalon glares at this daughter of Eve, who continues her tirade. It would behoove the mortal to silence herself. One would think when I shift my focus to her, she would realize her mistake and beg my forgiveness. She does not. It's not until the one named Trevor comprehends what has riled my ire and grabs the woman's arm that she pulls her attention from the now laughing lamb to the fool hissing at her.

"Are you an idiot?"

"What?" she hisses.

"Don't say the GD word in front of the riders, dumbass." Her eyes flick to me, and what I detect in them is her registering the grievous error she spoke. Her breathing increases, her lips tremble, and beads of perspiration form along her brow. Yet fury still narrows her eyes.

Avalon shakes her head at the woman before answering my question. "As I was saying, he doesn't just care for Renny. He loves his son."

"MY SON! Wayne, do something about this, or I will."

The one named Wayne sits a little straighter before he tells her in a flat, unemotional tone. "No. And you should know better than to make demands on me. I don't fucking care who you think you are."

"And he cares for the one named Greer?" I ask.

"She's kinda like his wife. So yeah, you can say he loves her as well." The one who claims she is the child's mother throws a knife in Avalon's direction. I will not permit her to kill the lamb for speaking the truth. I block the blade before sending my vines to retrieve her. Once she is yanked from her feet and pulled to me, I waste no time snapping her neck. One less mortal in the world and a threat removed.

"What the fuck are you doing?" Wayne yells.

"What my father sent me to do. What the lamb released me to do. Would you care to join her?" This mortal makes the wise decision to return to the seat he leaped out of when I killed this daughter of Eve.

"I see you're making friends everywhere you go, rider." I turn to see a most unwanted sight, and the reaction from the lamb mirrors this thought.

"Terrific, now it's an asshole-palooza."

~Avalon~

As IF THREE assholes filling this tent wasn't enough, the biggest one has to come strolling in the door. Raum. Why does it not surprise me these pricks are working with him.

"Jacob—"

"Wait, now you're Jacob. What happened to Jared? Did you forget who you're supposed to be?" They may think I'm laughing about what I said. The truth is, I'm imagining shoving a knife in his chest.

"Jacob, Jared, it's all the same. A tried-and-true name to throw off the *sheep* surrounding us, little lamb. As you were saying, Wayne."

"And who might those *sheep* be, Jackass—excuse me, Jared?"

"Jacob."

"We could always go back to the name I prefer calling you."

"I'm sure we could. Yet, something tells me, little lamb, you won't."

"You two know each other." Famine interrupts before I can say anything further. I'm unsure what Raum meant by this last part; however, if it could put my family at risk... he's right, I won't.

"Oh, me and the lamb go way back. Don't we, Amy?"

"Back to a time when I found you crying like a bitch in the middle of the road."

"An act, I assure you."

"Academy Award worthy. Or... is it possible you did run a fowl of the man who did things to you that you never thought could happen to a man? Oh, and that would be the bird fowl, not the afoul you imagine I meant. Get it, Birdy?"

"As amusing as always, I see. You also know this never happened. It's amazing this rider allows you to retain such a sharp tongue."

"You should not assume to know me, fallen."

Raum glares at Famine for a second before he turns his attention back to Wayne. "I'm here to collect what you promised."

"I–ah… I don't have her."

"And why not?"

"Sienna's off the table."

"Sienna?" Raum asks as he places his hands behind his back.

"Sin is the chick who's supposed to," he clears his throat while letting his gaze assess Famine for a second before finishing. "Entertain the crowds. She's the one we bargained for. She's the reason he's here. At least, I assume it's the reason. We haven't gotten that far yet."

"And why not?" Raum asks.

"Because I killed one of his companions."

"Do tell, rider."

"No." Famine's unyielding response leaves no room for further discussion.

"Well, c'est la vie."

"What's that supposed to mean?" Wayne's attempt at indifference is ridiculous since he keeps shifting in his chair while his eyes dart between Raum and Famine. Maybe I should tell the rider his brothers are looking for this jackass and the one sitting next to him. Do the world a favor and all.

"It means, my feeble-minded friend, she is under a rider's protection. If you attempt to retrieve her now, it's the rider you'll face, not a duped mother. However, we had a deal, and I will require recompense since I have delivered on everything promised."

"Of course, you would be in the middle of this, bird boy."

"Still not as funny as you believe," Raum said while leveling his focus on me.

"Oh, I don't know. I find your new name freaking hilarious. But I suppose we could return to jackass if you prefer."

"Shouldn't you be dead by either Pestilence's plague or War's sword by now?"

"Perks of befriending the riders."

"It seems one rider is unaffected by your charms."

"Can't please everyone, bird boy. I would have thought you figured this out by now."

"Your continued use of a name that means nothing is infuriating." If calling him a name infuriates him, let's see what this will do. I lift my hand and begin rubbing my forefinger on my thumb in a slow, circular motion.

"Why do you keep doing this with your fingers?" Raum asks while mimicking my actions. I almost want to laugh at him.

"Oh, this? Well, it's the world's smallest record player playing my heart bleeds for you."

"You make no sense, lamb," he snaps while pulling his hand back down and placing it behind his back. If a demon could blush, this one would be glowing bright.

"Neither do you."

"Your words, like your actions, are confusing."

"Do you understand this?" I ask, lifting my middle finger to kiss it prior to directing it at him. "Or are you still baffled?" He huffs his frustration while I smile. It's the little things in life, and where this demon is concerned, I'll take my victories where I can get them.

"I will assume the one named Sienna is under your protection. Hence making her no longer an option for this one to fulfill his agreement. Is this correct, Rider?"

"She is."

"Then I will require another. You would agree this is only fair. Correct?" Raum's focus moves from Wayne, who gives an apprehensive nod, to Famine, who does not respond. "I will take your silence as your agreement."

"Allow me to present some women we have—"

"No. Famine's interference altered our agreement, so I believe the replacement should come from the camp he has claimed as his."

"You will not take Sienna."

"We have already established this point. A fact I do not need to revisit."

"Fine. Who do you want?"

His lips twist up in a triumphant grin before he makes his demands.

"I want the lamb."

Chapter Twenty-Two: Come Again.

N O WAY DID I HEAR this asshole right. He thinks he can bargain with the rider for what? For me. My soul. What? I can assure you I'm no more on the table in this negotiation than Sin was. So, I would think my answer should come as no surprise. "Come again?"

"You have no use for her any longer, Rider."

"There is one seal left unbroken."

"Yes, but the word amongst our kind is you do not intend to allow the lamb to bring Thanatos here. So you have no more use of her, and since she has proven herself an adept opponent… I want her."

"Why?"

"Did you just ask him why?" I cut him off from receiving his answer. There shouldn't be a why, just an emphatic no.

"Seriously, Famine? This shouldn't even be a damn question," I said in a rush. However, they continued their conversation like I wasn't standing here.

The longer my head ping pongs from one asshole to the other while they continue debating who will retain control of me, the more the reality that this was what I wanted comes to mind. Wasn't this my plan to seek this asshole out? I still think he's the only one who will ensure I don't live long, meaning he'll send me straight to the rider I want to rescue from wherever his dad sent him. I'm getting ready to agree with his demands when he makes me rethink this whole him sending me to Thanatos thing with one damn sentence.

"She is a soul I look forward to breaking over many centuries." Centuries. How in the hell does he plan on torturing me for hundreds of years? Even though Raum directs his conversation to Famine, his focus is settled on me, and let me tell you, it's enough to make my skin crawl. "Unlike you, Rider, I believe in choices, so I'll give you a week to decide. Something tells me you'll have no issue handing her over to me."

"Is this so?"

"Yes. If you don't want the community where this Sienna lives destroyed."

"You don't want to test me, Fallen."

"And you don't want to push me because I am aware you cannot fulfill your task and remain in their community. After all, your talents are not as far-reaching as your brother's. Pestilence could remain within his chosen one's camp while sending out his tendrils to eliminate the surrounding mortal encampments. Whereas you must be present to control your vines. I believe it's clear the creator didn't want any of you to complete your task with ease. He wanted you to work for it. Do you think his secret hope is you will all fail?"

"Do you think I will allow you to continue drawing breath if you press this issue any further?"

"Now–now, rider, there's no need to get yourself all in a twist. We're all friends here."

"Friends?" If I spit this word any harder, my teeth would be scattered across the floor. "You do realize this prick tried to kill Pestilence, right?" Famine's eyes shoot towards Raum, and his reaction reveals two things. First, he did not know. And second, he is not happy about what I just said.

"You will need to elaborate upon what the lamb advised."

"I did no such thing."

"You fucking liar. You did. He did. If I hadn't stepped in, he would have dragged Pestilence's soul to hell to…what did you say, 'torture him until the end of time?'."

"You really expect this rider to believe you, a mere mortal, saved one of the riders?"

"Um, yeah. Since that's what happened," I said, taking a defiant step closer to him.

"These mortals and their fanciful imaginations. I mean, can you even imagine a pathetic daughter of Eve saving your brother?"

"I saved Death too. And you damn well know I saved Pess— Pestilence since the arrow I shot ripped through you and made you run like a scared little…little."

"Little what?" Raum asks with the same mocking tone he's used more than once. Something I can assure you pisses me off.

"A scared little daughter of Eve." I meant it as an insult, but the roar of laughter coming from him and the two dimwits doesn't bode well for it having the bite I intended. The issue is when I look over at Famine, it's clear that he doesn't believe anything I said. I suppose it's easier to believe a deceitful demon who has lied at every turn over me, someone who hasn't lied to him once. Yeah, I can see where this makes sense. Assholes, the lot of them.

This wouldn't be an issue if Famine would talk to his brothers. He would know what I've done for the riders. But no, he would rather isolate himself, keep me prisoner, and believe this damn demon.

"Now that your lamb has given us all a good laugh, I hoped to speak with you. In Private."

"No. Say what you came to say, so we may return to the business at hand."

"Fine. Allow me to offer you a trade instead. One I hope you will be intrigued by." Famine doesn't look intrigued he looks pissed. I would have to say he doesn't care for this demon or his theatrics. "I'm sure, as you know, there have been times when I crossed paths with your brothers since your arrival. They would prefer I refrain from inserting myself into your mission. Something I am happy to oblige with."

"For what?"

"This is why I like you, Famine. You're a being of few words, meaning we can get straight to the matter at hand."

"Let's get there faster," Famine's deep, commanding voice leaves little room for argument. Although why he's willing to hear this asshole out at all is something I don't understand.

"I will return to the underworld and allow you riders' carte blanche to fulfill your ride unencumbered by me or any of my kind. In exchange, I have offered these good men before you." I can't help but laugh at this comment. Good men? There isn't an ounce of goodness or morality in the lot of them. These assholes are rotten to the core, much like Sausage Fingers. Raum's pinched features inform me he still doesn't like it when a mere mortal interrupts him when he is going on one of his little morally ambiguous high road monologs. "A place within my ranks. You and your brothers will leave them unharassed and alive—"

"And physically unaltered," Trevor interrupts, making Raum huff his frustration before he includes this last bit.

"With the same physical attributes befitting men of their status." Trevor's gloating grin came a little too quick since what Raum asked for wasn't what Trevor intended. Maybe these assholes should have read the fine print before signing on the dotted line with a damn demon whose sole purpose is to remove humanity from this world. If Famine agrees to this shit, it leaves a lot of wiggle room for Pestilence, War, and Famine to show them what attributes befit their status. Besides, one thing I know for sure is even if Famine agrees with these ridiculous terms, his brothers haven't. And something tells me after what Trevor did to Ember, War won't be so agreeable with these terms or letting him live. Unless the status he feels Trevor deserves is death, then maybe it's something he could and would get behind. "They will work for me to deliver the souls who somehow escape your ride."

"You believe we will permit any survivors?"

"If the lamb has taught me nothing else, she has demonstrated how resourceful these vermin can be."

"I'll vermin you, asshole," I snap while pushing past Famine, who halts my approach by grabbing my arm. It really toasts my cookies that he has no issues accomplishing it. "Famine, I get you don't believe anything I have to say, but you should trust me about this one. Talk to your brothers before you make any deals with him or when it comes to these assholes. I think they might have some thoughts about it."

"They are not here at present, lamb, and since I care little for these sons of Adam or this inane conversation, I will choose for them. Do as you please with them; however, should they return to the community I have claimed as mine, I will send them back to you in pieces."

"I accept this." Raum's willingness to let Famine kill them if they fuck with Sienna's community must not align with Wayne and Trevor's plans for Sin's town since their mouths are currently collecting flies. "I am pleased to have allied myself with your course."

"This does not make us allies."

"Friends?"

"I have no friends. And if I did, a fallen angel cast aside by our father would not be where I start."

"Acquaintances with the same mission."

"Your desires to remove these sons and daughters have nothing to do with our ride. You and your lot have your own agenda, and don't pretend otherwise," Famine replies as he pushes past Raum.

"Just do your damn job then, Rider."

Famine's shoulders go rigid. He doesn't even flash a glance in Raum's direction. Before the demon realizes what is happening, he has already called his vines into action. Unlike the slower path I'm used to seeing with them, this time they have Raum wrapped up tight in seconds, restraining him so Famine can deliver his response without the demon's typical biting retort. "Do not presume to tell me my task, fallen."

Famine releases Raum, who is bent over panting like a rabid dog. I want nothing more than to laugh while declaring, "hurts, doesn't it," but Famine is dragging me back toward the flap to this mammoth damn tent.

"I can walk without your help," I snarl while trying to pull my arm out of his grasp. It's a ridiculous attempt, and the only thing it accomplishes is his flared nostrils and noisy breathing.

Something that only gets louder when Raum dares to speak again.

"Oh, Rider, I have one other thing I want."

"You are in no position to ask for anything else."

"Even so, it would befit you to consider it." Famine stops to give Raum his undivided attention. Something you shouldn't want to have with this rider.

"Enlighten me, Fallen. What is it you want?"

"O zyfl ltu hyrn." I have no damn clue what he asked for. Whatever his burning desire encompasses pisses off the rider. The issue is he is taking his frustration out on my arm.

"Mtachv iae nuhoucu iaesmuhw kytynhu, iae ysu zuhkaru la lydu tus yzyi wsar ru. Ow iae kyf."

"I suppose so, rider," Raum said. "Iacs Mouffy as ltu Hyrn…iae ktaoku nel afu zohh nu rofu."

Raum no sooner finishes whatever he had to say when he turns into the raven and—I would love to say scurries, but I don't think it's possible since what he does is—flies away. Fast. I think he was afraid of what Famine's response would be.

"I suppose I shall await your attempt, fallen."

Chapter Twenty-Three: Expiration Date.

~Sienna Late Winter 2027~

I DON'T KNOW WHY EVERYONE keeps looking at me like they are. Some people are giving me side-eyed glances or tight smiles. These are the people I grew up around. While others—the ones who joined Post Rider—look at me like I just kicked their puppy, or worse, refuse to look at me at all. It's confusing since I can't think of a single damn thing I could have done to piss them off or earn their sympathy.

"Um… mom. Is something going on I should know about?"

"Don't you worry about anything, Sin."

"I'm a grown woman now, Mom. I think I can handle whatever has them so upset. So how about you just tell me what's happening?"

"Gail, could I get your help over here?" Jerry's request gives her the respite she was hoping for because she gives me a quick *"We'll talk later"* before leaving me standing there mid-protest.

The longer the day wore on, the more I noticed people avoided any area where I might be working. The entire thing is not sitting well with me. I kind of wished I would have stayed in my damn little greenhouse. Their constant whispering to each other and avoiding eye contact only makes it more apparent until I can't take it any longer.

I can't help but feel something big is happening, and it seems I'm smack dab in the middle of it. So I search for the one person I know can't lie to me, my best friend, who also happens to be my sister.

"Sil, what the hell is going on with everyone today?"

"Not sure what you're talking about, Egghead."

"Come on, Goober, you can't tell me you haven't noticed how I'm being avoided like one of Pestilence's victims today."

Sylvia sighs before turning to face me. "It's nothing you've done, sis. It's just that some people aren't too happy about the rider who showed up at our gates since he seems content to stay here, or the raiders who, from all appearances, came to collect you?"

"Shit, they were here?" I ask as my eyes search the community for any signs of damage. The rider I can't do anything about, but Wayne's group and I had an understanding. An understanding that only had a six-week shelf life. Something that must have expired today since they came to call. The issue is after Famine showed up, I lost track of time and didn't realize the damn deal we made with Wayne and his camp had reached its deadline.

"When?"

"Hours ago."

"Hours? But they left… without me. Why in the hell would they leave without the person they bargained for?"

"Famine."

"Famine? What does the rider have to do with any of this?"

Sil gives me a soft smile while rubbing my arm before she heads off to talk with some of her friends. People I used to call friends, but now I help oversee their safety instead.

Sil and I are only three years apart, but after the world took a shit, I had to grow up much faster than she did. So, most of the friends I had back then now hang out with my little sister. While I watch her stroll over to where they wait, I'm left standing there, feeling alone, exasperated, and confused. I know I shouldn't let it get to me, but this is easier said than done most days.

And why would the rider interject himself in a human matter? He doesn't even like us.

I try to brush off all these swirling unanswered thoughts and focus on the task no one wants to do, preparing for the upcoming late winter storm. However, no matter how valiant my effort is to push these thoughts aside, the unease lingers like an unwelcome gnat flitting around in the back of my head. I can't help but feel something big is happening, and it seems I'm smack dab in the middle of it.

Later that evening, I'm sitting in my room, trying not to overthink the day's events until I can speak with someone who can fill in the gaps when a knock at the door ends all further debate. Because when I answer it, the being I find standing on the other side is none other than Famine.

"May I come in?" Famine asks. His posture is stiff, not that he is ever animated. His muscles almost look like they are jumping under his skin as they flex and relax, and his expression is pained. I'm not sure what has him so riled, but since I want to know what the hell is going on, there is no way I will deny his request.

"Mi casa su casa," I say, stepping aside to let him in.

Once he closes the door behind him, Famine gets straight to the point. "I need to talk with you about something." When he allows the silence to linger longer than any sane person would be comfortable with, I can't help but push the conversation along.

"What happened today?" I ask, feeling a knot form in my stomach.

"Did you make a bargain with a group of cretins west of your camp?"

My heart rate picks up as I gather the courage to ask. "What do you mean?"

"A man named Wayne sent men to collect you, so when the lamb and I went in your stead—"

"Wait, you did what?" I ask as the first wave of panic washes over me.

"What part of my words are you finding difficulty with?"

"All of them," I snap while the knot in my stomach becomes a ball. I feel like I've been punched in the gut. These people who I thought were my friends... hell, my allies kept this shit from me all damn day long. I can't believe they could do this to me or why he involved himself in it. "I don't see why you're worried about it."

"Because I have claimed this community as mine. The inhabitants who reside within the confines of it are under my protection, meaning you as well."

"But this happened before you came."

"Do you have any idea who you sold yourself to?"

"Two assholes. A guy named Wayne and his buddy Trevor. Oh, and a jerk named Jacob."

"No, the mortal simpletons were not who planned to claim you, and Jacob is much worse than a jerk."

"I'm confused. The deal I made was with Wayne, Trevor, and Jacob."

His huffed laugh confirms how clueless I am about what I got myself mixed up in. "Then I suppose you should thank me."

"Thanks. Now, care to tell me why?"

"Because the one who planned to take you is much worse than the two cretins you believed would hold your ropes."

"Ropes? Who said anything about ropes? I was supposed to fight for them. Nothing else. So, no ropes unless you're talking about the ones that would be around the ring they planned to put me in."

"Yes, because fighting is the reason they wanted you, an untrained scrawny—"

"Hey!"

"Mortal, who couldn't win if you had help."

"That's unnecessary."

"You were right about one thing though. The one to whom you gave your life to would have used chains…not ropes." The gasp I give him softens his tone for the rest of it. "Next time, don't be so quick to offer this…." his eyes travel the length of my body. Is this what he wanted to say? I'll never know because he changes it to "yourself, to one of my kind."

"Oh." This is the only response I can give him.

"They will not be returning. I have settled your debt." Famine says like he goes around making and breaking deals all the time. "Should they make any attempt, they will face me. The assurance I provided to these miscreants was simple. I will not stop with only one of them paying for their mistakes. Next time, none will return to their camp."

This is when the first waves of dread settle over me. Now, their reactions all make sense. The deal we made was supposed to remain between just the people who went, but within hours of our return—even with a damn rider showing up at our front door—the entire community knew. They also know, because I didn't go with Wayne's men, what this means for our long-term survival when a rider is no longer around to stop them. "But what happens when you leave? They'll attack this community."

"Who said I planned to leave?" Okay, now I'm more confused than when I started this conversation. Why would Famine want to stay? He's all about killing off humanity. If he didn't think it was beneath him, I have no problem imagining him carrying a sign reading '*Down with the damnable mortals*' and marching through the middle of town. Yeah, I can picture it now. Or let me rephrase. I can see him making Avalon do it cause he wouldn't want to taint his hands by carrying a sign displaying any words about the mortals he deems to be a lesser lifeform than him.

But I don't have time to ask for any follow-up since he leaves me alone in my room to contemplate his admission. It might be easier if I had all the facts. The issue is everyone is hellbent on keeping me in the damn dark. However, I know someone who should be able to fill in the shit no one else wants to say, the one he likes to call Little Lamb. This is a conversation I would love to have tonight, but it will have to wait until the morning.

As I climb into bed, I feel like I'm on the edge of a precipice, and one wrong move, one misstep could send me tumbling over the edge. Right now, I don't know what will happen next, but one thing is for sure…. Camp life is about to get a lot more complicated.

~Famine~

THIS DEMON HAS much to learn, starting with when I say no, I mean no. Raum's second request—made all the more infuriating by his use of our ancient language, something these mortals should not be permitted to hear—advised he wanted the lamb. To which I told him he was welcome to make an attempt at taking her if he could. This is when the vile creature pushed me beyond the point of reason when he told me I had to choose between Sienna and the lamb.

I contemplated killing every being in the room, but it would have put the lamb at risk. And she could not assist me while I dealt with the fools; it would have forced me to protect her. Something she may have mistaken for friendship.

Besides, every second I remained in their camp was another opportunity for one of the damnable mortals to retrieve the woman who has somehow garnered much of my fascination.

I suppose this is the reason they placed her in shackles. I should have realized they were up to something and refused the one who stopped us. There are always lessons to be learned in any situation. This is one I shall not soon forget.

During our visit to their camp, there was a conversation about the lamb saving two of my brothers. She was as resolute in the fact she helped them as the demon was that she didn't. I was reluctant to believe any mortal could or would assist the riders. However, the longer Raum spoke, the more I questioned if she did everything she claimed. The problem is one brother who could tell me the truth is well beyond my reach, while I have avoided the other two. It may be time to have the meeting Pestilence and War are pushing for.

But not today. Today, my only desire is to make sure Sienna is safe.

The instant she opened the door, I had the most unpleasant urge to pull her into my arms. There is something about this mortal I am drawn to, and no amount of denying it has helped so far. Something that is almost as infuriating as it is confusing.

Her calming presence opposes my pounding heart as I watch Sienna move around her room. Yet another thing to agitate me. Tiny beads of sweat dot my brow, and I fight the urge to clench my hands into fists. It's as if my body is at war with my mind, and I'm caught in the middle of the damnable battle.

My eyes track her every move, and I can't help but notice how the lamplight's soft glow only accentuates her body's shape. My fingers vibrate with the need to explore it. Every dip, every curve, every smooth place that lives in my imagination. After seeing what pleasure the lamb gave Thanatos, I never thought I would want to experience it.

But I do.

With her.

With Sienna, I want it all. Every moan, groan, and scream of my name. These are mortal reactions. Something I've never felt before, and I'm unsure if I like them. The thought of being vulnerable in any way is abhorrent to me, and yet, here I am, unable to resist the pull of this mortal woman.

When she looks at me with eyes as green as the vines I control, the warmth and kindness shining through them makes me want nothing more than to stare into them for the rest of my days. However, I drown in a sea of emotions when she grants me her timid, unsure smile. Especially with the nervous way she bites at her lip. This action makes me want to pull her into my arms to protect her and prove she will always be safe with me. In this instant, something clicks into place… like finding a missing piece of myself. Something I am unwilling to let go of.

Yet, I will not surrender to these emotions. Sienna's safety is my top priority, and I'll do whatever it takes to keep her out of harm's way. Even though I know this means putting my own feelings aside.

To do this, I remind myself this is not my purpose. I cannot give in to my escalating desires. I force myself to maintain a modicum of distance, but this last part is proving harder each day.

So I say what I came to tell her and turn to leave with the same icy demeanor I presented throughout this entire interaction.

When I left her room, the sense of longing did not abate. It's a feeling I had never experienced before, and it both alarms and intrigues me. I must find a way to quell these tumultuous emotions, which often feel insurmountable. Because the more time I spend with Sienna or around her, the more I feel myself falling under her spell.

No matter how much she stirs these unwanted emotions, I will maintain my composure in Sienna's presence. But more important than the woman who has bewitched this rider, I will display none of these emotions in front of….

The little lamb who will have no issues using it against me.

Chapter Twenty-Four:
Simple Truth.

I N WHAT HAS BECOME THIS damn rider's custom, he wakes me up at the ass crack of dawn so I can take my happy ass back out to tend to the shit no one else wants to do. It's like ditch duty all over again. Today I'm hauling shit to the garden to prepare for spring planting. And yes, I still know it's called fertilizer, and I still just don't care.

During my third trip to the garden, I encountered a girl around ten talking to Famine. I don't know the events that led up to their conversation, but for some damn reason, this kid is apologizing to the jackass who has taken over her community.

"I no–know you don't like me, and I'm sorry for whatever I did to you, Mr. Famine. Plea–please don't send your plants after me."

Famine's arms are crossed over his chest, glaring at the little girl. There's no wonder why she's terrified. After a second, he lifts his gaze toward the sky and huffs an aggravated sigh while shaking his head.

"Just go." His command leaves little room for misunderstanding, but for reasons I can't explain, she steps closer to him rather than running in the opposite direction. However, her slow approach ends when he brings his attention back to her.

"I'm leaving right now, Mr. Famine." The rider pulls his brows together while he watches the little girl scamper away. It's my turn to convey my irritation about how he handled the little girl… actually, how he dealt with the entire situation, which comes by way of a forced snort. "Won't happen again, Mr. Famine."

"Why does she keep calling me this?" Famine barks his question at me like I should have known it was something he didn't understand.

"Well, I'd like to think it's because she considers you old as dirt, but I think the actual reason she's doing it is to be freaking respectful—although I don't get why since you're acting like an ass—so how about you give her a break and stop being the dick you're proving yourself to be."

"I could have done without your extra commentary."

"If you don't like how I explain things, don't ask the one mortal who will tell you the truth about what something means. If you want shitted fluff, then I suppose you could ask…." I turn, looking over my shoulder, hoping to find one of the two idiots I would like to point out to him, and luck happens to be on my side today because the dimwitted bobblehead saunters around the corner. "Her."

"I would sooner resume the pointless conversation with the child who started this incident."

"If you don't like the people you travel with but continue doing so, what does that say about you?"

"I could ask you the same question, lamb."

"Not even remotely the same thing."

"How so?"

"You choose to ride with them. I'm forced by an ass of a rider to follow behind," I reply while I continue past him without waiting for his response. I'm sure it comprised some threats of death, hoity-toity words of superiority, and a slew of other shit I don't need to hear yet again. Trust me, once is enough.

When I round the corner, I discover a shocking sight. Sin whispering while lovingly stroking the horse I'm still trying to win over. Damn, I have to admit, seeing how he is with her makes me a little jealous. I pull the gloves off my hands and walk over to where they are standing.

"Hmm, I think he likes you. Don't ya, Eclipse," I say as I run my hand from his nose to the top of his head.

"Eclipse?"

"The name I've given Famine's companion."

"You mean his horse?"

"These magnificent creatures are not like normal horses. They're an extension of their rider. Loyal to them at the risk of their own life. And smart as hell. But this one here has taken me much longer to win over than the other rider's horses. Isn't that right, boy?" The horse gives a snort while pawing at the ground.

"Win over? Why would you even try?"

"Why wouldn't I?"

"I guess I thought their horses didn't like anyone."

"Normally, they don't."

"So why would you think he likes me?" she asks while stroking his mane, further proving my point. I don't think she realizes these amazing horses don't let anyone touch them if they don't like the person doing the touching. For example, if Cammie or Nevil come within fifty feet of Eclipse, he'll slam his foot on the ground, snort a warning, and if this doesn't halt their approach, he'll rear up and try to crush them. Just to be clear, I don't blame him. I wouldn't want Sausage or Bobble touching me either.

"I have my suspicions."

"Wanna clue in the clueless?" she asks with a laugh.

"These horses tend to protect the people the riders feel...." Okay, how do I tell Sin I think a particular rider has a growing attraction for her? "Strongly about."

"What do you mean, strongly? Like hate?"

"No... definitely not hate. They protect any person the horsemen care about. People, the riders themself, would protect if they thought they were in trouble."

"But that would mean." She hesitates with her brows furrowed as she contemplates what I just told her. It's a lot. I know. But I think it's time for her to understand why we're still here. Why her community is still intact, and why they are not withering and dying in his wake.

"It means Famine isn't as opposed to rider human relations as he claimed."

"Whoa, slow down. No damn way does Famine have feelings for me. He's just... just. Oh hell, I don't know, but he doesn't."

"Okay, Sienna, then you tell me why he's left your little community stand when much better, bigger, and more organized ones have fallen."

"Hey, our little place in the world might not be all big and showy, but it's still a great place to live."

"And I don't disagree; however, until we came across this place and '*you,*' he's never left one the same as it was before he found it."

"Well, shit," she said before plopping down on the hay bale behind her. I'll leave her to ponder what this means for her while I consider how I can use this to get my ass out of here so I can hunt down the damn demon I will force to send me to Thanatos.

*****

My eyes dart from one area to the next while my heart feels like a jackhammer in my chest. This is it. After what I can only imagine has been months, Famine has slipped and left me unguarded. Thank you Sin. And while I hate leaving these people to their own devices with him, something tells me they are in no danger from this rider. Provided nothing happens to Sienna.

If they treat her like she is the most precious person in the world—because to him, she is—he'll protect the town, which means they're also safe. So, if I ever wanted to run, now would be the time. I'm unsure what Death is facing, but I can't imagine it's all that pleasant for him.

The lack of light since the sun has set only helps me in this '*get your ass out of here*' mission. With my body pressed against the house, I keep my head on a pivot while I slip through the shadows. Each time there's a snapping twig, rustling leaves, a whisper of wind, or a distant laugh, my heart skips a beat. But it's just the wind, an animal scurrying through the underbrush, or the people I'm leaving in the hands of a rider I'm not fond of. I may have asked the almighty to look after them. My only hope is he's listening. I've already wasted more time than I should while waiting for the perfect opportunity, so I push forward with my plan.

My footsteps are silent but deliberate as I make my way towards the treeline and what I hope is my way out. Escaping this community is step one. Easy enough. Step two centers on finding a demon who has only ever sought me out. No problem there. Then the last phase is all about pissing him off enough to make him want to kill me more than torture me. Simple.

Yeah right.

When I reach the last house, I take one last look behind me prior to sprinting for the woods. Sin seems hellbent on testing my theory about the horse not letting just anyone touch him since Sylvia is picking her ass up off the ground after Eclipse put her there.

I kind of feel like shit about doing this. However, when it comes to Famine, I don't get many opportunities. I'm taking a chance tonight only because I realized he's too engrossed with watching the sisters interact with his companion to worry about little ol' me. Oblivious to what's happening around her and her role in my escape, Sin continues to stroke Eclipse's mane. I can't help but feel a pang of guilt for using her to aid in my exit, even if she doesn't realize it.

With my plan in place, I step out of the shadows and run straight into Nevil.

Chapter Twenty-Five:
Apple.

S ON OF A BITCH! OF all nights for this dipshit not to have Cammie wrapped around him, he had to pick tonight. If I were keeping score, it would be the assholes of the world: ninety-nine. Avalon: five. Okay, maybe ten. Either way, this luck shit is lopsided as hell.

"Well–well, looks like I arrived in the nick of time."

"Up yours, asshole. Shouldn't you be ass deep in the screaming idiot right now?"

"Are you offering, Avalon?"

"Not even if you were the last prick alive."

"Don't you mean dick?" he asks, grabbing his crotch to display the dick he's talking about.

"That too."

"Let's go. Time to tell Famine what the hell you've been up to." He grabs my arm to yank me into him, but I wrench it from his grasp.

"I'm not your fucking bobblehead. Don't touch me like that!" Nevil's eyes narrow a second before he brings his foot up to slam it into my abdomen, knocking me back into the house I was using to conceal myself. The force of the impact buckles my knees and sends my ass sprawling to the ground.

"You know, I really fucking hate it when you call her names."

I push up on my hands and knees, sucking in generous gulps of air, hoping to replenish what he knocked out of me. Through panted breaths, I somehow give him a typical snarky-ass Avalon response. "Good. Glad to know I can make you hate something else about me. You and her make the perfect fucking couple. Sausage and Bobble. Maybe you two should get matching tattoos."

"Maybe you should since it was because of you we're together."

"I didn't do shit other than find the bitch in a basement."

Nevil grabs my hair to wrench my head back, forcing me to look at him. "No, bitch. You brought us together when you cried to your fucking rider. The one who did this shit to my face."

"First, I didn't say anything to Death."

"Then how'd he find out what happened?"

"Because you're sloppy, and unlike you, he's not stupid."

"Keep it up, Lamb." The way he says this is both meant to mock and belittle. "and you won't have to worry about being Famine's prisoner anymore because I'll take care of you the same way I took care of the last fuckers who stood by while a rider thought he controlled me."

"What the hell is that supposed to mean?"

"It means after Cammie found me hanging from the side of the ravine we threw your ass into and nursed me back to health, I killed the useless pricks who didn't stop him."

"You're the one who destroyed the community we were staying in."

"Tell me you didn't think I would let any of those punk ass bitches live after they did nothing? My only regret was Xander and his fucking bitch wasn't there when I burnt it to the ground. I wanted to watch as their flesh melted from their bones. I figured it was only fair since Xander had no issues watching Death carve Bob and me up, beat us, and leave us for the vultures."

"First of all, Nevil, there weren't any vultures around there. Some bunnies, a deer or two, a dumbass raven, and more than a few jackasses, but no vultures. Second, the people who lived there had nothing to do with what happened to you. You three idiots did it to yourself," I snap, knocking his hand off me so I could return to full height. This prick loves to kick you when you're down. There's no way I want to make it any easier for him.

"See, Avalon, that's where you're fucking wrong. *Those people* are dead because you couldn't keep your damn legs closed."

"Fuck you, Asshole. I wasn't even there when you proved how much of a coward you are by killing a bunch of innocent people."

"Yes, and thank you for that. Because you left, Death followed, leaving those sheep all alone. They made perfect fucking fodder for this wolf's revenge."

"Now you're a wolf. You and the damn Bird Boy should become best fucked up friends."

"You know, Avalon, I had plenty of time to think about all the shit I wanted to do to repay you for what Death did to me, but none of it feels sufficient anymore. A bitch like you requires something special. You'll have to give me a little more time so I can figure it out."

"Yeah, well, while you're frying the few brain cells you have left in that lump you call a head, how bout you clue me in on why you helped bring another rider into our world? At the very least, you must be smart enough to know you won't be alive for long when Death returns."

"Oh, I have it on good authority that I don't have anything to worry about."

"Which makes you a bigger idiot than I already thought you were." His lip twists into a snarl, and his posture becomes stiff.

"I look forward to the day when you are on your knees begging me to end your miserable fucking life."

"I've already told you before, I don't fucking beg."

"Just know, Avalon, before you die, I promise to make you watch the people you love suffer. Suki among them." I move to hit him, but the action comes too late.

*****

I jerk my hands up to protect my face from the hit I know Nevil plans to deliver, but they don't get far because something stops them. What the hell? I peel my eyes open enough to realize my hands are bound and tied to the bookcase in Famine's room.

This can only mean one thing. Famine either knows what I did or will soon, which means I need to get my ass out of here before he shows up.

"I grant you freedom, and this is how you repay me. By attempting to flee." Too late. The prick is already here, and it seems he plans on pushing my damn buttons during this stupid exchange.

"Freedom. You call what you gave me freedom. I wasn't fucking free, Famine, and don't kid yourself that I was. You know your brother wants the prick who brought my ass back to you tonight dead, right?"

"I don't care."

"What the hell is that supposed to mean, Rider?"

"It means my goals no longer align with those of my father."

"What? You mean after all the shit I had to listen to you yammer on about over the last couple of months, you want us to live?"

"No, not humanity. Only one soul will survive my ride."

"You really think Sin—"

"DO NOT CALL HER THAT AGAIN!"

"Or."

"Or I will prove I no longer require the lamb. Besides, Sienna is not my only reason for coming to this conclusion."

"So what swayed the infamous and powerful Famine?"

"One should not mock when their life is held by another, but to answer your inquiry, my sole reason for existing is to annihilate the likes of you from this world. Once my task has been fulfilled, my usefulness to my father will be done. I prefer not meeting my brother's judgment or being forced back into our long slumber."

"How can you outright defy your father's will when Death couldn't?"

"Perhaps my brother is not the powerful being you mortals ascribe to him. Besides, may I remind you my other brothers have also strayed from their task?"

"Pestilence and War only did so after finding Greer and Ember. Are you telling me you found with Sienna," this time, I use extra emphasis when saying the damn name he demands we use, "what they found with the women they love?"

"No."

"So how are you defying him then? Because I happen to know Pessy—"

"Stop calling my brother that ridiculous name."

"Pessy and War could only do it when they admitted how much Greer and Ember meant to them."

"With a little help from my friends."

"Are you going to break out in song and dance next?" Yeah, so a certain Beatles song may have sprung to mind when he said this.

"Elaborate, mortal."

"Doesn't matter. Besides, I doubt what you said."

"Doubt they are the ones who help me defy my father?"

"Doubt you have friends." Famine throws his head back, laughing like War used to when he found something I said hilarious. I guess I haven't lost that comedian status. "So glad I can amuse you."

"I do enjoy that sharp wit of yours, Avalon."

"And I don't give a fuck what you like."

"Do you know once humanity is destroyed, our father will have no option but to release my brothers and me from our task? We will never slumber again while awaiting our father's decree."

"Did you get that shit from Raum? Been sipping his Kool-Aid?"

"Raum is an idiot, but it doesn't make his statement any less true. My kind will inherit the earth when humanity falls, and the riders will demand our release."

"Your kind?"

"His divine creations."

"Isn't Raum one of those godforsaken creations?"

"He is, so you can see why he would want your kind removed."

"What, he can't do it himself? Oh, wait a minute, is Raum the friend you spoke of?"

"His kind has tried since the day humanity fell from grace. The day temptation won out. As of yet, they haven't succeeded. Hence the reason for our creation."

"So is that a yes or no on the Raum being your friend thing?"

"I wonder if you will think you are funny when the people you love are nothing more than dust and bones."

"How about we cut the bullshit, and you just tell me what you came to say? Or did you just want to gloat?"

"There always has to be a bad *Apple* in the bunch." I jerk my head toward him after hearing his analogy. Does he know Death used to call me Apple?

"What the hell are you talking about?"

"Did my brother ever tell you why he called you this?" Well, I guess I have my answer to the whole—does he know his brother called me this—question.

"I'll take your silence as a solid no. It doesn't surprise me my other brothers would withhold this from you."

"Withhold what? Tell me why he called me that."

"It is partly because of your name. Avalon, which means the Isle of Fruit, or if you wish to be specific, The Isle of Apples. It's also a mystical place you mortal should know well. The place where humanity fell from his grace. Avalon is where the Tree of Knowledge, or the Tree of Good and Evil, can be found."

"What the hell is a Tree of Knowledge?" He laughs, but it is more in line with the, *you're an idiot* kind of laugh rather than *you're funny,* and just like that, I lost my comedian status. I wonder if they'll revoke my card.

"This admission comes as no shock to me, little Lamb. Even though you should know what it is, because it is the very one your Eve ate from and the one she tempted your Adam with."

"That still doesn't explain why he called me Apple."

"It's what you represented to him. Like the snake who tempted Eve with the apple. You represent the same." I imagine the shock on my face confirms my disbelief.

"You don't believe me?"

"Bullshit. Death called me Apple from the very beginning."

"He did because he knew the second you sacrificed your own safety for him what you represented and what you would be capable of doing."

"Which was?"

"Temptation. My brother always knew you would be his downfall."

"No one can know that fast."

"If we were discussing a mortal man, you would be correct, but we are talking about a being whose sole purpose is to judge humanity and determine your worth. It is why my father chose him to come. He hoped my brother would find what the rest of us would miss. This being...you are worthy of his forgiveness. If the being whose singular objective is to ferry the dead to their afterlife can be swayed, then he knew he would not need to wake the rest of us, and you served our father's objective well."

"I didn't sway anything."

"Didn't you? Are you certain of this?"

"Death left. Something you never do if you care about someone else."

"Or something you do when you love them enough to protect them." My heart races at hearing him say this. War and Pessy always told me Death cared, but I thought they said this to spare my feelings. To make me believe the only reason he left was because he loved me. An act of compassion since they couldn't bear to see me suffer. Something this rider would never do.

"If your saying is true, how could your father allow you riders access to our world, and why didn't Death stop it?"

"I was told our father is not the one who allowed it. You are responsible for our release. Not my father. Not my brother, and not the demon you like to blame. You and you alone broke the seal holding out at bay. A choice you made."

"I was tricked, asshole."

"So you say. Yet even if this were true, it was still a choice you made. Besides, you can only claim this for the first seal. If what I'm hearing is true, it was your decision to open War's."

"To save Pestilence."

"Ah, yes. The little lamb who saved a rider."

"Jealous that I would never do the same for you?" His only response is to smirk at me.

"Ya know, there is something else I don't understand about your ridiculous fable."

"Please proceed with your enlightened perception of the facts I provided."

"Everything the bible has taught humanity points to the Garden of Eden being in the Middle East."

"Who said it wasn't?"

"Then your explanation is bullshit because Avalon was some mystical made-up shit from King Arthur's time."

"It was."

"You're an idiot because both can't be true."

"Can't they? You mortals don't know half as much as you believe you do. Thanatos would have been better off if he had killed you the first day he met you. He could have saved himself a lot of turmoil."

"Fuck off."

"My brother has already done this. Yes?"

"You don't know half as much as you think you do."

"Oh, Apple, the entirety of all the realms suspects the little lamb meant to wake us brought my almighty brother to heel. Brought him to his knees, so to speak."

"Don't call me that."

"So you see, Apple…." He repeats my nickname, hoping to get under my skin. It works. "You are much the same as your Eve, accepting the forbidden fruit to destroy Adam's innocence. Only this time, a lamb did it to a rider."

Famine gets up to leave the room but stops just prior to exiting to give me one more fact, which damn near destroys me. "This is the reason our father has cast aside my brother. The reason he suffers in the dark and the reason he will lose his way. I'll leave you to consider that, Morte's mela."

Chapter Twenty-Six: Surprises

THE SUN HAS ONLY CRESTED the eastern sky when I make my way to the stables. After the battles we have fought over the past several days, we felt Storm and Red needed to rest for the evening. The least I can do for our companions before we force them out again is to tend to their needs.

The useless demon Raum continues to fight against us. Each day, when we ride out to find Famine, hordes of his undead are there to halt us. We fight until my sword is heavy and Pestilence's fingers bleed. The battle would be easier if he could use his plague, but the black death cannot kill what is already dead. I suppose this shouldn't surprise us since the one thing he has wanted for countless millennia is for us to complete our ride. I don't know what Raum hopes to gain from his actions. We plan to investigate it once we have released Thanatos, retrieved Avalon, and returned to the ones we had to leave behind.

At first, we believe Famine had accepted Raum's offer to aid him by distracting us from his ride; however, over the last several weeks, we have realized Famine is no longer moving. We don't know if something happened to him. If he is being detained by the high earl or if he fell to the sons of Adam. The ones determined to remove us from this realm. We don't know if he is suffering, if he stopped to regain his strength while he prepares for another push...or if he found what we found. The one thing Pestilence and I are confident about is that as long as the lamb travels with him, she will do everything in her power to stop him. To sway him. To save him. A task she will undertake until her body fails and she takes her last breath.

Something I will never allow.

The thought of this world without her in it is almost too much for me to bear. My eyes slip closed as I remember her smile. I love Ember. I do. She is the one bright spot in my life. Yet a tiny piece of me still longs to make u mo bella agnellu happy. Something I do my best to hide from my brothers and the rest of the world.

I remain rooted in place, enjoying my mouse's favorite time of the day. When the world is still dark and silent. When most mortal yet slumber, this is when she was most at peace. I wonder if she is awake and looking at the same sky I am now, asking herself if we will ever come for her. When the sun has crested the horizon, I turn to make my way to the barn, only to find Pestilence waiting for me. He looks up as I approach, his eyes filled with worry and dread. We both know what we are about to do will be difficult, but it must be done.

This is the day we have both been dreading. Today, we will not ride out to face Raum's undead. We will not continue our search for Famine. Today, we return to our realm to find out if Raphael found the means to release Thanatos. The real challenge lies in what will follow if he achieved his objective. We will have to tell our brother we failed to protect the lamb. My jaw aches at the thought of my last interaction with Thanatos regarding his Apple.

During the return trip to our realm, I cannot help but feel the burden of our failure weighing on me. We were supposed to protect Avalon, yet shielding her from her task is the furthest thing from what we did, and to top it off, we have failed to retrieve her from our brother. Something we will face the consequences of.

Even as our pursuit of Famine continues, we cannot figure out his plan. Is he avoiding us, as we suspect he is doing, or biding his time, waiting for the perfect opportunity to strike? We know he is a master manipulator, and although I am the strategist among my brothers, it would not be out of character for him to play the long game.

The thought of my mouse still traveling with him fills me with an urgency I'm unaccustomed to. For what feels like too long, our goal has been to find her and bring her to safety before any harm can befall her and halt any attempt from Raum to use her as a pawn.

We have failed.

Our last hope rests with an angel. It is imperative for Raphael to have discovered the key that will set Thanatos free from the prison where Michael encouraged our father to confine him. If not, our options for bringing him out are limited. It will fall to the lamb to break his seal. If she declines or if the worst comes to pass, Pestilence and I will tear the veil apart to bring him out of the void. Because the simple truth is we are desperate to save this world. Something I am no longer confident we can achieve without our eldest brother.

Which is the reason we mount our companions to return to our realm.

*****

"Raphael, tell us you have promising news."

"I'm afraid I cannot give you what you seek."

Raphael's words hit us hard. These nine infinitesimal words couldn't have been any more harsh than a punch to the gut. With our unsuccessful attempts at confronting Famine, we had placed much of our hopes on his ability to find a solution to releasing Thanatos, but it was all for naught.

I exchange a frustrated glance with Pestilence. Our silent communication is the only thing required to display our shared disappointment and concern. Still, I believe answers are necessary.

"What do you mean?" Pestilence asks, his voice laced with annoyance.

Raphael's heavy sigh aligns with our aggravation as the weight of our failure becomes apparent in his tired eyes. "I've searched from one end of our father's universe to the other, delved into ancient texts, and even consulted with those who oppose their annihilation. Yet none know of a way to release Thanatos from his prison."

My heart sinks. We had come so far and fought so hard, only to face what feels like an insurmountable obstacle. How could we have been so unsuccessful in our duty to our brother and the lamb? I can't help but feel a surge of anger toward the ones who put him there. Pestilence and I have no desire to release him with our worst-case scenario option because the simple truth is we are unsure of the ramifications it could cause in their world when the veil comes down.

Pestilence understands this fear all too well, knowing what he stands to lose. "You must have something, some lead to follow, some way we can reach him!"

Raphael opens his mouth to respond; however, Michael interrupts our conversation before he can provide any answers.

"What brings you to my realm, riders?" Michael asks.

"Your realm. Did I miss the memo our creator sent out announcing this?" I reply as I step closer to him. If he knows what is best, he will leave now since he is among the ones who sought Thanatos's removal.

"I doubt our father would hand over his greatest empire to a fool, brother," Pestilence says, his eyes narrowing. "But keep in mind, Brother, even fools have their uses."

"And what would his be?" I ask while lifting my lip in a snarl.

"He may yet show some intellect and advise us where we may find the lamb."

"I have no interest in the lamb," he replies, his words cold and final. "My only concern is fulfilling my purpose as his guiding warrior in a realm you should not be in."

"Then why are you here?" I demand, my hand tightening around the hilt of my sword.

"I am here because it is my responsibility as his trusted council. Something I can do from within this realm. You have no right to question my presence here."

A tense silence persists while he glares at me, and my stare dares him to push the subject. Neither of us will back down until Pestilence speaks.

"We come seeking—"

"Thanatos must return to his rightful role if you wish us to continue our ride," I interrupt.

"Continue? Have you even begun yet? From what I have witnessed, you first allowed the lamb to distract you, then another mortal you wanted to bed, and now you are hunting for the lamb again. Have I missed any facts related to your ride, War?"

"My ride is none of your concern, and it would serve you well to remember it, emuhumm." Calling him useless in our native language has him advancing on me, an act of aggression I plan to meet much the same.

"Our brother, Thanatos, has been cast into the void between worlds. We want him back. Now!" Pestilence adds, his voice laced with venom.

"It was his actions that placed him there," Michael retorts, his voice betraying the indifferent attitude he is attempting to achieve. "A sentence I have no intention of releasing him from."

"A choice you will soon regret. As the mortals are not the only souls we can reap," I snarl, my voice laced with the fury this being aspires to evoke. If not for my old friend stepping between us, Michael's soul would have been the first we claimed, followed shortly after by the one always at his side. And his comment has me wondering if it will be two souls we reap this day or three.

"I understand your pain, War. But sometimes, even the mightiest of warriors must accept their limitations. We cannot control everything, no matter how much we want to," Raphael says, shaking his head while his features twisted into a mask of pain.

I grit my teeth, unwilling to accept defeat. "We will never accept there is no way to break the chains that bind him."

Raphael's expression softens, and he places a hand on my shoulder. "War, sometimes the greatest act of love… is to let go. To trust that there is a higher plan at work. Thanatos may find his own path, his own redemption. And Avalon, she is stronger than you realize. She may yet surprise us all."

Anger boils within me. Why in all the realms is he saying this shit? Besides, how can he ask this of us? We are the horsemen, the bringers of chaos and destruction. We have faced countless challenges before, overcoming impossible odds, yet now we are powerless to protect the one person who means so much to us. And not just Thanatos, but the lamb as well.

"I believe it is past the time for you to return to your task," Michael's smug comment is followed by my fist becoming acquainted with his nose while Pestilence releases the black tendril that encircles them. I believe the three angels realize their misstep.

Michael's true colors are revealed as he and Gabriel back away. Only Raphael remains.

"Tell me, old friend," I growl this moniker. Fury courses through me because the one soul I believed I could trust, aside from my brothers and the few mortals who have proven themselves worthy, is now among the ones I call enemy. "Why do you remain?"

"Because even if you can't see it, I remain the title you hiss." Raphael waits until the useless angels is out of sight before he leans closer and mumbles, "I haven't given up. There may be one last option, but it comes with great risks."

"Do you believe we fear any risk?" Pestilence growls.

"No, but you should."

Pestilence and I exchange glances, both of us ready to do whatever it takes to save Avalon and release Thanatos from his torment.

"Tell us," Pestilence says, his voice steady.

Raphael takes a deep breath, steeling himself for what he is about to propose. "There is a forbidden ritual, a last resort. It involves tapping into the darkest powers, the ones that we have sworn never to use. But it might be our only chance if you are willing to accept the price you must pay."

I can feel the weight of his words, the gravity of the situation pressing down on us. We have always been bound by our duty and principles, but faced with the prospect of losing Avalon and leaving Thanatos trapped, they leave us with little choice.

"Does this ritual pose any threat to our families?" Pestilence asks.

"Your families?" Raphael did not need to ask this question. His raised brow conveys his thoughts on what my brother said. He will protect the sons and daughters in Avalon's realm because this is his assignment. It doesn't mean he understands our affinity for them.

"Yes, Raphael, our families."

"The mortals you care for…the ones you have chosen as your mates, will remain protected. You have my word."

"Then we will do whatever it takes," I say. My response is firm. Our determination is unwavering.

Pestilence nods in agreement, his resolve matching mine. "We will not let them suffer any longer."

Raphael's eyes soften. Appreciation mingles with sadness. "Your brother is fortunate he can count on you. But remember, the consequences of this ritual are dire. It could change everything."

We take a moment to let his words sink in, understanding the weight of our decision. But the risks become insignificant in the face of love and the bonds we hold dear.

"We are prepared for the consequences. Let us begin."

With our plan in place, we return to the mortal realm. Raphael will notify us the instant he has everything ready. In the meantime, we will continue searching for the lamb. If we wish to remain untouched by the taint his plan will bring, she is our last hope. A strategy that will either save our brother and the lamb or damn us all. A fate we are prepared to face if the outcome protects the ones we love. We allow the weight of our choice to surround us on our return trip, marked by the silence of what's to come. Perhaps we should have been discussing strategy because what we discover when we return to her world is most unexpected.

"Hello, brothers."

~Sienna, one month ago~

MY HEART IS pounding out of my chest as I approach Avalon. I need to know if all the things I believe are true, and something tells me she is the one person in this world who can answer this for me. Since they returned from Wayne's camp last week, I've wanted to ask her, but something happened. Avalon's entire demeanor has shifted, and I'm not sure what caused it. Whatever it is has something to do with Famine. And that something put her back in shackles.

"Hey, Avalon, are you busy?"

"I am, but I wouldn't oppose some company while I work, Sin—err, I mean Sienna."

"Sin's fine. All my friends call me Sin."

"Yeah, I think it's best if I refrain from calling you that." Damn. I realize we haven't known each other for a long, but I thought we were friends. Maybe asking her is the wrong choice. While Avalon continues loading bags of fertilizer and other supplies needed to tend to the garden, I stand there biting my lip, tapping my leg, and contemplate scrapping the whole thing.

"Up?"

"Huh," I mumble.

She smiles before repeating whatever I was too busy living in my head to hear. "I said, what's up?"

"Oh. Nothing really."

"So you came out here to ask if I was busy?"

Do I jump in with both feet or turn tail and run? This is the question I'm asking myself while I say something else to her. "Thanks for helping me plant the garden. Most of the time, people are gung ho on the first day, but by day three, it's just me, a shovel, and the cool spring air."

"Maybe you should give that thanks to Famine."

"What do you mean?"

"Doesn't matter. But you're welcome."

We worked in silence for the next fifteen minutes even though I started and stopped myself from enquiring what I came out here to ask more than once. Avalon makes the choice for me when she catches me watching the rider.

"What do you want to know about Famine?"

"I… I don't—umm."

"Is this about his growing interest in you?"

"He doesn't. I mean, he isn't… I'm sure he does the things he does for everyone." She laughs. No, not laughs; she falls over, holding her side as hysterics overtake her. "Um, why are you laughing?"

"You can't honestly believe that. Famine doesn't do shit for any of us mortals, with one exception. You."

"Why?"

"Because he likes you. It's something he doesn't understand, let alone how to handle the jumble of emotions it brings with it."

A swell of emotions courses through me upon hearing her confession. I never dreamed that Famine's actions could be driven by anything more than a passing interest in our community. Yet... Avalon's laughter, which is tinged with equal parts amusement and sorrow, shatters all thoughts of this. This new certainty brings a surge of fear, confusion, panic, and something else... curiosity.

"I don't understand why me?" In a hushed voice, I finally ask.

Avalon's laughter subsides, and she looks at me with a sympathetic smile. "I don't know. I suppose you're special."

"I don't feel so special. The truth is, I feel...."

"Confused, lost, scared... but maybe a little intrigued." I suck in a breath. How the hell could she know how I feel right down to the last emotion? "Don't worry, Sienna, your secret is safe with me. When it comes to the riders, it won't take long before you discover the connection with him. Even if none of us understands it. I will tell you this much: I'm willing to bet it's something that scares him almost as much as it terrifies you."

I may not want to acknowledge it, but she's right. And the worst part is it's something I've known but refused to admit for a while now. Yet, the time for hiding my head in the sand is at an end. I need to either explore what these feelings mean or shut this shit down. I think my choice should be clear with the following question as I discover a newfound determination to understand what's happening between the rider and me.

"Can you tell me more?"

Avalon hesitates while weighing her words with the utmost care and caution. "I can only tell you what I've observed. Famine has always been distant from his brothers and detached from his actions in our world. But since he met you, something has changed. He became more... compassionate. Almost human."

I hold my breath, hanging onto Avalon's every word. "What do you mean, more human?"

"He started showing emotions I suspect he had buried long ago and has since forgotten. Until you. Until every part of him wanted only to protect you, even if he didn't fully understand why. And trust me when I tell you, Sienna, it's not something he does for just anyone."

"You can call me Sin. I don't mind," I mumble while sitting on the fallen tree trunk before my trembling legs can give out altogether. My mind is spinning from her revelations and the implications it brings with it. Could Famine's actions be driven by more than duty and obligation alone? Could there be something more to him? Something deeper developing between us. Could whatever it is transcend our role as ended and ender?

"You might not, but he does. He's adamant no one is to call you by this name."

"What? How do you know?"

"He told me as much. In fact, he demanded I refrain from calling you this."

"Why in the hell would he care? People have called me Sin since I was a little kid. It's just a nickname."

"I don't think he sees it as a simple nickname."

"Meaning?"

"He doesn't like the connotation this word brings about. To him, my clueless little friend, you are anything but sinful. Because redemption can never come from sin."

Her words hang heavy in the air, filling me with a sense of responsibility and hope. If there's even a chance that I can help Famine find redemption, I cannot turn away from it. I owe it to him, myself, and the bonds forming between us.

"Tell me everything you know," I say, my voice steady. "I want to understand what this connection means and how it can help him."

Avalon gives me a slight nod, but her eyes tell another story. They're filled with a combination of understanding and concern. "Just be careful, Sin. The path to redemption is never easy and often comes with more than a few risks, not to mention sacrifices."

I take a deep breath, steeling myself for the trials I know I am about to undertake. "I'm ready," I say, my voice filled with the determination I feel.

As Avalon and I continue our conversation, I wonder what awaits us on this journey. Little did I know this conversation would put me on a path that would test my limits, challenge my beliefs, and lead me to discover the true power of love and redemption.

All at the hands of a rider sent to kill me.

Chapter Twenty-Seven: Ready Or Not.

~Sienna Spring 2027~

OVER THE LAST SEVERAL WEEKS, I have been working up the courage to do what I am preparing to do tonight. My conversation with Avalon was enlightening, but didn't tell me everything. So, during this time, I've watched, hoping to learn his routines. I've listened, trying to figure out what motivates him. And during this time, I discovered he watches me almost as much as I watch him and something tells me he does this to ensure my safety.

I also notice no one calls me Sin any longer. Something I plan to have Famine explain to me since Avalon was right, and he is the reason for it. If I were smart, I would avoid him like his brother's plague, but it's clear no one will mistake me for Eistein soon. So, in other words, I plan to march my happy ass up to him tonight and demand he tell me everything.

"Sienna, do you think this is the best idea?"

"No. I think this is a terrible idea, Sil."

"So, why are you doing it?"

"Because I need to know, and the only one who can give me the answers I need is him."

"What if you piss him off?"

"Then I suppose it's been nice knowing you."

"Don't say that, damn it! Don't even joke about it." Sylvia barks in her most demanding, authoritative tone while grabbing a different shirt from my closet. I'm unsure why my little sister thinks I need help getting dressed for the night, but she does. In fact, something tells me wild horses...no, wait, Famine's horse couldn't drag her away. And Eclipse has already done it a time or two while I was putting Avalon's theory to the test.

The entire time I'm putting on the shirt Sylvia handed me, I can't help but feel a mix of nerves and determination. Tonight is the night I confront Famine and demand answers. I need to know why he treats me different from everyone else. Why doesn't he want anyone to call me Sin? Why he looks at me the way he does. I need to know if the way I feel around him is what he feels. It's a puzzle I won't ignore any longer.

I need answers. Answers...I pray he will provide since only Famine holds the key to unlocking them.

Despite my attempt to steady myself with several deep breaths, my nerves persist despite the reassurance that I possess more information about this rider than anyone else. Well, maybe not Avalon, but she seems to have some bond with Famine none of us understands. I just have to keep repeating the following...I know him. Like Avalon, I know Famine's routines. I have observed his body language, which, if I'm right, will inform me if I'm pushing too hard. I have seen the way he watches over me like a silent guardian.

I take a deep breath and look at myself in the mirror, adjusting my shirt collar. Sylvia stands beside me, her worried expression mirrored in her eyes. She's never been the worrier in this family. That's my job. At least it has been since Dad left. But I can't let her fear or my uncertainty hold me back.

"Sil, I appreciate your concern, but I have to do this," I say, meeting her gaze in the mirror.

She sighs while her hand brushes a strand of hair behind my ear. "I know, Sienna. You've always been stubborn like that. Just promise me you'll be careful."

I nod, grateful for her understanding. "You have my word, little sister. I won't do anything reckless."

With one last glance in the mirror, I grab my jacket and head towards the door. I don't know if her following behind me or if she had let me leave without her would make me more nervous. So, for now, I will say her presence gives me the moral support I need. The instant we step outside, the cool night air embraces us, heightening my apprehension and sending it soaring straight to dread.

Sylvia looks at me with a jumble of worry and confusion. I can tell she wants to stop me. Hell, I'm shocked she hasn't run off to tell Mom. But I need to do this on my own. I need to face Famine, confront him, and demand the truth. So, if I don't want anyone interfering tonight, I need to put her at ease.

With a reassuring smile, I say, "I appreciate your concern, Sil, but I have to do this. I refuse to live in ignorance anymore. I need to know the truth, no matter what answers I receive.

Besides, what's he going to do to me in the middle of camp with everyone watching?"

"Um, send his damn vines to squeeze the life out of your insolent ass. I thought we covered this once before."

"You're being ridiculous, Sil."

"Tell that to the people who have had the displeasure of meeting his creepy crawlers."

"He doesn't have bugs."

"The hell he doesn't. I heard Avalon talking about his swarms of locusts. Last I checked, locusts are bugs, big sister. Just because we haven't seen them doesn't mean they don't exist."

"You need to relax."

"I don't trust him when he's in the middle of camp, so you can imagine how little I trust him to be alone with you, especially when your safety is in question."

"Even if you don't trust him. Trust me, Sil."

Sylvia's eyes soften, and she assesses me like she is trying to think of anything that will change my mind. What she must see is the determination in my expression. She knows how stubborn I can be when I set my mind to something. When she relents and nods in understanding, I know I won't have to worry about her trying to stop me. Deep down, I know she fears for my safety, but I'm betting so does Famine.

"Be careful."

"Always," I tell her, leaning over to kiss her cheek. I watch her walk away, praying I'm not making the worst mistake of my life.

The blustery winds and my knocking knees make my trek across our community towards Famine's place more difficult. The only thing keeping me moving is my conversations with Avalon playing on repeat. She's the only one in camp who doesn't think I'm crazy or in danger from him.

I take a deep breath, trying to steady my racing heart the closer I get to his door. I kind of wish I hadn't sent Sil away now. If Sylvia had walked with me, she would have squeezed my hand and given me a reassuring smile before walking away while nibbling on her thumbnail—something she does when she's nervous—to provide me with space to talk to him alone. It would be that little bit of reassurance I need during this trek across the square.

With one last breath, I pull my big girl panties on and raise my hand to knock on the door. The sound my knuckles make against the wood door echoes through the quiet night. Moments later, the door creaks open, revealing Famine's intense gaze. His eyes flicker with surprise as he takes in my determined expression.

"What do you want, Sienna?" he asks, his voice laced with a mixture of curiosity and caution.

I square my shoulders, ready to demand the truth. "We need to talk, rider."

Famine's expression shifts, a flicker of something unknown crossing his face. But instead of backing down, I stand my ground, refusing to let his enigmatic nature intimidate me any longer.

Tonight, I will uncover the secrets that have hounded me for weeks, no matter the consequences.

Even if it means risking everything I hold dear.

Chapter Twenty-Eight: Dangerous Things

~ Death Date unknown ~

THERE ARE TIMES LIKE RIGHT now when I wish I could knock the piss out of the part of myself I kept locked away. My other half is what you would expect of any demon. He's an insufferable pain in the ass.

"You know, if you quit bitching and started looking, we might find the damn exit faster."

"I tried to help, but you told me to piss off. Remember?"

"I recall you being an ass."

"My memories differ from yours," he retorts, leaning against the rock while I continue searching for this elusive damn portal keeping me locked away from her world. Exasperation caused by our lack of progress burns within me until I feel on the edge of exploding.

My demon counterpart isn't helping to curtail any of this. He should have learned by now to keep his snarky remarks to himself or risk being locked away again. Perhaps it would have been better not to give him any of my attention since I find him sporting a smug expression and relaxed posture, which only exacerbates my irritation. I don't know what pisses me off more, standing like this or how unfazed this dumbass is by the urgency of our situation.

I grit my teeth, trying to suppress the rising irritation. It's difficult dealing with this demon who wants to challenge me at every turn. His arrogance and unwillingness to cooperate only make our journey more difficult.

As I continue my search for the elusive portal, his voice cuts through the silence again. "You know, if you stopped being so damn stubborn, we might actually make some progress." He smirks. One thing is clear: he enjoys getting under my skin.

I shoot him a glare, my patience wearing thin. "And if you weren't such an insufferable pain, maybe I wouldn't have to be so stubborn."

He chuckles, seemingly unfazed by my irritation. "Ah, the classic blame game. Is this what the mortals call tit for tat?"

When I growl my frustration, he continues provoking rather than helping. "I was just pointing out the obvious."

"Obvious to whom?"

"Right now, the only one who matters. Me."

"You're a prick."

"A pleasant prick, and you're welcome since it seems I'm the only one who points out your annoying flaws, my crabby other half. Maybe now that you know the truth, it will help make you more likable."

"I'm not looking to be liked, and seriously, can you not be useful for once?" I snap, my patience wearing thin. "We need to find the exit, and you needling me at every turn isn't fucking helping."

He laughs again. It's a sound almost as infuriating as he is. "Oh, I'm sorry. Did I bruise your delicate ego by pointing out the obvious? Maybe if you started listening to me instead of shutting me out, we could have made some progress."

I shake my head, refusing to let his taunts distract me, opting to focus my attention on our surroundings. I scan every nook and cranny for any sign of the portal. The rocky terrain is unforgiving, but I'm determined to find a way out of this place and back to my Apple.

"You know, it wouldn't hurt to ask for my help. I have some knowledge about these things. Trust me."

I resist the urge to roll my eyes. Trusting my other half after I locked his ass away for so long is the last thing I want to do, but ignoring him is not getting us out of here any faster. I grit my teeth, hoping it will aid me in not barking my response. It doesn't work. "If you have any useful information, now would be a right proper fucking time to share it."

His smirk widens, a glimmer of satisfaction in his eyes. "Finally, you see reason. There's a hidden symbol on that wall over there. It might be the key to unlocking a rift between the worlds."

I follow his gaze and spot the faint etching on the rough surface. Despite my initial skepticism, I approach it, scanning my eyes over the intricate lines. A surge of anticipation courses through me when I realize he might have found the way out. Something I have no intention of sharing with him.

As I decipher the symbol's meaning, I can't help but feel a begrudging gratitude towards my demon counterpart. He may be a pain in the ass, but it seems, just this once, his presence might have proven helpful to aid in our quest for escape. Despite the tension between us, a glimmer of hope sparks within me, fueled by the possibility that this symbol might be our ticket out of the place our father placed us.

*****

After several hours, I have uncovered the entire incantation explaining how to open the door between this realm and any other my father has created. Is it possible this is how my father travels from one plane to another? The problem is that I risk tearing open the veil without the proper key. Something I do not possess. So, if I don't want this to happen, I will need to use extreme care.

I step back to study what I have uncovered. The answer must be here. I only need to find it. And then I see it. The one word I believe will release me.

It's quiet. To quiet…save for the distant echoes of dripping water. The rocky terrain beneath my feet is rough and uneven, throwing me off balance and digging into the soles of my shoes. A dim light filtering through the cracks in the cave's ceiling casts eerie shadows, adding to the sense of foreboding but confirming we are onto something.

The silence alone should have been my first clue that this might not have been the best idea, but my desire to return to my Apple overshadows everything else.

When I touch the etching, a faint tingling sensation travels up my arm, sending shivers down my spine. The air grows thick, and I can't tell if it's from my anticipation or a result of finding these ancient glyphs. Mossy, damp earth fills my nostrils and mixes with a hint of something metallic.

When the tingling increases, I try to pull my hand away but can't. With the first wave of pain crashing over me, I am aware of my demon's frantic shouts urging me to stop; however, it's too late.

The tearing sensation filling my chest is one I am not unfamiliar with. It's the same sensation I experience each time the lamb releases one of my brothers. The issue is Avalon has already called them there. Could this mean she has opened my seal as well?

Before this thought is complete, I'm thrown back away from the wall with the force of an explosion. As I crumple to the ground, the world goes gray, and reality slips away.

*****

The sound of my demon yelling brings me out of the foggy haze. It's an odd sensation because I don't so much open my eyes as it's like a mist lifting, letting me see for the first time.

What the hell am I doing here? I don't remember coming here or how I got here.

"Avalon," echoes through my head. This is when it all starts to come back to me.

I'm shocked to find my hands covered in scrapes, blood, and dust. I'm not sure if the explosion or something else caused it. When I look at the space where we discovered the symbols, what I find is a hole almost large enough for me to climb through.

I stagger forward to rest my hands on the inside of the hole, careful to avoid any of the etchings. I don't want a repeat performance of what happened the last time I touched it. It's odd how concentric the pattern is from the missing bricks. It's almost like someone took them out rather than an explosion blowing them out. There's another thing bothering me...my demon side is nowhere to be seen.

"Where are you?" I yell, scanning the cave for any signs of him. He will regret his choices if he slipped into Avalon's world without me.

"Answer me!"

"Seal it," his words echo not through the cave but in my head. "Seal it now, Death."

"What? Why would we seal our exit out of this place?"

"You need to listen to me." His words sound rushed, almost pained. "You have to seal it before you slip under again."

"What the hell? How long was I out?"

"You haven't been knocked out. You've been awake this whole time."

"Bullshit. The last thing I remember is touching the damn symbols you pointed out a few minutes ago."

"You've been awake and tearing at the hole. You also locked me back inside you."

"That can't be right. How long ago was the explosion?"

"Death, it was five days ago. You need to seal the opening to Avalon's world right fucking now!"

~ *Famine* ~

SHE IS STILL standing in my doorway, waiting for me to invite her in, but I would be within my rights to refuse and send her away. The thing is, I don't want to. I desire to understand what brought her to my door. I can sense how frazzled Sienna's nerves are, and the longer I make her wait, the more she questions why she's doing it.

"I want answers, Famine. Tell me everything. Why don't you want people calling me Sin? What's your connection to Avalon? But the more important question is, why does it feel like you're always protecting me?"

"Because I do."

"Do what?"

"Protect you."

"Why? I need you to tell me why." Her eyes trace the lines of my face, her teeth biting at the inside of her cheek. When she lifts her hand to push a stray piece of hair out of her face, I don't miss the slight tremble accompanying it.

The sigh I give her could be misconstrued as annoyance, and while this is not incorrect, it has nothing to do with her and everything to do with me. I'm aggravated I let this happen. I let a daughter of Eve make me question everything.

Sienna standing before me makes it hard to concentrate, bringing a mixture of frustration and desire surging through my veins, causing my heart to race and my breath to hitch. Her eyes fill with curiosity while her body trembles with anticipation. I understand these mortal emotions because they are the same familiar stirrings of hunger deep within me. It's a physical ache, a gnawing sensation that intensifies with each passing moment. My body craves what I believe she can give me.

The hunger intensifies into a tightness in my chest, like an invisible hand squeezing my heart. It radiates through my veins, causing my skin to prickle with an insatiable longing. It fuels my power, heightening my senses and sharpening my focus, but it also brings a certain level of discomfort…an unfamiliar turmoil brewing inside me.

And yet, despite the discomfort, I find myself drawn to her. Sienna's presence and vulnerability stir something profound within me, awakening a side of myself that I have tried to keep hidden for centuries.

It's a combination of protectiveness, desire, and a sense of responsibility that I don't comprehend. It's as if she has entwined my very existence with hers, and I cannot escape the pull she has on me.

Sienna's trembling fingers are a physical manifestation of her own emotions. The confusion swirling within her mirrors the chaos within me. Her gaze lingers on my face, searching for answers, and I can't help but feel a pang of guilt for the uncertainty I've brought into her world.

I meet her gaze and find a glimmer of understanding. There's a connection between us, something deeper than mere coincidence. It's an oath forged in the depths of my soul, a bond that transcends time and space. And it's this connection driving me to protect her.

Her hand reaches out and brushes against mine. The contact sends a jolt of electricity through me, causing a shiver to run down my spine. The hesitation, curiosity, and fear mingling in her gaze increases my need to protect her.

So, as the hunger continues to gnaw at my insides, I make a choice. I open the door wider, inviting Sienna into my world, knowing that this decision will only deepen the complexities of our entangled fates. But I cannot deny the pull any longer, for it's in her presence that I find a sense of purpose, a flicker of hope in a world consumed by darkness.

"You ask why I protect you," I finally speak, my voice laced with a mix of resignation and longing. "Because, Sienna, you are the one person who has made me question the nature of my existence. You have awakened emotions within me I did not believe possible."

Sienna's eyes widen, her breath catching in her throat. It's a dangerous admission, a vulnerability I rarely allow myself to show. But in this moment, as I stand before her, I can't help but let the truth spill from my lips.

"I owe my father my complete devotion, yet my connection to you overshadows any debt I feel to him. I cannot fully explain it, but there is something about you, something that draws me in. You are the one thing I can't explain, nor do I comprehend the surge of emotions you bring. But I want to."

Sienna's gaze softens, and her hand cups my cheek. The touch is gentle, filled with a tenderness that is both soothing and unsettling. The pull between us increases. It's an unspoken connection that defies logic and reason.

Our eyes lock, and our worlds collide. I realize Sienna has become integral to my existence, no matter how hard I tried to resist. And I can't help but wonder if, in protecting her, I am also discovering a part of myself that I never knew I wanted.

My feelings for her put the woman I care for in danger. Which means my focus has changed. I am no longer a rider hellbent on destroying all of humanity.

I am a rider hellbent on annihilating anyone who would take her from me.

Chapter Twenty-Nine: Here Goes Nothing

OVER THE LAST FEW WEEKS, I think about the ones I left behind more and more. Who knew I could be someone who would miss them so much that the thought I may never see them again brings nothing but crushing heartache washing over me? It's worse than the damn tsunami I endured when Famine arrived. I want to play hide-and-seek with Wren, watch how far Ellie has progressed with her archery lessons, and sing a song with Duck. I want to get drunk with Suk, Greer, and Ember. I want to ride on Ghost or Red and tell them how special they are. I want to tease Pestilence about his tender heart. And I want to hug War while he reminds me he's the fun one.

Yeah, who knew I would be capable of these emotions?

But I am.

Because of him.

Because of my rider…and the longer I'm away from War and Pessy, the greater the distance feels between Thanatos and me. When I'm with them, they talk about him. Something Famine refuses to do, at least with me.

Then there's the asshole and bobblehead I still have to contend with every damn day. These two idiot's mission is to make my life a living hell. I refuse to give in or let them know how much they bother me.

At least Eclipse has finally accepted me, even if his rider hasn't. It doesn't mean he'll be letting me gallop my happy ass out of here perched on his back anytime soon, but having a connection with him helps.

"Hi, Avalon." I spin to find Sienna standing behind me.

"Hey, Sin." Something I only call her when we are alone and only because she asked me to.

"Are you okay?" I could tell her how not okay I am, but why make my dark cloud her problem? So rather than dumping a bunch of shit on her she doesn't need to deal with, I return my attention to the task of brushing Eclipse and give her some half-hearted response.

"Peachy."

"Come on, A. I know better than that." Hearing her call me the nickname Suki gave me twists the vice settled around my chest a fraction tighter. "I know we've only known each other for a short time, but I would like to think it's been long enough for me to realize something's wrong."

"Just…you know…remembering."

"People you lost."

"Yeah."

"I get it. We've been fortunate here and haven't lost many of our people, but it doesn't mean we don't miss the people who are gone."

"I guess I'm lucky because my friends are still alive. At least they were before Famine...."

I know I said she didn't need to get weighed down by my shit, but it didn't feel right letting her think the people I miss were dead. It's almost like tempting fate, something I will not do when it comes to them. So I told her about Suk, the crazy but fiercely loyal redhead I call sister. I told her about Greer and her gentle, caring heart. Also, I informed her about Wren, Ellie, and Duck, the three littlest souls who have stolen my heart. I told her about Ember and how we hated each other until we found common ground—protecting the people we care about. I told her about Sophie, Nehra, Noll, and Hope. But it wasn't until I got to Pessy and War that I shocked her the most.

"Yes, I am, in fact, telling you they're my friends."

"But they're riders."

"I know. And it doesn't change how I feel about them."

"So you're saying...."

"Some of the individuals I care about and miss the most are the riders sent to end us."

"Okay, you just officially blew my mind with that confession," she exclaims, her eyes wide with astonishment. She continues to stare at me, mouth open for several seconds. I can see the question brewing in her eyes, and I know without a doubt what she wants to ask.

"I don't know how I feel about Famine. In a lot of ways, he isn't like his other brothers, but...in other ways, he is. I would like to think he is so unrelenting because he is loyal to a fault, but I can't say for sure."

"Can I ask you something else?"

"Sure."

"Do you think the riders could...you know...lov—err, I mean, care for one of us?"

"I know they can. Pestilence doesn't just care about Greer. He loves her, and War has chosen Ember."

"Does that mean the rumors I've heard about you and—"

"Please don't ask me about Death." Her face flushes from the heat of her embarrassment, and now I feel like an ass for the way I said it. "It's just…it was a long time ago. Death picked his path, and it wasn't me."

"Oh."

"Yeah, so as you can imagine, it's not something I want to talk about. Besides, I don't plan on seeing him again for a long, long time."

"I don't understand."

"Well, since Death is the being tasked with ferrying your soul when you—um-mmm—pass on, I don't plan on seeing him for a very long time."

"Why don't you return to them if you miss them so much?"

"Don't really have a choice right now, Sin."

"What do you mean?"

"It means I'm not here because I want to be here. I'm here because I'm a prisoner."

"What if I tell Famine to let you go home?"

"I don't think it would matter."

"Why not?"

"Because Nevil will never let me leave. He thinks it's his mission in life to see me in chains serving his stupid ass. Besides, he loves to torture me, so he would do anything in his power to convince Famine not to release me."

"Oh really? Well, I think it's high time this asshole learns his place," she says with a smirk before she spins on her heels and marches off to wherever she believes putting him in his place leads.

~ *Sienna* ~

I REALIZE THE whole time I'm storming away from Avalon without telling her what I am planning isn't the brightest idea, but something tells me she would have tried to stop me. Seeing the heartache in her eyes the entire time she told me about them broke something in my heart, right down to my soul.

It toasts my ass that Famine could disregard what she wants this much. Even if the dimwit traveling with them opposes her release. I can't believe some miserable prick like Nevil could have so much sway with Famine that the Rider would listen. But even if Nevil does, I'm willing to bet I hold more. And it's high time I put this theory to the test.

After Famine confessed how he felt about me, I did the mature thing or stupid, depending on what side of the fence you fall on regarding rider-human relations. What brilliant something did I do? I thanked him, spun on my heels, and left without saying another word. I'm not sure if his confession shocked me stupid or what.

Here I have a man who I have thought about more than once telling me he feels drawn to me, and my enlightened response is to thank him before Scooby-dooing my ass out the door. To make matters worse, I haven't seen him since then. I don't know if he's avoiding me. If he is, I can't say I blame him. One thing I know is I won't give him a chance to ignore me. Not when the issue we need to discuss is this big.

Chapter Thirty: Once In A Lifetime.

I DON'T KNOW WHO IS more shocked when I storm into his room without knocking, him…or me. Regardless, I'm here now, and I refuse to back down.

"If I asked you for a favor, would you do it for me?"

"Do you plan to run away again after I grant the requested favor?"

"I owe you an apology for how I handled everything the other night…and no, I won't run away again."

"Then my answer is I will do anything in my power."

"I want you to let Avalon go."

"Except that."

"Why?"

"Because the lamb will remain with me."

"She wants to return home."

"She has no home."

Unwilling to let him deter me, I push forward. "She wants to go home with your brothers, and I think she deserves it."

"No."

"This is your definitive answer?"

"It is."

"Then you leave me no other choice," I tell him as I move closer. It's time to put this attraction and subtle innuendos to rest. I think what I plan to do will not only put it to rest but shatter it when I skim my lips over his.

I had imagined this moment several times, and in my daydreams, he always swept me into a breathtaking kiss, not this. Rather than giving into the passion I know we both feel, he remains still, neither advancing nor retreating.

When I pull away long enough to look him in the eyes, his focus is only on me. If not for the rapid rise and fall of his chest, I would say my test was a monumental fail.

"What are you doing?"

"I'm not sure."

"Then why do it?"

"A question I'm asking myself," I say while running my tongue along his jaw before pulling his ear into my mouth.

"You need to…. Shit!"

"Do you want me to stop?"

"NO!" his swift response at least confirms he does not oppose the attention I am showing him.

"I'll make you a deal, Rider. If I can make you moan, you let Avalon go back to the other riders."

"No."

"No?" If Famine doesn't want to make this deal, he doesn't get to experience what I know he wants more than he will admit.

A truth I can say with absolute confidence because the evidence of his desire is pressed against me.

"Why have you stopped?"

"Because I made you an offer. One you declined. So I stopped."

"I wish you to proceed."

"You do?"

"Yes."

"Well, Famine, you know what you need to do then."

"Why is this so important to you?"

"Because just once, she deserves to have someone put her first. I think you could be the Rider to do it." He groans, but his vines streak out to halt my retreat when I walk away. I don't mutter so much a word of protest when he's behind me, pulling me back into his embrace.

"Does this mean?"

"I will make the arrangements after."

"After?"

"Yes, my beautiful angel, after," he tells me before his lips crash back down on mine. His hands roam over the curve of my hips until they have landed under my ass. When he pulls me against him, my body goes haywire as my head attempts to catch up with how easy it is for him to take control. So much for me seducing him.

Our kiss deepens, the passion fueling our desperate need. Famine's touch ignites a fire within me I no longer want to ignore. The way he worships my body leaves me weak in the knees and surrendering to his every touch and caress.

The room is cast in shadows, and the air is thick with anticipation, mixed with the scent of desire and musk. Our heavy breathing fills the silence, punctuated by soft moans and whispered pleas.

As Famine's lips explore mine, I feel a surge of electricity coursing through my veins. His touch is both gentle and commanding, launching shivers from the point of contact. Every caress, every movement of his hands on my body, sets me ablaze with a hunger I have only dreamed of.

I can taste the faint hint of mint on his tongue as it dances with mine, a bittersweet flavor that only intensifies the craving burning inside me. Lighting a blaze only he can feed. His grip on my hips is firm, pulling me closer to him. It's a magnetic force that I can't resist. He's my every desire come true, and I want to beg for more.

I'm lost in a whirlwind of sensations, my senses overwhelmed by the raw passion that consumes us. The way he explores every inch of my body, leaving a trail of heat in his wake, makes me wonder if he's done this before. Could Avalon and I have been mistaken? Has he mastered the art of seduction?

But in this moment, none of that matters. All that exists is the connection between us, the undeniable chemistry that ignites like wildfire. As our bodies move in sync, a mix of craving and longing, I realize that this is a dance we've both been waiting for, a dance of two souls entwined in a moment of pure bliss.

His hands explore every inch of my body, leaving a trail of desire in their wake. I can't help but moan against his lips, the pleasure building with each passing second. It's clear that Famine wants me just as much as I want him, and I no longer wish to deny the overwhelming chemistry between us.

The warmth of his fingers trailing soft circles along my breasts and brushing over my hard nipples electrifies my already sensitive skin, causing jolts of euphoria to rush everywhere he touches. His growls of desire for my body are a primal hunger that matches mine. As his lips explore me, I throw my head back, savoring the taste of him still lingering on my tongue.

With my shirt and bra now discarded on the ground, he's free to focus his attention on the nipples, waiting for the heat of his tongue. His fingers glide over the peaks, teasing and tugging, causing my breath to hitch and my body to arch towards him. Each time he grazes his finger over one of them, it sends a jolt of ecstasy straight to my core, intensifying the ache between my thighs.

Famine trails his lips down my neck, and his teeth graze my sensitive skin, leaving a trace of goosebumps in their wake. The combination of his gentle caresses and commanding grip awakens something inside me. I don't think I've ever been this wet before. If he doesn't fuck me soon, I might explode.

My hands find their way to his shirt, desperate to feel his bare skin against mine. With a swift motion, I strip him of it, revealing a chiseled chest that begs to be explored. The sight of his defined muscles and the heat radiating from his body only adds to the intoxicating mix of sensations flooding my senses.

"If I do anything you don't like—"

"No! Love…. Love everything you're doing. Don't stop," I pant while pawing at him to continue.

With one quick swipe, he rids me of my pants, leaving me bare for his viewing delight. His finger travels the space between my breasts, over my abdomen, but stops short of the soaking wet core he is responsible for.

"The scent of your arousal is intoxicating. I plan to taste you everywhere."

"Oh, hell. Yes, please."

With this plea, he slides the finger that had stopped just short of my goal over my clit and straight inside me. The gasp I give him and the sensation he causes buckle my knees. If not for quick reflexes, I would be on the ground.

As Famine holds me up, his finger continues to explore the depths of my desire. I can't help but moan as he thrusts in and out, matching the rhythm of my throbbing need. The sensation and pleasure are overwhelming, and I can feel my climax building within my core.

I'm so close to taking the ultimate step that will send me sailing over the edge, but Famine is not content with just his finger. He wants to taste…to devour every part of me. With a devilish grin, he lowers himself to his knees, his hungry eyes locked with mine. The anticipation of his lips on me is overwhelming when he spreads my legs apart, exposing my dripping core to his hungry gaze.

His tongue flicks across my swollen clit, and my hands land on the back of his head, desperate to have him closer. The mind-blowing sensation sends waves of heat coursing through my entire body. He explores every inch of my folds, his tongue delving deep inside my pussy. With expert precision, he finds every sensitive spot.

I twist my hands in his hair, unable to control the wild pleasure he is unleashing upon me. He continues to ravage my sex. His mouth and tongue work in perfect harmony, driving my body to the edge of oblivion. The room fills with the symphony of my moans, his groans, and the intoxicating scent of my arousal.

As my orgasm approaches, I can feel the tension building, coiling within me like a spring wound too tight. Famine knows it, so he increases the intensity of his ministrations. His fingers join his tongue, thrusting in and out, pushing me closer and closer to the brink.

And then, with one final flick of his tongue and a well-placed thrust of his fingers, I shatter into a million pieces. My body convulses with pleasure, my screams of ecstasy filling the room.

Famine continues sucking and licking my clit through my orgasm, prolonging the blissful release.

"I'm not done. You taste divine. A delicacy I plan to dine on all night long."

His words are like icy heat chilling my skin yet burning me from the inside, and I can't help but submit to his command. I trust him to take me to heights of pleasure I've never experienced before.

With a ravenous look in his eyes, he guides us towards the bed, our bodies still nothing more than a tangle of limbs. His mouth on mine, his tongue probing for entrance. Just as I opened myself for him before, I part my lips for him now, granting him access to my mouth, an act he doesn't squander.

Our tongues dance for dominance as my hand frees his rock-hard cock giving me my first indication of how large he is. Not letting a little thing like girth, length, or size deter what we both have longed for, I run my thumb over the thick head and along his shaft. His moans confirm he likes what I'm doing to him.

When we fall onto his bed, I am ready for him to slam inside the pussy he has pulsing with need, but Famine surprises me when he doesn't. Opting instead to position himself between my legs. His lips, hot and demanding, find their way back to my throbbing core. The sensation of his tongue swirling around my clit is electrifying, sending another round of pleasure coursing through my entire body.

I grip the sheets tight, unable to contain my moans as Famine works his magic. His tongue flicks and teases, driving me closer and closer to the edge. I can feel the familiar coil tightening deep within my core, ready to snap and send waves of utter bliss washing over me.

But just when I think I can't take it anymore, Famine stops. He looks up, and I find his eyes filled with a mix of desire and control. "Not yet," he says, his voice husky. "I want to savor you."

I whimper my disappointment, craving the release he has built back up, but I know that Famine's teasing will only make it that much sweeter when I finally reach the peak and find my release. I surrender myself to his every touch, every caress, knowing that he holds the power to bring me to the brink of ecstasy.

His lips continue exploring, trailing kisses along my inner thighs, leaving a trail of fire in their wake yet cooled by the dampness of my arousal. I arch my back, urging him to continue, to grant my every wish. And finally, after what feels like an eternity, he plunges his tongue back into my dripping core.

The ecstasy is overwhelming, and I can feel myself losing control. Famine's tongue dances and swirls inside me until I'm sent hurtling over the edge, my body convulsing with the force of my second orgasm.

I scream his name, my voice a fusion of rapture and satisfaction. Famine continues to lap at my core, turning my body to mush, until finally, I collapse onto the bed, spent and sated.

I try to catch my breath while Famine rises to his feet. A satisfied smile graces his beautiful face. His green eyes are so intense I swear they are glowing. His unrelenting, hunger-filled gaze makes me squirm. I didn't think I could be any more turned on until he spoke.

"That was just the beginning," he whispers, his voice filled with promise. His confession confirms that I'm in for a night of unforgettable ecstasy with him. One thing is clear: Famine is not just a lover but a master of pleasure. Something I am more than willing to submit to… to surrender to his every touch and caress.

My eyes trail his movements while he pushes his pants off. His hand lands on the erection that I am not opposed to begging him for. To slam himself inside my body before torturing me in all the best ways possible. I want him to punish me for all my transgressions as long as the device he uses to do it is the cock I am desperate for. I swallow my anticipation and watch him stroke his dick while his eyes focus on the damp core he was devouring seconds before. When he licks the rest of my climax from his lips, I can't help but run my tongue along mine while I imagine what he would taste like.

"Confession time, Sienna. How would you like me to make you find your release this time?"

"Hold that thought, Rider. Because I want…." I don't tell him what I want. I show him when I sit up and slide my tongue along his cock. He must like it because he slows the steady stroking and presses his arousal to my lips. It's my turn not to waste any time as I slide my mouth around him and take him as far as I can. As I take him deeper into my mouth, the weight of his erection pressed against my tongue sends waves of heat burning through my core. Every jerk and twitch of his dick, every drop of his pre-cum, drives me wild with an insatiable need to increase my pace until I taste him, just as he has done with me.

His hands find their way into my hair, guiding my movements with gentle pressure. I can sense his climax building, his body responding to my every action. His taste, both salt and sweet, fills my mouth, while his earthy scent surrounds me, igniting my senses.

I continue to suck and lick, my mouth working in sync with my hand, stroking him with a rhythm that matches the intensity of our connection. The moans that escape his lips fuel my own desire, spurring me on to take him deeper, to bring him closer to the edge.

An undeniable tension is building in him. His muscles tighten beneath my touch. His fist knotting in my hair is a silent plea for more. I respond by increasing the pressure, my lips working a fervent rhythm as I bring him closer to release.

His fingers glide over my nipples, giving me pleasure as I continue to push him to the brink. The room fills with our mingled moans, a fusion of desire. Sweat glistens on our bodies as we move together, our movements growing faster, more desperate.

The heat building within us is a wildfire consuming our bodies. Famine is unyielding when he pulls me closer, slamming his hips forward to force himself further down my throat. It's too much and yet not enough. When his forceful thrust makes me choke, he relents. His breaths are coming in ragged gasps. He is approaching his release, and even though I want him to fuck me, I cannot stop what is happening between us any more than I could halt a storm on the horizon.

I am ready to take every bit of what he will give when he flips me onto my back, pinning my body down with his. The touch of his hands on my skin sets off sparks of electricity, leaving me breathless and wanting more. His lips crash against mine with a kiss so fierce if I wasn't already panting, it would steal the breath from my chest.

He enters me with a force that sends shockwaves of pleasure through my body. Every thrust is an explosion, a collision of passion and need. I arch my back, meeting his every movement, craving the ecstasy only he can provide.

Time seems to stand still as we lose ourselves in each other, our bodies melding together in a dance of carnal desire. The bed creaks beneath us, a nonexistent clock ticks on the wall, and the world tumbles away until only Famine and I remain.

His eyes lock with mine, a primal hunger burning in their depths. If I wasn't already aware of his might at this moment, I could never deny the raw power coursing through him. A dominance that drives him. And for the first time in my life, I willingly surrender to another, giving myself over to him.

As he reaches his climax, his body tenses, muscles coiling like a predator ready to strike. I can feel the pulsating heat inside me, the waves of pleasure crashing over us both. We shatter together, lost in the euphoria of our shared release.

After we lie there, spent and breathless, our bodies entwined in a tangle of limbs and sweat-soaked sheets. The room is filled with the scent of our passion, a heady reminder of the night we will never forget. It was one of the once-in-a-lifetime kind of experience I'm hoping he wants to do again.

Soon.

Chapter Thirty-One: Reunion

TODAY, I'M FULFILLING MY PROMISE to Sienna by traveling to the camp where I will reunite with my brothers. I have to admit I look forward to seeing them after all this time. When I first arrived in this realm, I avoided them, fearing they would attempt to sway me from my task, just as they had been. I suppose the joke is on me since it was through constant moving to avoid them I encountered Sienna.

The woman who showed me what life could be like if I opened myself up to the possibilities. I should never have listened to Michael without talking to them first. It's something I will regret for years to come. Because this damn angel lied, he stole precious time I could have spent with them.

Upon arriving at the location where Pestilence and War made camp, I was disappointed to discover they were not there. I knew their absences could mean only one thing…they had traveled to our realm hoping to release our brother.

Pestilence and War must not have realized I had stopped moving. I made my decision the moment I met her. It was quite simple: I could not imagine not being around Sienna. I determined if they found me, I would attempt to convince them to leave my chosen and her community in peace. If they opted to press the issue, I was prepared to face them, and when they fell, the ones they loved would meet my vines.

This, in part, is why I understand they did what they felt they must. Pestilence and War recognize the only way to stop me would be to release Thanatos. They know just as I do when he arrives in this world, I will no more be able to defy him than they will be able. They possess the same knowledge I have regarding his arrival in this realm. Once the lamb releases Thanatos, my ability to resist his command will be as futile as theirs.

For all my strength, it pales in comparison to his. A weakness I don't disclose to anyone. This doesn't mean I don't want to release him from his prison, but I would be remiss if I didn't fear what it could mean to Sienna's safety. What if everything I have been told and shown is a lie? What if Avalon does not hold the sway over him they have led me to believe? How would we stop an unstoppable force?

I wonder if Pestilence and War thought about this. They must also be concerned since they each have their own version of Sienna. It almost makes me feel bad they haven't seen their chosen in months because they have been pursuing me. Almost. After all, they are the ones who have continued this inane hunt.

While I wait for them to return, I attend to my horse. The lamb believes I am unaware of the time she spends with him or the name she has given him. Eclipse. I do not oppose the moniker, although I have no intention of telling her this. She can continue to live in oblivion.

I feel their return before their physical form materializes, and the shock I witness covering their faces suggests they did not expect to find me here.

"Hello, brothers."

I don't know who is more shocked to find me standing here. Pestilence or War. But I know who is furious that I made them chase me. With a clenched jaw, narrowed eyes, and lips pulled in a taut line, War's gaze bores through me. Yeah, if he could hit me, he would without giving it a second thought. I am not naïve enough to believe he is incapable of putting me on my ass if I permitted such an assault. Unfortunately, he won't get the chance because he knows I'll release my vines to stop him.

"Where is she? Is she alive? Is she well?" War demands. When he drops to the ground, it shakes from his descent.

"Why do you care so much for the lamb, brother?"

"Because she showed us what it means to be human."

"And tell me, War, how does the brother you were preparing to release from the prison holding him feel about your fondness for his Apple?"

"If you come closer, brother, I'll be happy to explain." If I didn't know any better, I would say the murderous glint in his eyes is directed at me. I must be misinterpreting his reaction since none of us has ever lifted a finger to harm his brothers. It seems Pestilence agrees when he places his hands on his hips and drops his head while shaking it. War is not used to being defied, so my response will no doubt be distressing to him and his ego.

"If you wish to threaten me, little brother, I can return to my camp, and you can continue wondering if she is being taken care of."

"NO!" my brother growls as he takes a menacing step towards me, but Pestilence pulls him away.

"Always the pragmatic one. Thank you for putting yourself between him and me," I say, tilting my head. Pestilence moves his focus from War to me, and I do not miss the slight shift that occurs when his tendrils are pushing for release.

"I didn't do it for you. I did it for the lamb. She wouldn't want any of this."

"She is to be returned to us! Right fucking now, Famine," War snarls as he shoves Pestilence's hand off his shoulder.

"Is it possible the lamb is not a weakness for Thanatos alone?"

"Avalon is not a weakness," Pestilence intercedes before War can respond.

"I am not so certain. Perhaps it would be best if the lamb was removed from consideration."

"You will not harm her." This is the first time Pestilence loses some of his calm demeanor.

"Since you do not know where I hold her and Thanatos cannot return until she calls him here, it seems you are unable to stop me, brother."

"No, but I can," War snarls, pulling his sword from his baldrick.

"Nor should you mistake my loyalty as fear, Famine," Pestilence confirms while his black death slips free to twist around him.

"You know there is one thing I am curious about."

"Do you think I give a shit what interest you?" War snaps.

"You should if you want to see the lamb again."

"What do you want to know?" Pestilence inquires after placing himself between War and me.

"Where did the scars come from?"

"Scars?"

"On the Lamb. Were they a gift given by one of you, or was it Thanatos who put them there?"

"Information you would already have if Avalon wanted you to know," War snaps.

"You need to learn the art of negotiation, my militant brother."

"And you need to learn what I will do if you—" Again, Pestilence places himself in front of War before interrupting to give me a partial response.

"Most of them are from a time before our arrival, but men who traveled with our brother added to the ones she already had."

"Not Thanatos?"

"No. Why would you think our brother is capable of doing something like that?" When my only response is a half-hearted snort, it pushes War to once again jump to her defense.

"What the hell do you believe she could have done to merit that kind of abuse from him?" War's inability to have a civil conversation where the lamb is concerned confirms his feelings for her are not as benign as they should be.

"You have met her right, brother?" I ask with a laugh.

"Disparage her again and Pestilence's mercy for you will no longer matter."

"Truly?"

"Regardless of what you think about the lamb, no one deserves what they did to her," War says prior to spitting on the ground at my feet.

"Interesting how quick you are to jump to her defense. Tell me, do you do this for Ember as well, or is your sword reserved for the sole protection of the lamb?"

"Speak of Ember again, and you will find out."

"The lamb almost died because of it, didn't she?" I ask because knowing this will explain a lot about her need to protect the ones who cannot defend themself and the few individuals she feels close to. Which includes my brothers.

"Yes, and had they accomplished their goal and Avalon fell, Thanatos would have brought their godforsaken world down around them." Pestilence's emphasis on saying our brother's name was meant to dissuade my belief about how another rider feels about her. It does not.

"She is stronger than I give her credit for," I muse.

"She is stronger than most give her credit for. A mistake few make a second time," Pestilence confirms.

"Why don't you form your own opinion," War demands while crossing his arms over his chest. I laugh before mounting my horse to return home.

"My opinion of the lamb is that she is obstinate, infuriating, and when prudent logic dictates she should flee, she does the opposite and runs toward the threat. But I have also found she is capable of compassion, fortitude, and immense love. Which is surprising for a soul who has suffered as she has. In truth, I find her fascinating. Is this all you feel when you look at her, War?"

"It is."

"Well, that remains to be seen." War's desire to provide his thoughts on my last comment is cut off so I can advise them what I came to say. "I will deliver the lamb to you in two days."

"Why can we not have her now?"

"Because I said so. She has one last task to fulfill for me, but you have my word, War. I will bring her."

"But—"

"Two days from today, brother. No sooner."

"Will the task release Thanatos?" Pestilence asks as I spin Eclipse to leave.

"No. And you shouldn't be so keen to release him either."

"Why?"

"See you in two days, brothers."

~ Avalon ~

HERE I AM, minding my own business, and who has to show up to make my day turn to shit? None other than Bobblehead. With her damn stupid crooked grin plastered across her face, I know she's here to annoy the piss out of me.

"Hellooooo, Avalon." Her singsong voice is grating.

"What do you want, Cammie?" I snap without turning to give her the attention she wants. Bobble moves, trying to push herself between me and the shelf I'm putting the gardening supplies and tools on. Too bad for her, I'm done, so as she does her shuffling sidestep, I spin on my heels and head for the exit.

"I'm bored," she whines.

"I don't give a shit."

"Well, you should." She rushes to get in front of me when I refuse to respond and continue across the courtyard. Since she knows I have no intention of stopping or entertaining anything she wants to talk about, she spins and begins some stupid ass skipping—hopping—sideways shuffle. Something an idiot like this one should never do. Well, that is, if she likes to stay upright.

"You're going to end up on your ass if you're not careful."

"Oh, someone might be on their ass, but I don't think it's going to be me, Av—va—lon." She draws out my name, adding a hint of sarcasm. I want to ask her how old she is, but then she might think she got under my skin, which I can assure you she didn't.

"Yep, someone's gonna be crying soon." Don't respond, Avalon. Just ignore Bobble. Her head is so full of fluff that, in all likelihood, she doesn't realize how ridiculous or clueless she is. Really, I should feel sorry for her. It has to be difficult being so damn dumb.

"I wonder who will cry first. I know who I have my money on."

"You know what, Cammie? You and Sausage—"

"Don't call him that," she yells, whipping her hand out, missing my face by inches.

"You get one, but no more," I tell her in a low, threatening tone while I fist her shirt in my hand before I shove her away from me. As she struggles to keep her footing, I continue with what I was saying prior to her ridiculous act of aggression. "You and Sausage Fingers deserve one another."

"And you know what, stupid lamb? I can't wait until Nevil comes home and tells you all about it."

"All about what."

"Oh, wouldn't you like to know?"

"No, in reality, I could give a shit less what that asshole is doing," I say, pushing past her again so I can end this childish conversation and put some distance between me and this dimwit.

"I wonder if he'll kill him or her first." This stops me in my tracks, and my heart goes from a simple thud to a pounding jackhammer in my chest.

"What did you say?"

"I said I wonder if he'll kill him or her first," in true bobblehead style, she tilts her head from right to left when saying this last part, "My bet is on...."

"Who?" I snarl, taking a step closer to her.

"Oh, now you want to talk to me? Maybe you shouldn't have been such a bitch when I wanted to chat."

I'm past the point of tolerance for dealing with her shit. Whipping in the direction she standing with her arms crossed over her chest, the blood drains from her face when I storm back toward her. She spins, tries to run, but I'm on the dimwit faster than she can move with her shirt gripped tight in my clutches, so I jerk her closer.

"I asked you a fucking question."

"I don't care, Av-va—" I don't wait for her to finish my name before I shove her, and this time she doesn't stay upright.

"I told you if you weren't careful, you would end up on your ass." I don't wait for her response. Why bother? If I want to know where Nevil went, I'm sure Famine knows. I'll just find out from him. No sense dealing with a dimwit who doesn't know her ass from a hole in the ground.

"You know, you should really learn to look around before you discuss the ones you hold so near and goddamn dear to your rotted heart."

"Fuck off, Cammie."

"Here's hoping he lets the bitch watch while he kills Xander." I didn't think it was possible, but with one damn word, she extracted every molecule of oxygen from my lungs. I turn as she reaches full height, a smug expression covering her face. "Nevil wanted to thank you for telling him how much your little friend Suki and those brats mean to you. And since he has friends who hate that bitch almost as much as we do, he knows the riders left them all alone and unprotected. I wonder if they'll beg for the riders to save them?"

I don't see black.... This time, I see red.

Chapter Thirty-Two: Now or Never

I LOOK OUT MY BEDROOM window just in time to see Avalon pounce on Cammie, punching her several times with wild, bone-shattering swings. Cammie's screams echo off the buildings surrounding us. I don't know what the bitch did. One thing I can say is I have never seen Avalon like this. I spin and bolt out of my room, but by the time I burst through the door, Cammie is on the ground, a bloody crying mess, and Avalon is sprinting into the woods on the far side of our community.

Cammie I could give a shit less about; however, A is another story. So, while many of the residents tend to the bitch who caused this shit show, I race after Avalon.

I always thought I was fast, but the speed she is streaking through the dark woods has me falling further behind her. My only hope of catching up with her now is to take the shortcut and pray she continues in the direction she is veering.

The branches scrape against my arms and slap my face, stinging my flesh with each hit, but I continue racing through them in pitch darkness, determined to catch up with Avalon. I suck in one deep breath after another, navigating through the dense foliage. The rapid thud-thud-thud of my pulse pounding in my ear. My lungs burn, and my sides ache, but I don't stop. I can't because worry and determination are pushing me forward.

I know Avalon well enough to understand that something must have triggered this violent outburst. She's not one to lose control, but something about her reaction tonight tells me she's teetering on the edge, and one step could send her plummeting into an abyss I'm not sure she will ever come back from.

I'm driven by the urgency to reach Avalon before she does something she might regret, but the darkness enveloping the woods isn't helping. Thank god for the occasional patch of moonlight filtering through the thick canopy.

I finally glimpse Avalon up ahead, her figure a blur of movement. She's heading towards a drop-off she will never survive, forcing me to quicken my pace. My only hope is to intercept her before she reaches it.

"Avalon!" I call out, bursting into the only open space she might see me. My voice filled with a combination of concern and desperation. "Stop!"

She turns to face me, her eyes wild with rage but also pain. "Sienna, stay out of this. It's none of your business."

But I refuse to back down. I take a careful step closer. Taking an extra second to gauge her reaction. "Avalon, whatever happened, I can help you. You just have to trust me."

"Trust you?"

"Yeah, that's what friends do. They trust one another."

"Friends? Is that what we are?" She scoffs, a bitter sound raising goosebumps over my exposed skin. "Because if I was any kind of friend, I would tell you to run in the other goddamn direction. To continue running until you are as far away from me and my fucked up life as possible."

"I'm not leaving, Avalon. I'm right here, and I promise I will help you."

She doubles over, gasping for breath, her body trembling from a combination of the anger and grief consuming her. "Cammie...she said, Nevil...Nevil is going to kill them," she pants between choked breaths. "I have...have to get to them. Before...before he hurts them."

"Hurts who?" I take a deep breath, trying to process the information. "Tell me what she said."

Avalon's voice trembles as she speaks. "She said that Nevil knows about Suki and the others. Knows they're all alone and unprotected. He's going to kill them, and it's all my fucking fault."

Jesus Christ, no wonder she went ballistic. Suki is like her sister...and those innocent kids. Who the hell would threaten children? We have to find them, to protect them. But first, I need to calm Avalon down and tell Famine what the hell is happening. I know he rode out to meet with his brothers today, and if anyone can stop Nevil, my rider can.

"Listen, Avalon," I say, trying to keep my voice steady. If I have any hope in hell of convincing her to come back with me, I can't let any of my fear seep out in my response. "We need to tell Famine what happened. He went to see his brothers today. If we—"

"Wait, Famine went to see Pessy and War?"

"Yeah. He went—"

"They're here? Not at home with the people who traveled with us?"

"Yeah, I guess they've been tracking Famine since his arrival."

"No—no–no–no!"

"It's okay, Avalon. He went to tell them he was releasing you."

"Releasing me?"

"Famine was going to let you go home, Avalon. He went to make the arrangements with the other riders."

"I don't fucking care about me, Sienna! I need to get to my family before Nevil can hurt them." She spins to run again, but I grab her arm. If Nevil plans to attack her old camp, she'll never make it in time to stop him, at least not without a rider's aid.

"Avalon, he had a head start. If you hope to get there before he does, you'll need help. So, all we have to do is wait for Famine to return to camp. Then we'll find Nevil before he can get anywhere around Suki or the kids."

"Well, see, that just won't work for me." I spin to find Nevil and someone I didn't think I would ever have to face again.

"Jacob? What are you doing here and why are you with…. Him?" I examine Nevil, grappling with the impossibility of hiding my contempt for him. The issue is Jacob doesn't answer my question, and he addresses his comment to Avalon. What I find most surprising is her response to him.

"Tisk–tisk, Avalon, you were supposed to come alone."

"Raum!" I'm not sure what Avalon's hiss response means, but I can't worry about it right now because Jacob's sudden arrival can't mean anything good. His association with Nevil, who is equally unpleasant, only adds to the urgency of this situation.

"Jacob, what the hell are you doing here?" I bark, hoping to get some answers. Jacob's attention landed on me for a brief second before he snorted a laugh and returned his gaze to Avalon. "Jacob, I want to know—"

"This prick's name isn't Jacob. It's bird boy, isn't it Birdy?"

"Always with the quick tongue," the man I know of as Jacob taunts.

"Mind your goddamn manners, bitch."

Her eyes finally settle on the man responsible for her panic tonight. "I'm going to fucking kill you, Nevil."

"No, little lamb, I don't think you will. Allow me to introduce myself properly. My name is Raum, not Jacob."

"Why lie?"

"Who said I did, little fighter? I wasn't expecting you to be with the lamb tonight; however, this may work out in my favor."

"You'll have to excuse me because it seems you have me at a disadvantage," I reply while I circle closer to Avalon, who is back to seething. Raum takes a second to lean over and whisper something to Nevil. A nagging feeling at the back of my mind suggests this is far from a positive development. My instincts are screaming at me, warning the wise path here would be to gather Avalon and skedaddle our asses back home. But a deep part of me knows it's already too late.

"I am the one who you were supposed to be delivered to. There was no fighting ring, at least not the kind you envisioned. Until your rider rode in on his white horse...pardon me, black horse, and saved the day."

"Why in the hell would you want me?"

"Because he's a prick," Avalon interjects. I don't know what's more unnerving, seeing Avalon so irate or this Raum laughing.

"Well, there you go. The lamb has answered for me."

"I don't understand."

"A trait many of your kind suffer from."

"No point in asking him to elaborate because he'd just lie to you anyway," Avalon snaps.

"So, what do you want?" I ask.

"Ah, finally, we arrive at the apex of the evening events." I look from Raum, whose focus has not wavered from Avalon, to the prick who lured her out here, over to Avalon. Something tells me she already knows what he's doing here. The lack of conversation only punctuates the silence surrounding us. The world is silent. No flapping wings, clicking bats, scurrying rodents, or even the buzz of a bug flying in our direction penetrates the still night. Hell, even the wind has disappeared. It's like time stands still while we wait for his response. However, the answer doesn't come from the asshole standing in front of us. It comes from....

"Me." Avalon.

My head whips in her direction, which may prove to be a huge mistake because the instant I remove my eyes from the two pricks, Nevil charges me.

"I no longer need you," Raum snarls just as Nevil slams against my side, sending me hurling over the cliff.

~ Avalon ~

I DIVE, GRABBING her hand the second before she tumbles out of my reach. The impact from hitting the rocky terrain is jarring and damn near knocks the breath out of me. And somewhere in the back of my head, a little voice is screaming that Nevil may push us over the edge any second now. It's a rational fear I cannot think about right now.

"Hold on," I yell, straining to keep her hand from slipping out of my grip.

"Don't let me go, Avalon," Sienna screams, her nails digging painfully into my hands and wrist as she tries to pull herself back up from the brink.

"Quite the conundrum you have there, little lamb."

"Shut the fuck up, bird boy," I hiss. Sienna's flailing pulls my upper body further over the edge. "Sin, climb."

"I can't. I'm going to fall! Please don't let me fall, Avalon!"

"Yes, little lamb, don't let her fall."

"Just hold on," I tell her as I tighten my grip on her wrist. I muster every bit of strength I have to pull her up, but it's not enough as I slide further over the edge. There's a genuine possibility Sienna and I may die tonight because there is no fucking way I'm letting her go. The crunching rocks rip through my shirt, jabbing into the exposed skin underneath. Warm blood soaks my shirt as I try to dig my feet in, but the packed earth and rocky terrain don't offer much in the way of leverage. Then there's Sienna, who can't stop thrashing. I can't blame her, but she's not helping this situation by doing it.

"I could help, lamb. You know what you must do."

"Fuck. Off!" The grunted answer I give him turns into a howl of pain when the sharp edge of stone rips a long gash along my arm. The blood streams from the injury down over my hand, and for the first time, Sienna slides down until I am no longer holding her wrist.

"Avalon, I'm slipping," she screams, but her terrified eyes and frantic flailing as she tries to find leverage are horrible to witness.

"Say the words Avalon, and I pull her up."

"Sienna, you have to climb," I beg.

"I can't. Famine, help me," she cries. "I'm slipping. Oh god, I'm slipping. I'm going to die!"

"Whatever you do, don't you dare let go of my fucking hands, Sin." Her hand slips some more until only our fingers remain wrapped around each other. "I could use just a little fucking help here. Goddamn it!" I scream towards the heavens, knowing I only have a few more seconds.

"Say it, Avalon," Raum snarls.

"I'll go with you!" I scream, and a second later, the weight that was pulling me over is gone. And Sienna is lying on the ground next to me.

*****

Yeah, it's okay. You can say it. I'm an idiot because I don't disagree, but if I hadn't agreed to come with them, Sienna would have fallen, and what kind of person would that make me? I'll tell you…an asshole, much like the stupid prick trailing behind this damn demon.

I'm not sure where they are taking me. I don't reckon it will be some five-star penthouse in an abandoned hotel like Death once commandeered for us. For some reason, I see a dank, musty dungeon with lots and lots of chains in my future.

Raum gave Sienna a whopping sixty seconds to recover before he yanked her off the ground and told her it was time to go home. Real fucking knight in shining armor, that one. Although why I would expect anything else from a demon is ludicrous.

You would think at least one of these assholes who keeps forcing me to travel with them would think to bring a horse for me, but no. I'm left to trudge along behind them, much like I did with Famine.

The issue is the wound on my arm is still bleeding, making me woozy and fuzzy-headed, which explains why I question the validity of what I'm seeing when I look up and discover someone approaching us on a horse. I want to yell. Scream out to them to run in the other direction until the haze lifts enough for me to see them with semi-clear eyes. The instant I register who is approaching, I'm unsure if I want to yell…cry…or run. But I don't do any of these things. Instead, I whisper one word.

"Pessy?"

~ Famine ~

I KNOW SIENNA was upset with my decision to not take Avalon with me when I rode out this morning. She doesn't understand why I am reluctant to return the lamb to my brothers. The truth is, I'm unsure what will happen if we permit her to break the seal.

As for the lamb, she earned my respect long ago. The more I learn about her, the more I understand why my brothers are drawn to her. Avalon swings when she should hold, demands when she should relent, and pushes when she should recoil. These are all traits of someone deserving of more than what my father will grant her.

Although I wanted nothing more than to return to Sienna after leaving my brothers, there was another matter I had to attend to. I had to go back to our realm, my home, to confirm or dispel the rumors I had heard. A crucial piece of the puzzle before I release Avalon.

The predicament I now face is the assurance I desired is not the one I received. Quite the opposite. Damn it! This puts me in a difficult dilemma. One that leaves me both frustrated and uncertain about what to do next. If I keep her with me, I can assure it never comes to pass, but if she goes back with War and Pestilence, will they be as vigilant as I will be?

The journey to return home affords me one thing: time to grapple with what is right and what she desires. Sienna's pending disappointment lingers in the air, a palpable presence pricking at my conscience. The thought of breaking my promise to her fills me with dread and leaves me teetering on the edge. I fear the path I believe is the right choice will make her hate me. So, I am desperate for a solution that will not end with her walking away forever.

Stay or go. Keep or return. Imprison or release. Disappoint or live with regret.

The weight of my indecision presses down on me. It feels like a storm brewing within my body, something I am unaccustomed to. I never believed mortal conditions could afflict a rider until now. The throbbing in my temples, the tension radiating throughout me, and the guilt gnawing at me all manifest as a dull ache in the pit of my stomach.

My mind, once clear and focused, now feels clouded and muddled. Thoughts collide with one another, creating a whirlwind of uncertainty and doubt. The lines on my forehead deepen as I furrow my brow, trying to make sense of the tangled mess of emotions.

With each passing moment, the sense of urgency intensifies. It's as if time is slipping through my fingers, and I am running out of options. The fear of making the wrong choice consumes me. I know what must be done, and this certainty should settle my chaotic thoughts, yet the fear of Sienna's anger and disappointment looms, overshadowing any sense of clarity I find.

As I contemplate the repercussions of my decision, I can't help but feel a pang of guilt. The thought of betraying Sienna and breaking my promise to her fills me with soul-piercing sorrow. I know that doing what is right will push her away, shattering everything we have built.

In this tangled web of conflicting desires, I am left to wrestle with the burden of my choices. Every option presents its own set of consequences, and I am torn between loyalty, duty, and love. The path before me remains unclear, and I can only hope that amidst this turmoil, a solution will emerge that will not end with Sienna's departure from my side.

But for now, I must push these concerns aside because I have arrived back at her community. There is no point in worrying her until I have decided which path I will choose, so I let the tension of my indecision slide away. Until I discover her sprinting toward me. Her screams fill me with a pending sense of dread.

"He took her." I leap off my horse and run to catch her as she collapses.

"Breathe, Sienna. Who took who?" Her response sends icy tendrils racing up my spine.

"Raum! Raum took Avalon." Her confession ends all doubts about my choice as I spur my companion in the last direction she was known to be.

The lamb can never be free.

Chapter Thirty-Three:
Running Out Of Time

When an asshole tries to pull you
under, stand your ground and remind
them who you are. They can be the
rain.... While I remain the thunder.

~ *Avalon Late Spring 2027* ~

ALL THOUGHTS OF THIS BEING a rider dissipate after I shake my head again. I can see why people who don't know him like I do would confuse the person riding towards us for the white rider. They are similar in build, but where this individual is bulkier than the man he is pretending to be, Pessy is taller.

Could this be the prick who killed Ember's family?

The moment he removes his hood, it eliminates all doubt and answers my question.

"Of fucking course it would be you, because why wouldn't it?" His stupid response is to grin at me like the asshole he is. "Tell me, did you kill them because you desired her?"

"What can I say? When I encounter something I want, I am relentless when pursuing it, and nothing will impede me from acquiring the object of my desire. Even a beloved family member."

"Were you just too chickenshit to approach her as you? Had to pretend to be a rider to make you feel more important?"

"No, Avalon, I presented as that fucker to ensure I would have the following I wanted."

"You're a prick, Trevor."

"Why do you care, Avalon? If my memories are correct, she tried to kill you."

"Because of something you fucking did. You never deserved her. Ember is way too fucking good for the likes of a miserable prick like you."

"Ember was nothing more than a pleasant distraction. My ultimate aspiration was to eradicate those fucking riders from this world."

"So you hang your hat on a demon. You really are an idiot."

"Careful, you don't have a rider to protect you, LITTLE LAMB." His mocking tone doesn't intimidate me like he was hoping it would. It pisses me off. I am preparing to offer him a retort when someone else speaks up and ends his fake-ass bravado. I don't know if I'm more disturbed by what he says or does.

"What is it you believe you will do to the lamb under my protection? Threaten what I desire most in the world again, and it is my might you will meet, MORTAL." Raum delivers his response with the same mocking tone Trevor gave me seconds prior. If this wasn't enough to rattle me, the disturbing part comes when he pulls me atop his horse and plops me in front of him. It reminds me of how War often made me ride. Despite the distress caused when War did it, finding myself in this situation with the demon who instigated all this shit infuriates me. Where's my damn dagger when I need it?

I don't know what game the asshole responsible for the world falling into chaos is playing, but he should know I don't follow the rules. Not for the riders and certainly not for assholes who threatened the people—and horsemen—I care about.

Right now, I need to figure out how to get my ass out of this shit situation because no one else will. After Raum placed me on his horse, he spurred the poor thing with merciless strikes until we were streaking through the night. Moving us further away from the rider who never liked me.

*****

Several days later, I find myself back in the damn cement underground bunker I was in when Nevil forced me to call Famine here. Unlike my last visit to this place, where I only had to deal with one asshole, now I'm stuck with managing four of them. Raum, Nevil, Wayne, and Trevor. The self-proclaimed prick of a leader, Wayne, was here when we arrived. While this doesn't bode well for me, at least it means Sienna's community will be safe from now on.

Within minutes of our arrival here, I'm tied up so the four dumbasses can leave me unattended to finalize their plans. I suppose it's no surprise that I am secured to the same place Nevil tied me last time. I don't think I need to tell you how fucking tired I am of assholes doing this shit to me. Hell, I still bear the scars that were left from when Famine did it.

Like every other time a jailor has done this to me, I'm busy trying to pull my hands free so I can get my ass out of here while the getting's good. With adrenaline flooding my veins, I strain against the restraints until my muscles burn and blood drips from the wounds I ripped back open. The rough, unforgiving cords dig into my wrists, but I push through the pain, refusing to believe this is how things end.

Sweat beads along my forehead as I twist and turn, my mind racing for a way out. But the instant I feel the rope give way, the door creaks open, shattering my momentary triumph. My escape attempt will have to be placed on hold since the four assholes saunter in. Do they believe their sinister grins intimidate me? Because I can assure each of them they don't scare me. The only thing that could claim this emotion is if I thought they were out there with the people I love, but since they're here, my family is safe, and they just lost their leverage against me. The best part is these assholes don't realize it. Something I don't plan on sharing with them.

"I still say we could have avoided all this bullshit if you had told us a rider had gotten so close to our camp," Wayne huffs from just outside the door.

"I told you what you require to complete your job. Nothing more, nothing less."

"You were supposed to tell us if we had a rider baring down on our asses. What if it hadn't been Famine? What if it had been those other two fucks?"

"Then you would be dead, and I wouldn't have to endure this mundane conversation," Raum replies with the same holier-than-thou attitude.

"Then, at the very fucking least, you could have told us she's the bitch responsible for calling the damn riders here. We could have killed her and spared ourselves the hassle of dealing with another one."

"And now you know why I didn't tell you."

"You wanted another rider here. What if Famine fucking killed us before you came strolling into the tent that day?"

"Once again, you would be dead."

"Why? Why not tell us what the hell was going on?" Trevor asks.

"Because I want the lamb."

"Then take the bitch, fuck her, and get over it." The sound of a fist hitting flesh carries to me, followed by someone slamming to the ground. One guess who that might be.

"I suggest you stop while you're ahead. Now, if you please, we have a lamb waiting for us. A lamb who is listening to your whining right now. Do you really wish to give her more ammunition to use against you?"

As each irritating dumbass enters, my eyes never leave theirs. I don't bow my head. Nor do I avert my eyes. I refuse to wilt and wither in their presence. Quite the opposite...I stand tall. If I had the strength to resist Calvin and the fortitude to oppose the riders, what the hell do they think their presence will do?

Nevil's expression narrows with sadistic glee. Wayne sneers like a predator about to pounce. Trevor's fists clench with violent anticipation. And Raum...well, Raum is the worst. He watches with a gaze full of twisted amusement.

I find it funny Wayne is rubbing his jaw. Dumbass.

"Too late, bullets collected," I say with a sneer directed at each of them. It seems they're too damn dumb to understand the reason Raum told them to shut up, which leads us into the next round of stupid ass conversation with pricks I can't stand.

"I think it's high time we break a lamb," Wayne says, with his eyes focused on my breasts.

"She is resilient and will refuse to be broken, even when you try to fuck her into submission. Trust me, I tried. Isn't that right, Avalon?"

"Go to hell, Sausage." Raum's jaw tightens, hearing the last part of Nevil's retort while he moves his focus from me to Sausage. The dimwit who may yet find out how unreliable this demon's promises are.

"I say we kill the bitch right here, right fucking now," Trevor interrupts with what I believe could end up receiving a painful retort from Raum while he continues to flex his hands in anticipation.

"I didn't ask you for your opinion."

"But—"

"Leave. Now!" When Trevor is the only one who turns to exit the room, Raum clarifies his directive. "All of you."

They are at least smart enough to do as he says because he's not a rider, meaning he has zero honor and will have no issue killing them, even if they have a deal.

"Those are some special friends you surrounded yourself with."

"They each serve a purpose."

"And when they finish said purpose, what happens then?" He doesn't respond. He doesn't have to. I know what will happen to those idiots. If I liked them, I would fill them in, but they've each made their beds so they can learn what fate has in store for them all by themselves.

"Why did you infiltrate Sienna's community?"

"I knew there would be a daughter of Eve out there somewhere who could halt his ride. So, while Famine was out decimating humanity, I searched for the one who would sway him. The instant I entered her town, I knew Sienna was the woman I sought."

"So what…you were hoping to have her removed before she could stop him?"

"It was my intention. I wanted her removed from the equation long before he stumbled across the town she lived in."

"Yet one more thing you failed at." He lifts his eyes, glaring at me for my insolence. You would think these assholes would figure out I'm not the cowering type. And Raum, being the alpha macho ass he is, wants to pretend I didn't get under his skin with my last comment.

"Who knew he would drive you so hard to avoid his brothers?"

"Apparently, not you."

"I'll concede my intimate knowledge of these riders pales in comparison to yours."

"What the hell is that supposed to mean?" Of course, he doesn't answer, giving me nothing more than the sneer I despise. When I adjust my hands to get some blood back into them, Raum's focus moves from my face to the bloody ropes holding me. His response is to give me his stupid tongue clucks while waggling his finger back and forth.

"What is it with bastards thinking they have the right to tie me up?"

"Devine supremacy."

"Asshole." His laugh doesn't give me the warm fuzzies, but it fuels the fire building within me. "Of course, you and Famine would be the ones who would actually go through with it."

"I believe two other riders had you tied up on more than one occasion. If memory serves several of those times when Death did it to you, you rather enjoyed it."

"Watching that close, were you?"

"There is little else to do while I wait for these damn riders to remove the irritants keeping me from claiming my new realm."

"Do the three dumbasses who swore an oath to you know this part of your plan?"

"They know what they need to know to fulfill their role and nothing more."

"Yeah, well, I call bullshit on the whole watching me part."

"Don't believe me? I observed you quite often."

"I knew every time you showed up, Bird Boy."

"Truly? Did you see me in the room with you when you shared the house on the hill with a rider sent to kill you? You should know the bath was his way of removing the pesky clothes you often wore. Not out of any kindness, as you believed. It gave me a rush watching you finally drop to your knees for one of my kind. Although I must admit, the roar of laughter when you called out another man's name almost gave away my presence. Had Death not been so distracted by a warm wet pussy, he would have sensed me."

"You watched while Death—"

"Fucked the little lamb? I did," He interrupts as a vile grin crosses his face. "I bet you can still feel him pressed between those thighs."

"Your observation, not mine."

"Yes, Avalon, it is my observation." He steps closer, burying his face in my hair and inhaling a deep breath before he whispers, "Would you like to know how much I enjoyed watching you on your knees?"

"Sure, right around the time I bury my foot in your ass."

"I can assure you this is not what I think of when I imagine burying something. Perhaps one day it will be my cock you are on your knees for."

Jerking my head away from him, I snap, "Never gonna happen."

"Never say never, little lamb."

"I suppose you're right. There is one way it could happen."

"Now you have piqued my interest. Do tell, Apple."

"In your fucking dreams! Other than that, I can promise you it will…." I lean as close as the ropes permit before providing the rest in a low, determined tone. "Never. Fucking. Happen. Oh, and don't ever call me that again."

"Make your declaration again so I can prove how wrong you are." Glaring at him, I doubt there is anything he can hold over me right now to make me give in and satisfy this asshole's sexual needs. Even so, there's no point in pushing my luck because one thing is clear from this little conversation…I don't know half as much as I thought I did.

Clicking his tongue, he presses against me, his finger skimming along my side. "Shame. I had hoped you would force my hand."

"You don't even like us mortals. Why in the hell would you want to sleep with one?"

"Because I want to prove to these riders they can use your flesh how they see fit without allowing some useless fucking emotion like love—or was it only lust your rider felt—to sway them from their task."

"You're a prick."

"Keep talking to me like that, Morte's Mela—"

"Don't know what that means. Don't care."

"Then there is no reason for me to tell you. Regardless of the name I said, you should know that if you speak to me like this again, you will leave me with only one forgone conclusion."

"Which is?"

"Fucking you is exactly what you want me to do."

"You know, Bird Boy, I think you envy the riders. You want what they have, but you're not man enough to do anything about it."

"First, I'm no man. Second, what you said sounds like a challenge. And third, if you do it again, I'll prove how incorrect you are when I bend you over and take you where you stand."

After this, our conversation ends, but he doesn't leave. No, the asshole walks over to a chair and sits down before plopping his feet on the small table next to it. It's like a silent stand-off between him and me. Who will break the oppressive silence first? I can assure him it won't be me.

I don't know how long we remained like this, but the dripping water somewhere from deep within this place acts as the timer, where every drop is another tick of the clock. I wish he would at least drop his gaze because it would afford me time to survey my surroundings. If I have any hope of escaping this predicament, I need a plan. To do this, I need to know the lay of the land. Something I can't do when I refuse to remove my eyes from him.

I wish this prick would just say whatever shit he wants to say. I should have learned by now to be careful what you wish for because my only wish now is to return to the staring match when he finally breaks the silence to make his demand.

"I would like to play your answer game."

"What the hell are you talking about? What answer game?"

"The one where you get to ask a question only if you answer one first."

"It's not a game, asshole."

"Nevertheless, you will play. So you can proceed with the first question, or I will." A small part of me wants to do it because I have some questions of my own. Yet the apprehension of what questions he may have lined up for me overshadows my curiosity. Something tells me they will not be as innocent as the riders.

"Why?"

"I'm unsure which 'why' you are asking, so I'll answer the ones I believe it could be. However, this is the only time I will grant this for the remainder of our game."

"Still not a game, asshole."

"To my kind, everything you mortals do is nothing more than child's play. And what is child's play if not a game?" I roll my eyes, irritated by the amount of superiority he conveyed in this response. "The reason I want to play your *game* is that I have questions only you can answer. My purpose for permitting you to go first is because I recall you once told a rider the saying is, ladies before gentlemen." He dips his head to show he believes he is the gentleman in this scenario. I bet my response will prove he isn't.

"Let's make one thing clear you are the furthest thing possible from a gentleman," I interject before he can ramble on with the rest of his stupid-ass monolog.

"Tisk-tisk, little lamb, you know how much I despise being interrupted. Regardless, my only question is, will you willingly submit to this game, or will you force my hand to make you answer? If force is required, be prepared for a one-sided interrogation where you're the sole source providing the answers."

"Fine. I'll start. Will you untie me?"

"Certainly." He says, and to my surprise, he doesn't give some stupid response like "after we have finished the game" or "if you're a good little lamb," he just does it. The relief of not having my arms dangling above me is instant, followed almost as quick by the pins and needles sensation. He stands there watching me rub my arms before I dab my shirt at the mangled mess I left my wrist in during my escape attempt, then he does something only an idiot would do…. He backs away. I admit his first question is not what I expected. "Do you enjoy teaching?"

"I don't know what you're talking about. Do you like being a miserable prick?"

"One of us needs to take on this role. Allow me to rephrase my previous question. Did you enjoy teaching Thanatos how women like to be pleased?"

"He read most of what he needed from my books. I don't suppose you would consider pissing off back to the hellhole you call home?"

"My realm is not the fire and brimstone they have led you mortals to believe. To answer your question, I will not. When your hand finds its way down to your pussy, whose face do you fantasize about?"

"One thing's for sure…it's not yours. Tell me where the last seal is?"

"You wound me, apple, and the seal is safe. Did you always want Thanatos, or did this happen only after he tied you up?"

"Death tied me up to prevent me from leaving again, and if you're so damn interested in what happened between the rider and me, why don't you stop beating around the bush and ask what you really want to know."

"Okay—" I cut him off before he could answer this because it wasn't the question I wanted to ask, and the truth is I didn't want to waste one of my turns on something I couldn't care less about.

"Why are you so damn afraid of me calling him here?"

"Who said I'm afraid?"

"The way you cringe whenever you're near them is the answer to this stupid question. Now, how about you give me a response to mine and not a question, or will this be the briefest question-and-answer session I've had to sit through with one of your father's other creations?" I refuse to say your kind because my opinion is the riders and this prick are nothing alike.

"We have not yet concluded our game. The reason for my reluctance is that I required the truth before allowing you to fulfill your task. Once I am confident, you are most welcome to call the last rider to your realm. As for your previous request for directness…when you were fucking the rider, what did you enjoy most?

"How is it possible one of the riders hasn't killed you yet?"

"You owe me an answer first."

"What I liked most about it was the fact it wasn't you."

"Very funny, lamb."

"Haven't you heard? I'm a funny person."

"A misnomer perpetuated by the riders, I presume."

"I don't know, bird boy, I thought it was pretty freaking hilarious."

"The reason they don't kill me is that they are forbidden. Why would you subject yourself to the rider's mission? May I assume it was because you like certain attributes the riders possess?"

"That's two questions. To answer your first one, it wasn't my choice, and what the hell is your stupid answer supposed to mean?"

"It means if they kill one of the high Earls, which includes me, they risk an all-out war between what you mortals call heaven and hell. My second question still stands."

"One dick isn't any different from another." Of course, this is all a lie, but I'm sick of his line of questions. Maybe this will put an end to them. "Why would they care about a war with the likes of you when they don't seem to care about it with us?"

"First, there is no war with your kind, only annihilation. They hesitate with *'my kind'* because the creator is not so keen to break the treaty, and with my responses, you now owe me two answers. First question: would you like me to prove how wrong your last response was?"

"Not hardly."

His snorted laugh pisses me off. "Second question: Tell me what you taste like."

"That's not a question. It's a request."

"Fine. Allow me to rephrase. Will you tell me what you taste like?"

"You think I fucking know?

"Yes, since you tasted it on the rider's tongue. Now answer the question."

"Me. I taste like me. If they can't touch you, then why have I heard them threaten you?"

"The treaty does not prevent them from speaking their mind. So they can bark about killing me all they want, but the truth is they won't risk what this would mean for this world or theirs. What would you say if I asked you to remove your clothes?"

"I would tell you to fuck off. Back in the field before you turned me over to Wayne, why couldn't the riders sense me since I was only a few feet away from them?"

"One of my many gifts. How did you think I could remain hidden from view yet still watch your travels?"

"Can't say I ever really gave it much thought since I didn't fucking know you were there. Watching. Like a pervert. How does your quote-unquote gift work?"

"I have the ability to camouflage your essence. Provided they cannot see you with their eyes, they will not be able to sense you with their divine abilities. A gift bestowed on me by our father."

"Doubt that. You know what, Raum, I think everything you have said today is a bunch of bullshit. In my opinion, you're nothing more than a scared little demon praying to stay one step ahead of the riders who make you shit your pants. You need them to do what you never could."

"And what's that, little lamb?"

"End humanity."

"I will topple this God-forsaken world, and when I do, I will make sure the riders can never find your lost soul, Avalon."

"Give it your best shot, bird boy, because I will do anything to stop you."

"Anything?"

"If it involves me kicking the shit out of you, then yes, anything. Just like I promise, whatever little fantasy you have playing out in that head of yours will never happen."

"How do you propose to kick the shit out of me, let alone halt any of my minuscule desires?"

"Tell me where Death's seal is, and you'll find out."

"I have it right here," he says, pulling the parchment from his pocket and laying it on the table before backing away, hauling the chair he occupied along with him. The scraping sound it makes as he drags it behind him is grating. Why the hell doesn't he just pick the damn thing up? I suppose the answer is because he's a dramatic a–hole. With the table out of range, he props his feet on the only other furniture in here, a piece of shit broken-down cot.

With his retreat, he leaves the seal at an equal distance between us. Is he testing me? Taunting me? Tricking me? If I charge over to snap the damn thing, what will he do to stop me? Will I even make it, or will he be on me before I take my first step? Rather than finding out, I offer a response to his desire, but I can't pull my eyes off the scrap of paper I have wanted in my hands since I opened the first seal.

"It takes two people to fulfill a fantasy."

"That it does. I hear Thanatos was an excellent student. Had you screaming his name often and with such exuberance."

"You keep bringing up what happened between Death and me, so not only do I think you enjoyed the show, asshole, I believe you're a tad bit jealous."

"Are you offering, Avalon?"

"Not even fucking close."

"In that case, I was not the only one who envied your rider."

"I'm not so sure about that. Especially since you sure seem to know a lot of the fucking details."

Clicking his tongue, he tilts his head before telling me, "Sadly, the envy is shared by his brother. However, the more time I spend with you, the more I understand the appeal. To be so close to the chosen lamb. Your scent is extremely… Alluring. Even I find it hard to resist. I imagine it could be near impossible for one of my kind. I suppose this is why War was so envious that the rider you taught those lessons to was his brother and not him, little lamb."

"You can stop calling me lamb anytime now, asshole."

"Like a sheep to the slaughter, the little lamb does beckon the wolf."

"Now you're a wolf? Been sipping the asshole's Kool-aid?"

"I'm whatever I aspire to be. I'll tell you what," he says with a mischievous grin. "I'll make you an irresistible offer. One you may not want to refuse."

"Not interested."

"You have yet to hear it." When I don't give my typical snarky retort, Bird Boy must assume he should proceed with the offer I'll never accept. "Return to my realm and swear you will remain with me for all eternity. If you do this, I will stop what you could not thus far."

"What's that?"

"Halt their ride."

"I have no intentions of being your slave for a day, let alone all eternity."

"Slave is a relative term. There are so many things you can do to serve me."

"You have got to be shitting me, Bird Boy. If you think I'm going to fuck you, you're crazy."

"Fuck me is precisely what you will do. Every day until the end of time, you will bend to my will while I defile the lamb he selected. I want to prove to the riders and their father how much the lamb enjoys one of his fallen."

"He's your father too."

"Tomato. Tomahto."

"Why does every asshole in this world have to repeat this stupid as fuck saying to me?"

"Divine—"

"Supremacy. Yeah, we covered that shit once already."

"My offer is this.... I want the lamb our father has chosen. Together, we will prove him wrong yet again. Besides, I want Death to see you on your knees before me. So my request is simple...turn from your riders, and humanity will live. Stay, and I will make it my mission to destroy your world."

"Go to hell, Raum. You don't have anything I want."

For the first time since he sat back down, he drops his feet in a heavy thud to the ground and leans forward to rest his enormous arms on his thighs to deliver his response. "It is my belief you require some much-needed attention, Morte's Mela. Attention your rider is incapable of providing. I am merely offering my services in his stead."

"I don't want or need anything you have to offer. Least of all your dick. I would rather have cobwebs fill my shriveled-up lady bits than let you anywhere near me."

"The clock is ticking, little lamb. Famine will never permit you to break Death's seal. He no longer wants to release his brother because he doesn't want the little fighter to meet her end. If he had taken me up on my offer, I would have allowed what he wanted, but the damn rider has not yet learned the error of his ways. So he will suffer the same future as the other riders."

"What future?"

"The loss of their chosen when Death topples your world, and I will enjoy watching it happen."

"Yeah? Well, there's one thing you're forgetting."

"What's that?"

"He'll listen to me." I snarl as I rush forward and crush the paper in my hand, destroying the final seal. The one I know will bring my rider back.

"Ah, he did love you, didn't he?"

"Yes," I say with a triumphant grin. Since Raum made no move to stop me and is only now standing to approach me, I smile, knowing I have won, but if I did, why the hell is there a smile forming on his face?

"Well, Apple, there is something I know you do not."

"Which is?" Raum walks right in front of me. His eyes alight with fire. His hand skims along my side, leaving goosebumps and waves of revulsion in his wake. I know he wants me to look down and follow the path his hand is traveling, but I refuse.

Famine's vines arrive seconds before he streaks into the room. "Stop, Avalon! Don't open my brother's seal."

But it's too late. I have already cracked what I believe is the most crucial one. Cracked it. Hell, I obliterated it. There's nothing anyone can say or do now to halt his arrival. Something I do not regret because I know he once loved me, and I'll use that love to stop his slaughter.

It feels like everything is moving in slow motion. Famine's vines no longer seek a target, his face ashen as his gaze falls to the hand still holding Death's seal. If Famine's expression alone wasn't enough to send my heart into overdrive, Raum's mouth hovering inches from my ear so he can tell me what I've done certainly does.

Raum presses closer to my body with his hand still resting against my skin and whispers. "He will retain none of the memories from his last visit to your world. Which means…."

Raum pulls back far enough for me to see the sadistic grin covering his face as the world trembles and quakes around us.

"He won't remember you."

Coming Soon

Also by Marcelle Valentine

Start Reading

Scarred by Fate Series

Ritual Nightmare
Breaking Purgatory
Fate's Ritual
Opposing Tartarus
Sacrificial Endings

The Ash Rock Series

Shadow's Moon Season One
Shadow's Moon Season Two
Shadow's Moon Season Three
Shadow's Moon Season Four

Arrival of the Four Horsemen Series

Death's Inquest
Pestilence's Judgment
War's Verdict
Famine's Punishment
Coming Soon: Avalon's Answer

Vella

Shadow's Moon Season One through Four
Seized by Sin
Silverwood Throne

Teaser Ritual Nightmares

What do you do when a demon is chasing you?

Fall in love with a supernatural who is hellbent on saving you.

Amidst the chaos of my life, I question whether I am a demon's gift or Logan's everything.

I have spent most of my life running from the demon my father summoned, and now I find myself in a small town. This simple life is a welcomed change from the endless hum of dread that has been my constant companion. I pray I can stay longer than a few months this time, however my past tells me these prayers will go unanswered.

Until I stumble across Logan, and everything changes. His presence is consuming, and I can't help but be drawn to him. His shifting eyes are both thrilling and mesmerizing. The feeling of safety that washes over me when I'm with him is unlike anything I have ever experienced. It's as if I'm finally home after years of wandering.

Keep reading for a brief excerpt from Ritual Nightmares.

Ritual Nightmares Excerpt

I pull into my usual spot at work, thinking back over the last month and a half working here. It seems like I am a part of the gang now. Well, except for Priscilla, who still hates me for reasons unknown. After Priscilla had done such a bang-up job of making me feel inadequate on my first night, I changed my entire wardrobe.

Tonight I am wearing a form-fitting shirt with a plunging neckline that I now realize reveals entirely too much cleavage. I pull at the shirt, trying to cover myself better, and wonder what I was thinking when I put this thing on. I'm irritated at myself for ever letting that woman rile me. The result has me here like this, pulling at my shirt, only making my breasts more prominent. A quick check of my watch tells me there is no way I will have enough time to drive home and change, so I'm stuck wearing this.

I head in, finding Kat and Gabe in their normal positions at the bar. Kat keeps poking his nose as Gabe tries to stop her, although he isn't trying too hard. If you ask me, I think he might like Kat.

Logan and his crew are already sitting in the VIP section. He turns as I make my way up to the bar, and his eyes slide down to my overly exposed cleavage. I watch his tongue glide over his lips, and sweet holy baby Jesus, I think I need to change my panties. His eyes slide back up, focusing on my mouth. Here's the thing: logic tells me I should look away, but my eyes betray me for some unknown reason as they begin their slow descent to enjoy the sights of one of the finest physiques I have ever seen.

I get the full image with his shirt pulled tight, outlining the muscles begging to be touched, or maybe it's just me begging to touch them. In my mind, I see my little Id jumping up and down, yelling, it's me, it's me, I want to touch them. Thank you for that, Freud. I should not be doing this, and I definitely shouldn't be wishing he was not sitting down right now because I imagine those jeans look amazing.

This brings another image flooding my already sex-riddled brain, catching my breath mid-inhale. I imagine Logan standing there with no shirt, wearing only those jeans. His well-defined abs are out for my viewing delight. Even better is his perfect V dipping into his low-slung pants, down to much more exciting but equally large parts of his anatomy. Yes, I have noticed his impressive-looking man parts, and unless he stuffs a sock in his pants, which I highly doubt, he has nothing to be ashamed of in that department.

I bite the side of my lip, suppressing the groan building inside me, and force my eyes back up, but I take my time to enjoy the show. His biceps bulge and ripple when he leans forward with his arms crossed in front of his chest. I would be lying if I didn't admit I wish I could run my hands along them. I fantasize about what it would feel like to have those arms wrapped around me, pulling me close.

Warmth spreads through my stomach and settles between my thighs, making me shift just enough to take the pressure off. Logan lifts his left arm, resting his hand on the side of his face. I watch two of his fingers drop under his mouth to tap the stubble, beckoning me to touch it. Jesus, why can't I stop my eyes from following his every movement?

All questions for another day because I couldn't tear my gaze off him if I tried.

Continuing my eye assault, I move up to his perfect lips. Like the stubble, they also seem to call to me, enticing me to experience them for myself. This interaction only stops when my eyes lock on his. The side of his mouth hitches up, revealing that sexy little grin and cue the dimples.

His buddies are having a loud debate about who the best baseball player of all time is, and one of them, a guy named Cash, hits his shoulder to weigh in on their conversation. My cheeks flush, knowing he had just caught me checking him out, but worse, I think he was doing the same thing to me. His grin increases as he shifts back in his chair, ignoring Cash altogether. Before I can embarrass myself any further, Kat sticks her face in mine.

"Whatcha looking at, chica?" Which is her way of telling me she knows exactly what I was looking at. I clear my throat and look down at the bar as she sings, "K-I-S-S-I-N-G... first comes—"

I slap my hand over her mouth, making her mumble the rest of it, "For the love of God, Kat, please don't." She mumbles something else under my hand but then goes silent. "Are you done?"

She nods her head, but when I remove my hand, she sings, "Bom chicka wow-wow."

I groan, put my head down on the bar, and hit it repeatedly. Maybe it might knock some sense into me. "He's still watching, chica." She whispers to me in her sing-song voice.

"Lightning, Lava, Earthquake, Tsunami...."

"Oh, I know things that kill!"

"Nope, things that I wish would happen right now to get me out of this hell."

"Oh, so drooling over boss man is hell?"

"Kat, just drop it!"

"Okay, I guess I won't tell you that Logan and I weren't the only ones to see you mentally undressing him."

I pull my arms on top of the bar, resting them on both sides of my head as I make little crying noises. "Please don't tell me all the guys saw it too. I don't think I could face any of them ever again." I groan as I lift my head just enough to look at Kat.

"Nope, they are all completely oblivious to your totally hot fantasy."

When I pull my eyebrows together and scrunch my face, she takes my chin in her hand and turns my head to look at one very pissed-off Priscilla staring back at me. For the first time since the day of my birth, I'm happy that laser death ray eyes are not a thing, or your girl would be toast. After getting her point across, she turns and stomps back towards the break room.

Acknowledgment

The last seal is broken, and Avalon has to face the harsh reality that it may have been her biggest mistake yet. Will Death be the Rider to end our world? Stay tuned for the final book in the Rider series.

As always, my deepest heartfelt thanks go out to every reader who decided a post-apocalyptic romance with the four horsemen was their jam. If you love one series, I hope you might try the others, and if you like them, perhaps you'll let other readers know.

I could not have completed this series without those who supported me, including my beta readers, my niece Ashley, my mom, and my daughter Melanie. While this book did not feature anyone I took inspiration from, I believe the ones you have read about Wren, Ellie, and Duck will pop back up in the final entry for this series.

I have several projects in progress. Book five in the Horsemen series is in the early stages of writing. I also have a Vella underway about a certain fae prince, which readers of my Ash Rock series may recognize. My standalone serial killer novella will be available in select markets soon. Readers of my other series may find an Easter egg about the next series I have planned within the pages of this book. And for lovers of YA series, I may have one that is in the planning stage. This will take us to a small town where demons and the like abound.

Thank you to my husband and family, who have been my biggest cheerleaders. I love every one of you.

And finally, to every author who has ever put pen to paper and fingers to keyboard, whose work only inspired me more to follow this dream, I hope I do not disappoint.

Thank you Marcelle

Newsletter

Consider visiting my website and signing up for my newsletter to receive updates on this series and all my future projects.

https://www. marcellevalentine. com

Please consider leaving a review if you enjoyed the book. Any thoughts are appreciated and will only help me improve the story. Reviews also provide new readers with a way to find my books.

You can also follow me on social media:

Facebook
Goodreads
Instagram
TikTok

Marcelle Valentine

About the Author

Marcelle Valentine has long been an admirer of creating worlds where people can get lost. From a young age, her active imagination took her on epic journeys to faraway places where troubles and friendships abound. After discovering the intriguing world of Paranormal/Fantasy Romance, which stirred up memories of all those distant places and friends, her desire to write returned. She invites you to travel with her during these journeys and get lost in a world with friends, enemies, and lovers, all firmly rooted in the supernatural realm. Marcelle is the author of the Scarred by Fate Series and the episodic series Shadow's Moon. She lives in Ohio with her husband. She has two children, three grandchildren, and one lovable, lazy Great Dane.